LARCOMBE MANOR

TED TAYLER

BOOKS

Vinci Books

vinci-books.com

Published by Vinci Books Ltd in 2026

1

Copyright © Ted Tayler 2018

The author has asserted their moral right to be identified as the author of this work in accordance with the Copyright, Designs and Patents Act 1988. This work is a work of fiction. Names, characters, places and incidents are the product of the author's imagination or are used fictitiously. Any resemblance to actual persons, living or dead, places and incidents is entirely coincidental.

All rights reserved. No part of this publication may be copied, reproduced, distributed, stored in any retrieval system, or transmitted in any form or by any means, including photocopying, recording, or other electronic or mechanical methods, nor used as a source for any form of machine learning including AI datasets, without the prior written permission of the publisher.

The publisher and the author have made every effort to obtain permissions for any third party material used in this book and to comply with copyright law. Any queries in this respect should be brought to the attention of the publisher and any omissions will be corrected in future editions.

A CIP catalogue record for this book is available from the British Library.

Paperback ISBN: 9781036700607

The EU GPSR authorised representative is Logos Europe, 9 rue Nicolas Poussion, 17000 La Rochelle, France
contact@logoseurope.eu

By Ted Tayler

The Phoenix

The Olympus Project
Gold, Silver and Bombs
Nothing Is Ever Forever
In the Lap of the Gods
The Price of Treachery
A New Dawn
Something Wicked Draws Near
Evil Always Finds A Way
Revenge Comes in Many Colours
Three Weeks in September
A Frequent Peal of Bells
Larcombe Manor

The Freeman Files

Fatal Decision
Last Orders
Pressure Point
Deadly Formula
Final Deal
Barking Mad
Creature Discomforts

Silent Terror
Night Train
All Things Bright
Buried Secrets
A Genuine Mistake
Strange Beginnings
Dead Reckoning
A Normal November
Into the Sunlight
Tame the Storm
One True Friend
Whispered Truths
A Morning Murder
Quick to Anger
Red Herring Season
Gathering Clouds
Still Standing

Chapter One

Monday, 5th January 2015

It was the best of times; it was the worst of times.

Phoenix drove through the entrance to the place he had called home since the first of July four and a half years ago. Stone pillars loomed out of the mist like dark sentinels in a Hammer horror film. The magnificent grounds of Larcombe Manor stretched before him as he rattled across the cattle grid. Damp clouds hugging the ground masked the familiar, welcoming sight of the old buildings and lights of home.

His wife Athena and their daughter Hope would be fast asleep. Friends and colleagues who lived on-site were sleeping or hard at work in the underground facilities of the ice-house. Operations undertaken by the Olympus Project are carried out twenty-four hours a day, seven days a week throughout the year. It was ever thus. Organised crime and terrorism never took a break. So, those who opposed them must remain vigilant.

Phoenix was returning from yet another mission against the Grid. A fact-finding mission on this occasion. One which he carried out alone. Security for Olympus agents had been an issue recently, and Phoenix was mindful of the need for extreme caution.

The car's headlights fought a losing battle with a dense patch of mist. He slowed to a crawl. He negotiated this sweeping driveway so often that he couldn't believe he struggled to find his way home. Maybe nature was telling him troubled times lay ahead.

Phoenix shook his head. There was nothing new there. He couldn't recall an occasion in the past four and a half years without troubling times. Olympus could only hope they took two steps forward and one step back more often than the reverse. A tumultuous year just ended. What more evidence did they need than to consider how the final six weeks alone turned out?

Phoenix attended three Larcombe ceremonies in the last two weeks of November. First, Henry Case and Sarah married. So too, did his best friend, Rusty Scott and Artemis. Next, Sarah Case blessed Giles Burke and Maria Elena's wedding after their official ceremony in Spain.

The old Georgian manor house filled with couples; Erebus would have loved that. At present, he and Athena were the only ones with a child. Could it be that they needed to convert one of the many rooms into a creche? If so, it promised to keep Maria Elena busy.

Elsewhere, on the first day of December, attention focussed on Westminster. A handful of MPs missed the vote on the motion of no confidence tabled ten days earlier. This vote followed two audacious robberies that shocked the British public. They were the work of the Grid, a network of organised crime gangs that held a stranglehold on every facet of the nation's illegal activities.

Police appeared helpless to prevent these robberies, nor did they make progress in finding those responsible. Terror attacks across the country added to the unease felt by the public; who ran this country? Who could guarantee the public's protection? What had happened to the rule of law? The nation looked to Westminster for answers.

Both sides worked hard to secure success in the days before the vote. Both expected their efforts to allow them to claim victory. Instead, polls suggested a slight edge in favour of the Government suffering a damaging defeat.

Public clamour for action against organised crime and the threat of terror attacks was undiminished. Riots and looting became less prevalent, but chatter on social media remained as caustic as ever. Commentators in the media set the scene for the millions waiting for the result on TV and radio. Wise heads counselled that however the vote went, t was likely to be just the start of the drama, not the end.

When they counted and recounted the votes late into the evening, the Government survived the no-confidence motion by a mere four votes. But, for now, the Tory whips had reined in enough of their rebels to survive.

On the second of December, the Government discussed its response to the severe criticism of its handling of the crisis. A series of riots broke out in Leeds, Liverpool, and Manchester. The Grid orchestrated these to encourage a response in other towns and cities. There was minor damage, and casualties were few.

What caused this failure to ignite a nationwide fire of rebellion was unclear. Perhaps, it was apathy, or it may have been an acceptance that the margin of victory had been so narrow the Government had survived by a whisker.

Pundits predicted a General Election in the spring. Nothing controversial was put before Parliament when things got this bad for the ruling party. They only hoped to limp along until their advisors assessed they at least stood half a chance of winning at the polls.

In Scotland, Sir James Grant-Nicholls languished in HMP Shotts alongside five hundred other criminals. They rebuilt the maximum-security facility in 2012. After his arrest, they detained Sir James there while tests continued on the remains uncovered on his estate.

As Orion predicted, he had helped find Sir James's missing wife, Fiona. The tests also confirmed Sir James had murdered his wife. The happy occasion of the October wedding of Sir James to Elizabeth, the Duchess of Lochalsh, was a distant memory. A joyful event enjoyed by the Olympus hierarchy, which now had dealt a severe blow to the organisation.

The man Phoenix knew as Heracles got remanded in custody due to the serious nature of the case. There was no question of bail. Heracles would appear in court to face the Sheriff and a jury before the end of February. Olympus had to accept the financial benefactor they welcomed among their number from the outset was not the man they thought.

Sir James's new wife, Aphrodite, had started divorce proceedings. She was distraught, but her upper-class background provided her with resilience to such setbacks. She would regroup and recover. Elizabeth's close family gathered to shield her from the gutter press, foraging for a sensational story. Her wider Olympus family made her aware she was welcome to return to the fold whenever possible. Phoenix didn't expect to see her on Wednesday at the next meeting, but he knew it wouldn't be long before she resurfaced.

In the first weeks of December, the hustle and bustle of furniture arriving in various apartments meant the main corridors were never quiet for long. Athena and Phoenix were unaffected, but Geoffrey's move allowed them to concentrate on domestic matters. While Maria Elena Burke decorated her new home, Hope spent more time with her parents. The nanny took over when Giles Burke worked in the ice-house on a day shift. Athena and Phoenix made good use of their free time. Since Geoffrey moved from London to stay with them, their time alone suffered.

Geoffrey's absence eased matters somewhat in other areas too. They were free to discuss Olympus' business. Athena's father had a knack for appearing just as they talked of a proposed mission or debriefed a completed one.

A week before Christmas, they had returned from the bedroom for a late breakfast.

"If we can grab Henry later," said Athena, "we can get him to overhaul our security again. Instigate more frequent patrols of the estate perimeters. Beef up our cybersecurity and allow us to intercept overflying drones before they cross our boundaries."

"Good idea," Phoenix agreed.

A sharp crack interrupted Phoenix's reminiscences as he manoeuvred the car past the walled entrance to the transport section. The mist had continued to confuse him, and the nearside wing mirror paid the penalty.

"Damn," said Phoenix, "oh well, there's a first time for everything."

He left a note of apology for the transport crew chief under the windscreen wiper and returned to the main house. He felt tired, cold and damp, and his bed awaited him; thoughts of the past weeks needed to stop.

Athena stirred when he slipped into bed, but she didn't

wake. Phoenix heard Hope snuffling in the nursery. Before he fell asleep, Phoenix wondered how old Sharron was before she could respond to being asked to blow her nose.

It was so long ago now he had forgotten. He had lost count of the number of times he and Karen wiped her nose with a tissue. He remembered using a wet flannel to remove dried snot smeared across Sharon's chubby cheeks, her eyes and even in her hair.

When Phoenix awoke, it was after eight. The silence told him both Athena and Hope were no longer in bed. He knew he should get up, but memories that seemed so important last night soon crowded into his head, clamouring for attention.

Everyone had gathered together at Larcombe on the Tuesday before Christmas for a party. The general mood typified many companies and organisations across the country when the holiday season approached.

Festivities had begun at six in the evening. A large bonfire burned on the edge of the lawn. Guests watched from the dining room as it turned from a smoking pile into a flourishing warmth-giving spectacle. After eating, they walked outside onto the patio and then took the steps onto the main lawn.

"The manor house is so beautiful, isn't it, darling?" said Athena.

Phoenix carried Hope on his shoulders. He turned to look at the building. The lighting installed by Erebus a decade ago cast a delicate blue light over the stonework from the ground floor to the rooftops. The more discreet lighting further up the gardens were there for security reasons. But it offered the guests a vast expanse of lawns, trees and bushes to admire.

"It's magical," he replied.

There was a loud bang. Hope, who faced the house too, screamed and cried.

"It's okay, poppet," said Athena, "it's only the fireworks."

The stewards had organised a brief display. Hope, now back on terra firma, hid behind her father's legs and peeked at the array of bright colours in the night sky. Someone should have warned me, she thought.

Sarah Case had found little spare time since the wedding. When she and Henry weren't furnishing their apartment, she carried out duties in her new parish on the other side of Bath. Sarah discovered a church choir with a good number of young choristers.

A final skyrocket that produced a thousand glittering crystals and a loud thunderclap signalled the end of the firework display. Hope was more prepared this time, and as the echo faded, the boys and girls launched into Christmas carols in the dining room.

The guests made their way back from the garden. The bonfire still burned well, but the chill of a December night took its toll. There were smiling faces of people happy to be in the warm. When the carols ended, and Sarah had said a prayer, it was time to enjoy the rest of the evening. Mulled wine for the grown-ups, hot mince-pies, and squash for the young choristers.

Phoenix stood by the patio doors and took in the view.

"It doesn't get much better than this," he said aloud, "I wouldn't want to be anywhere else right now."

"I know what you mean," said Rusty, who had spotted Phoenix and wandered over to join him. "When we're together, having fun, it's easy to forget forces are at work who wish to tear all this from us."

"While we have breath..." said Phoenix as he saw Artemis heading their way.

"The fireworks are over, boys," she laughed, grabbing her husband's arm and dragging him towards the centre of the room. Rusty groaned as he realised Sarah was arranging party games until the parents arrived to collect the boys and girls of the choir.

Phoenix looked at the dying embers of the bonfire.

"If only," he thought.

"Time to say goodnight to a tired tot," said Athena. Hope was half asleep on her mother's shoulder, sucking a thumb.

"We should have invited Geoffrey over tonight," said Phoenix, "he would have enjoyed this."

"He's wrapped up warm indoors for the night," said Athena, "I called earlier to remind him we're collecting him tomorrow. I can't believe it's Christmas Eve."

They tucked Hope into bed, stood, and watched from the nursery door as she settled.

"Forget Christmas Eve coming around so soon," whispered Phoenix, "New Year's Eve will be on us before we know it. A first birthday. Yet another celebration."

Athena kissed him on the cheek.

"Come on," she said, "let's get back to our guests. The youngsters from Sarah's parish will leave in a few minutes, and we can relax in front of that big fireplace."

"Exactly," said Phoenix. "Give it an hour, and we'll take turns to stifle a big yawn until they take the hint."

"What did you have in mind?" asked Athena.

"An early night," replied Phoenix.

Now, as he lay in bed, he smiled at the memory.

The transport section sent a car to collect Geoffrey Fox from his seaside bungalow in Burnham on Christmas Eve.

The family then had a pleasant time over the Christmas holidays. Geoffrey enjoyed watching Hope tear open presents, some were her own and others their parents, but it kept her amused. He smiled a lot too.

It was the first Christmas without his beloved Grace, and Athena knew it was essential to keep him occupied and let him know how much he was loved. She knew the memories would return, but the less time her father had to think, the better. That night, she shed a tear as she recalled the happy Christmases they shared in London. Phoenix had gathered her in his arms. They needed no words.

Hope didn't give her grandfather much peace when they returned to Burnham on Boxing Day. She wanted to walk around the bungalow and gardens to ensure he was safe and sound. The family walked to the beach in the afternoon and let the fresh air buffet them from one end of the promenade to the other. It blew the cobwebs away from Christmas Day and sharpened the appetite for a meal out in town. In the early evening, they visited a restaurant that Geoffrey discovered on his occasional forays into Burnham.

When they said their goodbyes at the bungalow, Athena drove back to Larcombe because Phoenix had joined his father-in-law in a large brandy.

"Only because it's Christmas, Phoenix," Geoffrey said. "It's rare I touch the stuff these days."

The wink he gave Phoenix when Athena wasn't watching said everything.

As they drew up by the main building at ten o'clock, they bumped into Henry and Sarah Case. While the two female university friends chatted over church services, soft furnishings and the weather, Phoenix took Henry to one side.

"Have you revisited the security protocols yet, Henry?" he asked.

"Already done, Phoenix," replied Henry. "We had a wake-up call with these drones and that Gonzalez fellow. We reassessed every aspect of how we keep Larcombe safe. Giles and his crew are introducing technical innovations from tonight that will give us an early warning of any imminent incursions. The foot patrols will increase throughout the day and night."

"That's terrific, Henry. I can sleep easy tonight."

"More to the point, Phoenix, Athena can stop fretting."

Phoenix had smiled at that comment. Sarah and Athena's conversation ended.

"Everything OK?" asked Athena.

"Time will tell," said Henry.

Phoenix rolled over in bed and stared at the alarm clock. How did it get to be ten o'clock already? His reverie needed to stop. He got up, showered and made ready to face the day.

As he reached the door to the lounge, he heard Hope's laughter.

"That's what I like to hear," he said as he entered. He was surprised to see Giles Burke making his daughter giggle. Maria Elena was in the kitchen. Athena was absent.

"Hello, Giles," he said, "I didn't expect to see you. Hope seems to enjoy your company, though?"

Maria Elena came through from the kitchen with a drink for Hope.

"Giles can pull funny faces," she said, raising her eyebrows, "at least they're funny for a young child."

"Have you seen Athena?" asked Phoenix.

"You're not in her good books, Phoenix," said Giles, "she meant us to have a morning meeting. Athena told us you got back late. She still expected you to be ready for nine o'clock, given events overnight."

"Ah, the broken wing mirror. I hit the wall in the fog last night. I took one of the best cars on my recce trip yesterday. We've had far too many reported sightings of dark blue or black vans with two agents on board. I reckoned we should vary our transport more."

Giles gave Phoenix a quizzical look.

"No, nothing like that. Nobody knows about the wing mirror except the guys in the garage."

"What was it then?" asked Phoenix.

"The increased foot patrols proved successful. Henry has a guest in an interrogation room in the ice-house. They found evidence of his various hiding places from previous nights. Until last night he had always moved position when they tried to surprise him. His final spot was in the bell tower of the estate church. As the patrol passed, an owl darted away from the tower ledge. The lads must have spooked it. Our unwelcome visitor got a bigger shock as it must have flown past his face, and he couldn't stifle a string of swear words. The two agents lay in wait until he returned to ground level just before dawn and brought him in without a fuss."

"I'd better get over there to see what Henry has learned."

"Up to you, Phoenix, but Athena is watching proceedings from behind the one-way mirror."

"Imagining me trussed up in the chair," said Phoenix, "ah well, I've got to face the music sometime."

As he turned to leave the room, he had a thought: -

"Is Artemis working in the ice-house? As you're here with Maria Elena?"

"No, she was with me when we pitched up to the

meeting room. She and Rusty disappeared after Athena cancelled the meeting."

"I won't disturb them then," smiled Phoenix. "It will only upset me more if I interrupt them having fun. It might be the spare room for me tonight. I don't need more grief."

Hope giggled as he left the room.

No, thought Phoenix, it had to be Giles and another funny face. No way could she be finding my discomfort a laughing matter at her age.

Phoenix began the long walk along the corridors, down the elegant staircase to the ground floor and then outside to battle his way against the freshening winds. No chance of a repeat of a foggy night tonight.

He reminisced about the days following Boxing Day. Across the country, few families ever complained when Christmas Day fell on a Thursday. It meant a free weekend tacked onto the seasonal celebrations. The gap to New Year that followed was so brief that many had kept holiday entitlements in reserve to avoid returning to work until today.

Phoenix made his way along the path past the orangery and headed towards the stable block. He recalled reading reports from Minos and Alastor on events around the country. The only people working hard were the emergency services and the criminal fraternity.

When New Year's Eve arrived, there was the usual anticipation of a fresh start. As if the time between eleven fifty-nine and midnight was more significant on the year's final day than any other. Phoenix had suffered over forty-five disappointments in his lifetime. Nevertheless, it was just another day until last year when Athena went into labour earlier than predicted.

Phoenix had heard Hope's first cry when the crowds in London counted from ten towards midnight. He first set eyes on Athena with their daughter in her arms as the chimes of Big Ben boomed out across the Thames and the firework display began.

Hope was unaware of last Wednesday night's importance. As soon as she was born, Athena told him she wanted to celebrate the birth of their daughter at the same time. First thing Wednesday morning was wrong, as was first thing New Year's Day. Phoenix had been so keen to sleep after a week of night feeds that he agreed without protest.

So, Maria Elena and Athena contrived to tinker with Hope's routine to have her bright-eyed and bushy-tailed in her party dress at eleven-thirty at night. First, hope attacked the wrapping paper on her presents with gusto. Next, she devoured her jelly and ice cream. Maria Elena carried the birthday cake and one candle from the kitchen and set it on the table in front of the birthday girl.

Rusty, Artemis, Henry, Sarah and Giles had joined the proud parents to celebrate a birthday and another fresh start. Geoffrey Fox elected not to come. He was suffering from a heavy cold, which he blamed on the Boxing Day walk along the promenade. Hope stopped looking at her presents when she heard her mother sing.

Everyone joined in with her singing, 'Happy Birthday', and Maria Elena lit the candle. When they stopped, Hope clapped and then she paused. All eyes turned towards her, wondering what she would do next.

Her nose twitched, and a tremendous sneeze extinguished the burning candle.

"I think someone has caught Grandad's cold, don't you?" said Athena, as everyone collapsed in fits of laughter.

While Maria Elena cut the cake, Phoenix wiped Hope's nose and dabbed at her party dress. Athena switched on the television, and the scenes from the Thames embankment and Trafalgar Square echoed the events of twelve months earlier. As Hope dug into her slice of cake, the others raised a glass to 2015.

The following four days had seen little activity in the UK, but at Larcombe Manor, there had been sleepless nights for Phoenix and Athena. Hope's cold saw to that. She was on the mend now, thank goodness, Phoenix thought, as he reached the entrance to the ice-house.

He descended to Level Three. Henry Case was in Interrogation Room Two; Phoenix entered the observation room next door. Athena sat in a chair alone, her hands steepled under her chin as she rested on the window ledge. Their prisoner looked mid-twenties, possibly from a Mediterranean or South American origin.

"You got up at last, then?" Athena asked.

"It was a tiring journey after a long day," Phoenix replied, taking a seat beside her, "who have we got here and what has he told Henry so far?"

"This is Miguel Fernando, twenty-five, currently living in London. He moved south from Sheffield."

"Have we learned anything important?"

Athena sat back in her chair.

"Henry has just started, Phoenix, don't be so impatient. After our security patrol discovered him, they brought him below and left him in darkness for two hours. Henry treated him to occasional periods of your favourite music at excruciatingly high volume for an hour. Now, he's peeling back each layer of the onion. They need me in the administration offices. If you wish to stay here to watch, you can. I'll see you at lunchtime."

With that, Athena stood and headed for the door.

"I'm sorry," said Phoenix.

"I know you are," said Athena. But, she stepped away

from the door and kissed her husband's forehead, "these first few days of 2015 have left us on edge. Something momentous is looming on the horizon, and I don't know whether Olympus can counter it."

"We must take each day as it comes, Athena. Our cause is. Our intentions are pure. We must respond to whatever the Grid throws at us in equal measure for as long as we can. If the terror threat grows, then that too will need us to oppose it with as much vigour as we can muster."

The door closed behind his wife, and Henry Case continued to interrogate Miguel Fernando in the next room.

Phoenix wondered whether this young man was to be another resident in the pet cemetery.

Chapter Two

Tuesday, 6th January 2015

After the false start yesterday, things got back to normal for the Larcombe Manor senior staff today. Athena chaired the morning meeting, and everyone arrived by nine o'clock. The main items on the agenda were Miguel Fernando, the Olympus meeting in Birmingham tomorrow and Phoenix's report on his fact-finding mission.

"Can you bring us up to speed on your progress with our guest, Henry?" asked Athena.

"Fernando wasn't the hardest nut I've had to crack," replied Henry. "Giles found his juvenile records in South Yorkshire easily, a frequent truant from the various schools he attended before they excluded him. He often appeared in court on burglary charges when he wasn't in class. When he left home and moved to London, they held a street party."

"A typical teenager, based on the latest news reports," said Alastor with a wry grin.

"Fernando found employment soon enough," Henry continued, "he preferred two wheels to four to get around the city. He worked for Domino's pizzas, did courier work and flirted with the first moped gangs. Before long, he reverted to type. He's been helping dismantle stolen, used cars for parts. The gang Miguel works for creates bogus hire companies and then loans prestige cars. The parts are exported in container loads heading for Africa and the Far East. I convinced him he should tell me about this organisation. Perhaps we could visit them?"

"Give me everything you have, Henry," said Rusty, "I'll put together a proposal for direct action."

"This is minor stuff, Henry," said Phoenix, "okay, this gang has to belong to the Grid. There have been no independent operators since their last cull, but why did Fernando carry out surveillance on Olympus? Surely, they didn't plan to steal our vehicles?"

"That's unlikely," said Henry, "but this young man has had his eyes on you for a while."

Phoenix sat up, straighter in his chair, at that piece of information.

"He photographed you in October when you were in St John's Wood. You were outside the police station. You dropped off the rider and pillion passenger of the gang that attacked those Japanese tourists."

"I get it now," said Rusty. "Tyrone O'Riordan put the word out, looking to identify the people disrupting Grid affairs across the country."

"That's it," Henry continued. "There was a reward for information offered by the Grid's leaders that spread like wildfire around the boroughs. Young Fernando moonlighted with a spot of courier work that evening. He spotted you on the M25, tailed you to the station on his moped, and then lost track of you. He got his reward, but Tyrone O'Riordan wanted much more than the photographs once he had his hooks in him. Fernando came here to replace Simon Gonzalez. He's been snapping away, taking shots of people and vehicle movements since the middle of November."

"We should be thankful his time with us coincided with so many non-Olympus related matters," said Minos. "Apart from weddings and the holiday season, there won't have been anything critical to our operations."

"If you discount the contribution those photos make in establishing our strength in personnel and transportation, then I would agree," said Athena. "Any scrap of knowledge that falls into the hands of our enemies is one scrap too much."

"Fair comment," said Minos.

"How often did Fernando report back to O'Riordan," asked Phoenix.

"Every twenty-four hours," said Henry.

"So, Tyrone will know the surveillance was compromised," said Rusty.

"I bought us time," said Henry, "O'Riordan doesn't sit by the phone waiting for Fernando to call. Instead, he picks up his messages at the Glencairn Bank at lunchtime when he arrives for work on a weekday. At weekends he has been known to answer, but he's often not in his penthouse apartment. He enjoys the social whirl of the nightclubs and casinos."

"Did Fernando agree to send a message to his boss?" asked Athena.

"After a little persuasion," said Henry. "I required him to say, 'It's quiet here', and he managed it perfectly. Losing a little finger has little or no effect on the vocal chords."

"Well, it has been quiet here, as Minos suggested," said Artemis.

"I thought it an appropriate comment, given the circumstance," said Henry.

Phoenix looked up from the tabletop where he had been gazing. He now knew the answer to his question from yesterday. Miguel Fernando lay in the pet cemetery. Hidden deep in the woods at the bottom of the gardens, it was a quiet spot.

"I take it we can move on, Henry?" asked Athena.

"We shall have no further problem from Fernando," said Henry, "as for the Grid, who knows what their response will be? The extra security patrols and technical initiatives will stay in place until they reduce the threat level."

"Or it's eliminated," said Rusty.

"Minos will be in the chair tomorrow morning," said Athena. "Phoenix and I are attending the Olympus meeting in Birmingham."

"A different venue?" asked Alastor.

"Zeus wished to reduce the distances Gods travel," said Athena. "He selected a suitable place near the heart of the country."

"Zeus had no idea Heracles and Aphrodite might be absent for different reasons," said Phoenix.

The room fell silent for a moment. There would be no forgiveness for Heracles and his betrayal. Aphrodite, though, was a firm favourite. She may have been a member of the aristocracy, but she was a warm-hearted, generous person, both of her time and her enormous wealth.

"Do you have the agenda for tomorrow?" asked Henry Case.

"We make the final decision on appointing two new members," said Athena. "I shall tell Zeus that we eliminated two spies working on behalf of the Grid. Other items to be addressed concern the Irregulars. How many can we get into the field? Where should they target?"

"Which brings us to my contribution for today," said Phoenix, shaking himself awake.

Rusty allowed himself a grin. He hadn't seen much of his best friend over the holiday season, but he knew Phoenix hated sitting and waiting. He was a man of action. Meetings were a chore to be endured, not enjoyed.

"On Sunday afternoon, I drove to Northamptonshire," said Phoenix, "on a fact-finding mission."

"Was this trip driven by any perceived threat from the Grid to target Olympus?" asked Alastor.

"No," said Athena, "we stuck a pin in a map covered with a sheet of greaseproof paper. If we asked a member of the public whether they believed crime levels were rising or falling in their locality, many would say it was rising. As for the national picture, they would say it's definitely on the increase."

"My first contact was with a shop owner on a retail park outside Northampton," said Phoenix. "He had been in business in the town for twenty years. In the past three months, a woman was held at gunpoint in a jewellery shop in the town centre. A female drug addict threatened to throw acid at a young assistant if he didn't hand over cash. He knew of numerous cases of anti-social behaviour on the estate where he lived."

"Anecdotal evidence flies in the face of the official statistics," said Athena. "According to the Office of National Statistics, crime has been steadily declining for two decades."

"It was a pure chance the pin found this rural county,"

Phoenix continued. "The county's official drop of one-fifth is the sharpest fall across the country. So we thought it worthwhile to see if we could understand why the perception and the statistics differed so much."

"This is something Alastor and I have analysed," said Minos. "In part, it's related to how crimes feature in the media. After the recession hit hard, there were cuts in public spending, unemployment rose, and incomes squeezed. The natural response might have been for crime figures to rise, but they didn't. The number of recorded offences fell."

"In rural counties such as Northamptonshire, criminals target the border areas because they assume they will not have as much police presence as large towns and cities," said Giles Burke. "In the ice-house, police teams in the affected counties have access to automatic number plate recognition. The ANPR cameras allow them to spot known criminals as they drive into their patch. These roaming organised crime gangs have thrived in recent years."

"Northampton, Kettering, and Wellingborough have issues with gangs," said Phoenix, "it didn't take long to spot them. The expensive cars and the bling mark them. Locals didn't want to describe the make-up of the gangs in any specifics. Still, it's easy to hear whispers of sexual exploitation, drug dealers setting up in the homes of vulnerable people, guns and ammunition, machetes and swords. Extreme violence is only one street from anywhere you wish to visit."

"Did your fact-finding trip encourage you to mount a direct action against any outfit in particular?" asked Henry Case.

"The intimidation suffered by students at the university spiked my interest," replied Phoenix. "Gang members dealing drugs have ramped up their efforts to target the twelve thousand students on the two campus sites. I suggest we get Hugh Fraser to identify Irregulars capable of mingling with the students and highlighting these vermin. Then, Rusty and I can lead a team to remove the problem."

"Isn't there a danger the Grid will merely replace these drug dealers with people from nearby counties," asked Alastor, "if these roaming gangs are everywhere?"

"Doing nothing is not an option," said Athena. "We must keep delivering a blow to the Grid's operations wherever and whenever we can. We know it's likely to force them to make reciprocal strikes against Olympus, but we've increased our security levels, and every agent knows it's vital to be on the alert."

"I won't hold my breath," said Minos, "but we hope for a sea-change in the government's strategy on crime. If the police and the judiciary swung into action to take our place, they could decimate the number of criminals on our streets. But, at present, that help is light-years away."

"Certainly, it won't happen in our lifetime," said Rusty. "I look forward to visiting Northampton and its environs, Phoenix. Is there a priority attached to this proposed mission as yet?"

Phoenix shook his head.

"We may sort out Miguel Fernando's car gang first. Athena and I will let Zeus and the others attribute priority tomorrow."

"Thanks to Minos and Alastor's background checks, we have the information to figure out which two people to recommend to Zeus and the others tomorrow," said Athena. "Byron Paterson, the forty-year-old Californian, has the skills and the financial clout to help Olympus, and there were no red flags to discount him. However, he's not enough of a people person to match the new dynamic in the Olympus hierarchy. Raymond Ferreira, the thirty-two-year-old Irishman, passed every check, and his charity work with disaster emergency makes him stand out."

"He offers far less in financial terms than Patterson," said Artemis.

"True," said Athena, "but we believe his empathy will resonate with more of the other senior Olympians. Patterson's abrasive American approach might have been too strident."

"Another Donald Trump, you mean?" said Rusty.

"At least Trump's never shown much inclination to go into politics," laughed Minos.

Athena wanted to keep things moving.

"Lily Chan, our lone female candidate, is a thirty-six-year-old married mother of two. Everything checked out in her past, and we desperately need another female at the top table. Two great assets will become our new Olympians, *Chronos* and *Hebe*. Is there anything anyone has to contribute this morning?"

"We noted two statements from government sources recently," said Minos. "It's clear the panic in the ranks after the no-confidence motion inspired them. One spokesperson wanted the public to know tackling terrorism was a national priority. That provoked an announcement that extra resources would be in place following the Charlie Hebdo attack in Paris. Another leaked document reported that they thwarted three terror plots in the recent past."

"More, if you include those that Olympus had a hand in," said Rusty.

"You're on good form today," said Phoenix, "married life suits you."

"It suits us both," said Artemis.

"Especially when you get unexpected free time?" asked Phoenix, raising an eyebrow.

Artemis blushed, and Rusty smiled.

"Touché," he added.

Athena concluded the meeting, and she and Phoenix returned to their apartment. Maria Elena sat, cuddling Hope. Their daughter's cold had run its course, but she played on her recent illness. After several days where her parents had cared for her more often than their usual work schedule allowed, Hope had realised things were back to normal today.

"Oh, dear, are we having a relapse?" asked Athena.

"I think not," said Maria Elena, "her temperature is back to normal, and her appetite is fine. It's just that she missed you."

"We were only away for three hours?" scoffed Phoenix. Maria Elena stood and handed him her charge. Phoenix gathered his daughter in his arms; Hope clung to him like a limpet.

"You remind me of an advert I used to see on TV," he told Hope as he stared at her cheeky face. "When you grow up, you're going to be a proper little madam."

Hope didn't know what he meant, but having her father's arms around her felt good. But something told her everything would not stay the same here much longer.

"I wish we could stay here with you all day," Phoenix told her, "we have to get lunch and get work done this afternoon."

"She won't want to hear we're driving up to Birmingham in the morning either," sighed Athena.

"Sorry, Maria Elena," said Phoenix, "that will mean another early start for you. I hoped Les Biggar might ferry us to and from this Olympus meeting. He's otherwise engaged."

"I don't mind," said Maria Elena, "Giles is on a late shift today. He'll return to our apartment at six, so the bed will remain warm."

"Early mornings in the first week of January can be hard for everyone," laughed Athena. "It was no bed of roses last year when we had sleepless nights with this tiny tot."

Athena ruffled the hair on her daughter's head. Hope had stopped clinging now and half-turned, so she could watch and listen as her nanny talked with her mother.

"She doesn't miss much, does she?" said Phoenix, "every conversation we have, she takes in every word. I reckon she understands a damn sight more than we give her credit for, despite her only a year old."

"I'll get that lunch started," said Maria Elena.

Phoenix handed Hope to her mother.

"Fair's fair," he said, "give your mother a big hug for a while. Then we'll think of something we can do together on Thursday or Friday. Perhaps, a drive into Bath to visit the shops? There are bound to be sales campaigns to tempt us to buy clothes or toys we don't need. What do you say?"

If it keeps you both out of danger, it works for me, thought Hope, as she laid her head on her mother's shoulder.

Wednesday, 7th January 2015

The insistent alarm clock had Phoenix and Athena out of bed before half-past six. They were on the road towards Bath and onwards to the motorway system before seven-thirty. Phoenix drove them. Athena didn't mention that the near-side wing mirror appeared out of alignment. Phoenix wondered if he could remember to tell the transport chief to adjust the replacement when they returned home later tonight.

The meeting room suite on level one of the Library of Birmingham in Broad Street offered four high-spec, flexible meeting rooms, including rooms suitable for up to seventy delegates. The meeting rooms benefited from natural daylight and views over Centenary Square. There was nothing to complain of for any of the Olympians. As they arrived for a prompt ten o'clock start, they saw the ideal facilities for their needs.

As usual, Zeus and Hera were there before the others appeared. They had travelled up yesterday afternoon from their home set in the rolling countryside. The Eliot family had occupied Barley Mill in Kent for centuries.

Duncan and his wife Celia may have been in their late sixties, but they remained highly alert and active. Zeus had organised the agents on duty to ensure they swept the room for bugs; or anything that interrupted the flow of planned proceedings. So he didn't need to remind them to check for things that went bang or recording devices that would allow their enemies to eavesdrop on Olympus' business.

Hera had liaised with the venue staff to have refreshments delivered before the meeting began. Once the doors closed behind the last arrival, no one entered or left until Zeus said business had concluded.

Phoenix and Athena still sought a spare spot in the car park when Ambrosia burst into the meeting room. Piya Adani, the pocket-rocket from Leeds, was on a mission. She had called her lover, Hugh Fraser before she drove south. Of course, Hugh wasn't best pleased to be awake at such an ungodly hour, but Piya was unapologetic. She reminded Hugh his bosses in the manor house would already be wide awake and preparing to travel to the Midlands.

"Today's the day I make a big push to elevate my standing in the Olympus hierarchy," she had reminded him, "you should wish me luck."

"If I've learned anything since you came into my life," Hugh replied, "it's that you don't rely on luck. Force of will usually gets you what you want."

"I don't recall having to force you to make love, darling," Ambrosia had replied.

Hugh Fraser was coming around to the idea he had succumbed like a lamb to the slaughter. He was sure she was using him, but he didn't want to spoil the party. Life with Ambrosia was never dull, and when she discarded her crusading shield to reveal her more romantic side, Hugh was happy to go along for the ride.

"What's so funny?" asked Ambrosia, as Hugh realised he could have used a better phrase to describe matters.

"Nothing, sorry," he replied, "I stifled a yawn. I had a late night. Athena asked for an update on the Irregulars numbers. She wanted to take details with her today on any recruits we could put into the field. On his latest fact-finding trip, Phoenix uncovered another can of worms in the countryside."

"I hope to have something to bring to bear on Phoenix and how prized he is within the Olympus hierarchy," muttered Ambrosia.

"Tread with care, my love," said Hugh, "they are a powerful couple. Take on one, and you take on both."

"Don't worry, Hugh, I know what I'm doing. Before I go, can you tell me what figures you passed to Athena? It will not harm my cause if I can inform Hera before the meeting. She will have ample time to frame the proper response. I suggest that the numbers are too few and the proposed locations are misjudged. It will help chip away at the formidable foundations they have built around their reputations."

As Ambrosia arrived, Hera checked the name cards on the main table to see that the Olympians sat where she and Zeus wished. Her husband sat at the head of the table, with her on his left-hand side. Ambrosia was to sit next to her. Hera paused as she reached the chair Heracles occupied at the last meeting in Curzon Street. That position lay vacant on this occasion. Once his replacement was named, she would complete the blank cards. A new male God would take the chair next to Aphrodite. Her great friend, Elizabeth, the Duchess of Lochalsh, had missed this meeting. Hera wondered how long it might take to recover from a broken heart. None of them had ever dreamed what a black-hearted rogue Heracles had been. They had danced the night away at the Dorchester only three months ago to celebrate the couple's wedding.

"Ah, there you are, Hera. It's good to see you."

The elderly lady was surprised at the speed with which the latest arrival crossed the room. She found herself hugged and kissed on both cheeks as Ambrosia struck the meeting room in a whirlwind. Then, without a pause for breath, the newcomer told her everything Hugh had passed on concerning the Irregulars. She added no too subtle hints; it was too little or too late.

"Yes, dear, I'm sure you're right," Hera said, hoping to get away from her for a while. She still had the other cards to double-check.

Zeus noticed his wife was flustered and crossed the room

to rescue her. The door opened, and in strode Apollo and Dionysus.

"Good morning, gentlemen," said Zeus, "did you have a good journey?"

Dionysus, the retired civil servant, put a hand on Apollo's shoulder.

"Thanks to this fellow," he said, "we came up from London together."

"I was up in London for two days," Apollo explained. The former world boxing champion had a considerable property portfolio, and although he lived in Salisbury, he often travelled to the capital on business.

"I don't want the news to get out," said Sir Malcolm Dunseith, "but I made one of my infrequent visits to the House of Lords yesterday. My wife entertained most of the members of the Women's Institute from Moreton-in-Marsh, where we live. Westminster is a place of sanctuary for me on such occasions. I can't bear the Grange being full of the 'Jam and Jerusalem' brigade."

"You'll never know whether they kept their clothes on throughout the day, Dionysus," laughed Apollo.

"How's Louise now?" asked Hera.

Zeus gave his wife a stare. The poor chap didn't need reminding how drunk she'd been that night at the Dorchester. The memory of her sliding off her chair and disappearing under the table would stay with him forever.

"Much the same," replied Sir Malcolm.

Hera and Zeus shared a glance. Surely, he hadn't meant that sobriety and Louise had been strangers since October?

The door opened again, and their last four visitors entered. Achilles was deep in conversation with Athena. Behind them, Phoenix was getting on famously with Daedalus. It shouldn't have come as any great surprise.

Phoenix had realised that night at the Dorchester that Daedalus had increased his good friend count to eleven.

"Good," said Zeus, "everyone's here. So we can get started on time."

"We should raise a glass to absent friends," said Phoenix as he poured glasses of orange squash for himself and Athena at the refreshment table.

"I hope Elizabeth is alright," said Hera, "what a terrible thing to happen. She was so happy."

"She's stronger than most," said Apollo. "I don't think it will be long before she returns to the fold."

"The sooner we get the matter of the new Olympians decided, the better," said Zeus. "I wish to erase the memory of Heracles as soon as possible."

"I see you left a gap for a new person between Ambrosia and Aphrodite," said Athena. "We carried out our due diligence on the candidates proposed last time. Therefore, we recommend Raymond Ferreira becomes Chronos with immediate effect."

"Very wise," said Daedalus, "and very British," it was clear the move amused the French inventor.

"He's the best male candidate by far," said Athena, "why do you find his elevation amusing, Daedalus?"

"You misunderstand me, Athena. Heracles and Aphrodite represented the same generation. Their doomed relationship began around a table such as this at an Olympus meeting. Given her present situation, a young man in his early thirties would be of little interest. In France, a cultured, older woman such as the Duchess might see Chronos as challenging. Another example of how different our two nations are."

"Tell Zeus how you got here today, Daedalus," said Phoenix.

"Achilles drove across from Brecon and picked me up from our home in Monmouth. I told you when we walked from the car park."

"I think I'm safe, Phoenix," laughed Achilles, "his Gallic charm is wasted on me."

Athena sat on the right-hand side of their leader, Zeus. Phoenix had automatically taken the chair next to her. Because of their new friendship, Daedalus was his companion. Opposite them sat Apollo, who had found himself seated next to Aphrodite at recent meetings.

Dionysus had gravitated to the end of the table opposite Zeus. It didn't represent seniority, but he became the longest-serving Olympian after Erebus's murder. Ludovic Tremayne, the director of various oil and gas exploration companies, was happy to move to sit next to the former Private Secretary.

"Who did we decide should be the right person for the vacant chair?" asked Achilles, indicating the gap between himself and Daedalus.

"Lily Chan passed our checks," Athena confirmed, "we recommend she becomes Hebe."

"The goddess of youth and the cupbearer for the Gods," said Achilles. "She's married with two children, am I correct?"

"You are, Achilles," said Phoenix, "we should remember that the names from which Erebus selected the Olympian alter ego took no account of the relationships that existed in myth."

"Hebe was our daughter," said Hera.

"She married Heracles," added Zeus.

"Hebe served up nectar and ambrosia to the Gods," said Phoenix, smiling at the ambitious woman glaring in his direction. "It's only a name to protect her identity from the outside world. I think it's perfect. So have we agreed Lily Chan fills the twelfth and final chair?"

There were no objections. Ambrosia had to bite her tongue; she could bide her time. Phoenix may have won that round. She saw how the Olympians were now seated around the table; the battle lines were in place.

The fight had many rounds left yet.

Chapter Three

The weather outside the conference room windows was more changeable now. Dark clouds scudded across the sky, driven by strengthening winds. Hera switched on the lights. Nobody passed a comment.

The atmosphere around the table was packed with as much menace as the skies above. Zeus moved to the next item on his list. However, he was keen not to let this mood fester. Although only nine Olympians were present, they had regained the necessary twelve he and Erebus agreed at the initial meeting to establish the Olympus Project.

The balance of seven men to five women when they next met in London was more acceptable. Hera and Athena had their allies in Ambrosia and Aphrodite. Hebe was her own woman. Which of the female factions she aligned with would emerge over the coming months? Who knew? She may even be attracted to the older Olympians with wisdom gained through experience.

Phoenix had his allies. Apollo and Daedalus stood in his camp, but Achilles and Dionysus were inclined to stick with their more moderate leader. Chronos was an unknown quantity. This is because he was so much younger, less than half Zeus's age.

Zeus presented the latest financial statement. It wasn't pleasant reading compared to last October, following the Heracles debacle: -

"Sir James received a message in prison; his association with the Project ends with immediate effect. Secrecy is paramount. When the case comes to court, there must be no mention of Olympus or his contributions to the fighting fund."

"Did you stress the penalty for an unwise comment?" asked Dionysus.

"I had to be very careful with my wording," said Zeus, "but he's aware that even inside a high-security prison, we can reach him. So I've taken the precaution of having one of our agents infiltrate the defence team. One whisper of Sir James trying to squirm out of this by making a deal that involves revealing the truth behind the Olympus Project will mean he will die."

"I suggest we never mention this matter again," said Athena, "especially once Aphrodite returns. She's suffered enough."

"Agreed," said Zeus. "If we must take drastic action, we'll ensure it looks like a violent prisoner going rogue. Heracles will appear to have been in the wrong place at the wrong time. Is that acceptable to everyone?"

Once again, there were no dissenting voices.

Losing new monies from the Grant-Mitchell coffers would leave a large hole. Whatever Chronos and Hebe contributed, it fell well short of the sums Heracles provided in the past. As the others studied the numbers Zeus submitted, Ambrosia seized her chance.

"I will be more than happy to increase my contribution," she said. "Our cause is just. We cannot allow one setback to divert us from our mission. I'm sure the rest of you will match whatever I can bring to the table?"

"We have been doing that for much longer than you, Ambrosia," Zeus reminded her. "However, Hera and I will look at how much more we can offer."

"There is one among us whose financial input seems lacking," said Ambrosia. "I have studied the figures since 2007 and can't find anything attributed to you, Phoenix?"

Zeus glanced at his wife. She must have given Ambrosia access to this level of detail. He recalled Ambrosia calling into their home before Christmas to deliver cards and gifts. Then, while working in his study, the two women disappeared for a few hours. He hadn't realised this was the real reason behind the visit. Hera said nothing.

Athena was livid. Phoenix saw she was ready to explode. He laid a hand on his wife's arm to persuade her to calm her rage. An angry reaction was what this little minx hoped to achieve.

Apollo spoke first.

"Ambrosia, you are still wet behind the ears as an Olympian," he cautioned. "Erebus introduced Phoenix to Olympus only four years ago. The world believes the man he was before that day is dead. His fortune is in bank accounts in Switzerland and the Cayman Islands until seven years have elapsed. The money can then transfer in full into Olympus funds. Phoenix promised his mentor Erebus that he would work with the Project for as long as possible. There has never been a question of how committed he is to our cause."

Zeus saw this admonishment strike home. But he felt deceived by the devious manner by which Ambrosia uncovered what she believed to be a stain against the character of an Olympian who opposed her. There had always been power struggles among the Olympians, with the different factions vying for control.

It was apparent Ambrosia held ambitions for the top job. He and Hera couldn't continue forever. Athena was the next leader-in-waiting. When she and Phoenix combined, Erebus often spoke to Zeus of the strengths they brought to the table once the older couple stepped aside. However, Zeus wasn't ready to give up control just yet. He must make Hera realise he wouldn't stand by while Ambrosia manipulates her into promoting her chances of being his successor.

"You appear to think everything with Olympus is governed by money, Ambrosia," he said.

Athena couldn't remember Zeus using such a stern tone.

"We need money to achieve our goals," wailed Ambrosia.

"As you're so good with figures, can you quantify the benefits Phoenix has generated through his direct actions? He's the only one around this table who killed criminals bleeding this country dry with their activities. The country owes people like him and Rusty Scott a debt of gratitude, but they'll never know of their deeds. If they die in service, as many of our agents have, they will not mark their graves with a record of what they achieved. Heracles left us with a shortfall. Those of us around this table will give what we can. I will continue to do what I had begun; to approach our silent partners for extra donations. Many support our cause but never come out of the shadows. They continue to give while the Project delivers on its promises. If Erebus's spirit is diluted, the financial impact will be far greater than what we've suffered in recent months. We stand or fall together, Ambrosia. They will oppose any disruptive influence with great vigour. Is that clear?"

The room fell silent; the message was plain. Ambrosia was quiet; the dark clouds lifted outside, but heavy rain lashed against the windows.

"Time to discuss the next round of missions," said Zeus. "I have read the report from the security chief at Larcombe. We will wipe out the car gang that Miguel Fernando used to work for within the next seven days. After that, if the opportunity arises to use the Irregulars available, we should do so, but I need as many as possible assigned to the county of Northamptonshire. Even from the preliminary report I received late last night, it warrants immediate action. I trust you can cope with the planning and execution of both missions, Phoenix?"

"The London mission will be brief," replied Phoenix, "but we will face logistical problems with a large, rural county. Access to a band of Irregulars to gather intelligence will be vital."

"Hugh Fraser gave me details of how many operatives we could put into the field in the next fourteen days," said Athena. "I wish there were more than five, but Phoenix will select his targets with his customary precision."

Ambrosia found something fascinating on the table in front of her, and her eyes never lifted to see Athena directing every word in her direction.

"We can't wage outright war on the Grid's gangs across the whole county," said Phoenix. "The action will focus on taking out those criminals that will have the most damaging effect on their operations. The Grid will regroup. They always do, but even a few days will cost them a huge sum of money."

"Safe home from your missions, Phoenix," said Zeus.

"Our next meeting in Curzon Street, London, will be on Wednesday, the eleventh of March. That will be your chance to welcome Chronos and Hebe to the Olympus hierarchy. In addition, we pray Aphrodite will feel ready to return. The timing of the meeting is deliberate. Heracles will have had his day in court by then, and being amongst friends will prove a welcome distraction for our good friend, Elizabeth."

With the meeting at an end, Apollo was the first to leave. He had more portfolio business to pursue in London. Phoenix wanted to thank him for leaping to his defence, but Apollo was a man on a mission. Phoenix saw Athena move to the end of the table to chat with Dionysus.

"We can drop you off in Moreton-in-Marsh, Dionysus," said Athena, "it's on our way home."

"Many thanks," replied Dionysus, "time to face the music, I suppose. My few days of freedom are at an end."

This will be a fun journey, thought Phoenix. He noticed Zeus, deep in conversation with Hera. It was an attempt to steer her away from the clutches of Ambrosia. The diminutive Piya Adani was hovering, but Daedalus had noticed the situation too. He intercepted her and switched the light of his Gallic charm on full beam.

Phoenix heard him congratulating her on the work of the Irregulars. What a great idea it had been. Daedalus told her not to fret over events this morning. The Olympians always had a healthy appetite for lively debate. It would be water under the bridge by the time they next met.

"Ever the optimist," muttered Phoenix, but Daedalus achieved the desired effect. Zeus and Hera were gone. They escaped with Achilles.

"Are we ready?" asked Athena.

Phoenix nodded. They headed for the conference room

exit with their passenger. Daedalus had manoeuvred Ambrosia towards the refreshment table, and she had her back to them as they escaped. Jean-Paul acknowledged Phoenix as he passed.

"It's difficult to read that man sometimes," said Dionysus. "The French have a range of unique facial expressions, don't they?"

"They do," replied Phoenix, as they made their way downstairs to the car park, "but, in this case, I know what he said. So I owe him one."

"Well, what a lively meeting," said Athena. They had delivered Sir Malcolm Dunseith to his large, country pile on the outskirts of the Cotswolds town he and his family called home. They saw no sign of his wife, Louise, which cheered up their passenger no end.

"I wanted to thank Apollo for his intervention," said Phoenix, "but he was out of that room faster than a rat up a drainpipe. He stopped you from scratching Ambrosia's eyes out, at least."

"When she brought up your history, I thought that a low blow," said Athena. "I can't understand what Hera was thinking, handing information over without a word to Zeus. Ambrosia will use any trick in the book to make her way to the summit."

"Like father, like daughter," said Phoenix. "He wasn't averse to trampling on friends or relatives as he built his empire."

"Zeus pulled no punches in his response either, did he?" laughed Athena. "I can't recall him ever getting so angry."

"Ambrosia might rein in her ambitions for a while," suggested Phoenix. "The task ahead for Olympus looks difficult enough without wasting our efforts on fighting amongst ourselves."

"These storm clouds remind me of the look on Ambrosia's face when we left the room. I'll never know how Daedalus kept chatting to her as if they were discussing the merits of different varieties of champagne."

"I'll call him later," said Phoenix, "to check he escaped without injury."

An hour later, Athena and Phoenix reached the gates to Larcombe Manor. They were home safe, for now.

"I don't like it," said Colleen O'Riordan.

"I'm none too keen on the idea either, mother," said Tyrone.

"Why did you get them involved? Surely, you learned your lesson with the other foreign mob? They ripped us off to the tune of at least ten million. People with old money who don't want the status quo threatened are now a better bet. Even if they never mix with the likes of us."

"These Russians are guys you don't say 'no' to," said Tyrone, "but I can handle them. If they step out of line, I've got more than enough firepower to eliminate them. Some jobs need particular expertise. The Albanians delivered more than enough cash to the Grid through the skills they brought to the party. Even if they stole a few million quid off the top, these Russians could help me take things to the next level."

"I wish you hadn't arranged to meet this Vasiliev here, in your apartment. Scum like him, you want to keep at arm's length. Meet them on neutral ground. Tommy would never have let them into our home. He wouldn't even have let them visit the social club, despite everyone inside being one of us."

"I'm not my father," said Tyrone.

"Don't I know it, but please, be careful, Tyrone," said Colleen. "These are dangerous people."

Tyrone knew only too well that Leonid Vasiliev was a vital member of a ruthless gang of Russian criminals that ran brutal protection rackets and vice rings. Using violence to keep control of the trades they were involved in came as second nature.

In recent weeks, Tyrone had lost contact with Gonzo and Miguel, the two young men he sent to conduct surveillance at Larcombe Manor. They had been in the countryside, on the outskirts of Bath, for heaven's sake. Not in an inner-city with a reputation for high levels of crime. Yet, they disappeared and were presumed dead — time for action.

"We can be dangerous too, mother," Tyrone told Colleen. "We can't sit on our hands while these Olympus people carry on their business as if we don't exist. We gathered data before our watchers disappeared on people who came and went. They're well-protected within the boundaries of the Manor. I plan to hurt them in other ways."

Colleen went to the beauty salon to sulk her way through another day. Tyrone believed the Russians were a calculated risk. As for the other hidden approach he'd received after the two major robberies, that was another matter.

When Hugo Hanigan ran the Grid, he concentrated on the money over everything else. He wanted vast personal wealth but shunned personal relationships. Nevertheless, he still related everything he achieved to those seven bloody streets in Dublin where their dirt-poor Irish families had lived. Hugo never thought of what his money and the connections it made available might achieve.

Tyrone knew his mother didn't have a vision either. He

did. Tyrone wanted people to know who he was and what he was. He needed to influence higher places than the gutter, where his criminal fraternity spent their lives first. The Russians would help him hurt Olympus. Then, when he scratched that annoying itch, he could move on to the next phase of the game.

Thursday, 8th January 2015

While Athena, Phoenix and the others gathered for the morning meeting in the main house, Orion parked his car after an eventful drive from home. The weather was dreadful. High winds buffeted him throughout the eight-mile journey. A journey that took twice as long as usual due to minor accidents and the caution of younger drivers unused to handling extreme weather.

He didn't envy Erica tackling the school run this morning. The roads were tough enough to negotiate with the potholes that littered the surface of the city's streets. It became a whole new ball game when you added torrential rain, gale-force winds and the threat of falling branches.

Orion battled his way to the door to the stable block and made for the relative calm of his office. In the corridor, he met Hugh Fraser. Hugh sensed the weather wasn't Orion's only concern. That worried frown had been on his face since Monday.

"Do you want to talk about it?" asked Hugh.

"Come on in, Hugh," said Phil Hounsell, "it may be nothing, but my ex-copper's nose tells me something's wrong,"

"Are you still thinking of your former colleague?" asked

Hugh, "I passed that information on as soon as you told me. Rusty Scott promised to act as soon as possible."

"No," sighed Phil, "not poor Wayne and Bridie, although their deaths are still on my mind. Since we returned after New Year, I've suspected I'm being tailed. I spotted a dark saloon car, three vehicles behind me this morning. You had to be a mug to be out driving in this unless you had to. The car joined the traffic behind me, approaching Cleveland Bridge and then turned off half a mile before turning into the lane leading to the Manor. I had to stop twenty yards further on because a wheelie-bin blew into the road. I looked back to see the car exiting the side road and indicating to turn left, back towards Bath."

"Had you spotted this same car earlier?" asked Hugh.

"Maybe, on Monday evening," said Phil, "hard to be sure in the dark. There was a dark-coloured van behind me on the way in on Tuesday, which I then noticed following me home the same night."

"I'll arrange for someone to follow you this evening when you leave here," said Hugh, "better safe than sorry."

"We may need to keep tabs on Erica, my wife too," said Phil. "She saw someone sitting in a car a hundred yards up the road from our house yesterday morning. She reckoned the same car had been there every day this week."

"Leave it with me. I'll talk to Henry Case."

"You won't know this, Hugh," Phil Hounsell continued, "but a killer kidnapped my wife when I was still a copper. He snatched her right off the street here in Bath. I can't let her go through that again."

"Of course not," said Hugh, "look, let's take this one step at a time; it might be nothing. We'll look after you and your family; it worked out last time. How did you get her back? Was it a ransom he wanted?"

"He treated her well. No, there was no ransom demand. He wanted me to stop chasing him, so he could carry on killing the criminals he'd targeted. He was on a one-person vigilante crusade."

"What happened?" asked Hugh.

"Good police work found the place he held Erica captive. We rescued her while he was away in London. When he returned to Bath that evening, we caught up with him. I tackled him, but he drowned in Pulteney Weir after a fight in the water. I was lucky to survive. My DS saved my life."

"I had no idea. What an ordeal that must have been for you and your family."

"It's funny how things turn out," said Phil, "my DS just got married. After she left the police, she came here to work. She used to be Zara Wheeler. You know her as Artemis."

"You're kidding me? Who was this killer? Have I heard of him?" asked Hugh.

"Colin Bailey? I doubt it. He was responsible for over fifteen murders. I never had enough to bring him in for questioning, let alone charge him. I knew he had done them and why. For most of those deaths, I would have held his coat while he did the deed, but it was still murder in the eyes of the law."

"At least he's dead. So you needn't worry that he's tailing you and your wife."

Hugh looked as if he was leaving, but Phil stopped him.

"You don't have to answer this," said Phil, "but why are people here assigned a code name while others carry on with their given name? Why did it become necessary for Zara to become Artemis, for instance?"

"When the Project started, it was important to protect the identity of the people who contributed to and operated within the organisation. The connections those people had in the outside world included many who disapproved of their motives. So, the founder, Erebus, hid the identities of those who wanted to sever connections with their old life by naming them after Greek deities."

"Are you saying Artemis wanted that?" asked Phil.

"You would have to ask her that question," replied Hugh.

"I never had a choice," said Phil. "I automatically got dubbed Orion when I agreed to work from Larcombe instead of from my office in Bath."

"It works both ways, Orion," said Hugh, with a wry grin, "to the outside world, you are still Phil Hounsell, former DCI of the Avon and Somerset Police. Your colleagues would disapprove of the tasks you perform for Olympus. So everything you do for the Project is under the banner of your code name. That guarantees no paper trail or digital record connecting you to a criminal act. A police check would only uncover that you liaise with family members of ex-servicemen treated here for PTSD and trace relatives where our patients have lost touch."

"I had no idea my cover was so elaborate," said Phil.

"Erebus was a knowledgeable man," said Hugh. "I never met him, but he was a stickler for those protocols he established at the outset. There must have been something special in Phoenix's case. None of the agents I've worked with know what he did before he arrived. Even the code name Erebus gave him suggests a rebirth. The older man took Phoenix under his wing and mentored him. The rumour mill says he opposed the relationship with Athena at first. Once it blossomed, he promoted the couple as a team to the senior levels of the Project. They are next in line to assume total control. Phoenix is a born leader, brave as a lion. He got me here to help plan Olympus missions, but he's far better at the job than I'll ever be. He doesn't miss a trick."

Hugh Fraser realised he had said more than enough. Ambrosia was keen to prevent automatic succession from taking place. Hugh wanted to hear from her, to discover how yesterday's meeting went and whether she'd made any progress. It surprised him not to have heard from her last night.

"Anyway," said Hugh, "I've taken up enough of your time. I'll let you get on with your work."

With that, he left Phil alone in his office, staring at the trees blowing in the wind.

Phil Hounsell's mind raced. His crazy one-night fling with Zara couldn't have influenced her decision to go into hiding at Larcombe Manor. That night had been inevitable ever since they met in Durham. So, why did she become Artemis? Was it only to mask the fact she lived with Rusty Scott? She understood he didn't have a problem with that. Was it another person at Larcombe that needed protection? Somebody who persuaded her to adopt a code name?

That made Hugh's admission of his confusion over the origins of this Phoenix character more interesting. Phil had realised that the layout of this office prevented him from seeing what was going on. Hayden Vincent was his only real point of contact. Hayden fed him enough information to tackle the tasks he passed on to him but offered little else. Was it to prevent him from meeting someone from the past?

Hugh's comments triggered a memory.

That niggle he experienced when he spotted Phoenix unloading the car by the front door as he drove home one time something that haunted him ever since. Of course, he'd bumped into Phoenix at Glastonbury, which muddied the waters. Phil didn't recognise the face then, so why did it seem familiar that evening? It had been enough to mention it to Wayne when they talked only days before he died.

Phil went through the possibilities. Could it have something to do with him and Zara? The idea it might relate to a case they worked on together seemed impossible. No way Phoenix could ever be Colin Bailey. They never found his body. How could he discover when this Erebus chap introduced Phoenix to the Project? When did he arrive here at Larcombe Manor? Had his facial features altered so much that he was unrecognisable from the man he knew?

Phil Hounsell didn't hear the knock on the door as Hayden Vincent entered the room with an armful of folders.

"Here's a stack of investigative work to keep you busy until Easter, Orion," he said, dropping them into the in-tray on the desk. "Sorry, did I wake you?"

Phil shook his head. No, he was wide awake. He had to uncover the truth. How could he believe Zara was complicit in protecting Colin Bailey? He must be mistaken.

For a minute, he thought he'd rediscovered his nemesis, alive and well, only a few miles from where he died. Phil Hounsell looked through the office window at the wind-blown trees. He shook his head at the fantastic thought, and as Orion, he set to work on the next batch of cases demanding his attention.

Chapter Four

Friday, 9th January 2015

"Do you have anything new to report, Henry," asked Athena.

Another Friday morning meeting had arrived. Each one came around quicker than the last. Did the pressures of the trials and tribulations that faced Olympus cause that? She felt delicate this morning.

"Hugh Fraser advised me of a potential security problem, " Henry Case replied. "Orion reckons someone's followed him several times this week. His wife has also noticed the possibility that someone is watching the house."

"What action do you propose?" asked Phoenix.

"We escorted him home yesterday evening. A man in a van will call at the house this morning. Anyone who sees that will think it's time for a boiler service. Our man will beef up the locks on doors and windows and install cameras."

"Did he get followed in this morning?" asked Athena.

"Our driver saw nothing suspicious," said Henry, "but we'll monitor the situation."

"The Grid may have switched their focus," said Artemis. "We've made it difficult for them to get to our people here at Larcombe. However, Orion travels here daily, and therefore he's become a person of interest."

Athena glanced at Phoenix.

"That's a good point," she said. "We've warned our agents around the country, but people like my father are vulnerable. The Grid's surveillance would have captured visitors such as him and Orion. They could have become targets."

"I'll send someone to Burnham today," said Henry. "Geoffrey won't know we're there, I promise."

"What if you find he's under surveillance?" asked Athena.

"He won't know they've gone," said Henry with a grin.

"Alastor," said Athena, "what's the latest on this weather?"

"Hurricane-force winds gusted to over one hundred miles per hour," said Alastor, "and left a swathe of damage across the north overnight, bringing down trees and power lines. There was widespread disruption to road and ferry travel, and domestic train services have been suspended in Scotland this morning. Around seventy-five thousand homes lost power in the Highlands. It has been the worst winter storm so far, causing structural damage to buildings."

"Is this storm due to head south?" asked Giles Burke. "It's already been windy here, and the rain keeps falling. So flooding has to be a distinct possibility."

"The winds are forecast to ease over the weekend," said Alastor, "but they'll be back with a vengeance next week."

"Will this impede the missions we have planned?" asked Athena.

"We must allow extra travelling time to negotiate the M4 on Monday," said Rusty, "but it will take more than wind and rain to stop us."

While the morning meeting ground to a close, Hugh Fraser reflected on the conversation he had just had with Ambrosia. He found it impossible to get hold of her yesterday. She wouldn't take his calls.

This morning, she called him to apologise. The meeting in Birmingham had been a disaster. She misjudged the reaction to her exposure regarding the lack of input by Phoenix to the Project's finances.

"I went in too hard," she cried, "I won't make that mistake again. Can you forgive me for ignoring you yesterday?"

"Of course," he replied. "We'll have to put our heads together and devise a better plan."

"I like the sound of that," purred Ambrosia, "can you drive up to see me this weekend?"

"Weather permitting, I'll be there," said Hugh.

In the office next door, Orion studied the clock. He wanted to get away by one o'clock today. He knew Henry Case had arranged for work to be carried out at home but had no idea how long it would take.

Erica had called to tell him she'd let the agent indoors before taking the kids to school. She was going to her job at the building society straight after. So, he needed to get home to see the guy off the premises, check everything was secure and collect the kids from school.

Once he'd done that, the Hounsell family could look forward to a quiet weekend.

Larcombe Manor

At the Cotswold Airport, near Kemble, Les Biggar sat in his office, reading the newspaper. The weather reports weren't encouraging when he checked earlier. He'd flown in worse conditions in combat zones, but today was supposed to be a pleasure trip.

Biggles had more than enough flying hours under his belt to cope with most things the British climate threw at him. The weather was a serious consideration for helicopter performance and safety. It restricted visibility and affected take-off and landing. Things might look great at take-off, then a storm blows up, and matters turn hairy at the other end.

This rain might not affect them today, but it hurt visibility. The wind was always present, so Biggles had to learn how it affected flight and how to work with or counter winds during a trip. Especially if winds swirled around and changed direction as they did today.

As he waited for his passengers, he checked his projected route. First, they wanted to fly over the Roman city of Bath; an aerial view of the Royal Crescent was a must. Next, their destination was Old Sarum airfield, two miles from Salisbury. The last must-see on their wish list was Stonehenge.

Biggles reckoned the flight would take an hour. He was expecting a family of four: two parents and two pre-teen children. The money was better than good; it was great, which swayed him to take the booking. But, unfortunately, Biggles didn't recognise the name. There were so many oligarchs in charge of football clubs that he'd lost track these days.

A maroon limousine moved alongside the helicopter outside the office. The tinted windows prevented him from seeing its passengers. Les Biggar folded his newspaper, collected his kit and walked outside to greet them. A man emerged from the car's passenger door and stood, waiting by the doorway.

"Mr Mikhailov?" asked Biggles.

The man looked in his early forties, with typical Russian features and a solid build. He wore a heavy jacket, jeans and a thick woollen beanie. Biggles had imagined oligarchs always wore expensive suits. Perhaps this guy owned a lower-league football club? Or maybe something got lost in translation over the phone.

Biggles hoped the wife and kids weren't overweight too, or he may have underestimated the load he would be carrying. Why hadn't the kids gotten out and climbed inside? That was his experience with most kids of that age. They couldn't wait to get in the air. Then at least one of them puked in the first ten minutes. He kept reminding himself the money was excellent.

"Are we good to go?" asked Mikhailov.

"I'm happy to fly in this weather if you and your family still wish to travel," said Biggles.

Biggles opened the door and climbed inside the helicopter.

"Let's get everyone seated," he said, "then I'll run through the safety checks, and we can be on our way."

The rear passenger door of the limousine opened, and an older man climbed out. He lumbered towards the doorway. The man mountain looked like trouble.

"Change of plan," said Mikhailov, "Sergei will look after you while I pilot this thing."

Biggles turned. He was staring at the barrel of a GSh-18, the close-combat handgun the Russian Special Forces used in the Nineties. Before he could think of an escape plan, the giant Sergei had pinned his arms behind his back. He found himself face down on the floor of the helicopter.

Mikhailov's driver delivered something from the boot of the limousine. Things looked bad.

"Lie back and enjoy the flight," said Mikhailov. "Don't worry. We're sticking to the flight plan you logged. You are a very experienced flyer, yes? They call you Biggles? I, too, am an experienced pilot. I flew Hips on many missions in the Second Chechen War. We'll be passing over the beautiful Royal Crescent in around thirty minutes. Sergei will help you so that you can take in the view."

Les Biggar couldn't answer. Sergei had stuffed a cloth in his mouth and wrapped duck tape around his face. The fabric from the boot now enclosed his body and feet in a cocoon. The ropes tightened, and he could not budge his arms or legs. Then, as they arrived over Bath, Sergei levered him up so his head was level with the window.

"We are descending now," Mikhailov shouted above the roar of the engines, "we are paying your friends a surprise visit."

Les Biggar recognised the terrain. They were approaching Larcombe Manor.

"My driver is making for Old Sarum. We might have to hang around for thirty minutes until we go home. I'm looking forward to seeing Stonehenge from the air. I'm afraid you won't see it; we've reached your stop."

Sergei opened the door.

Hayden Vincent was leaving the stable block; he fancied an hour's exercise in the pool. Kelly was resting; her pregnancy was progressing well. A deep, throbbing sound rose over the sound of the wind; he looked skywards. It was a helicopter Hayden knew well. He hadn't realised Biggles was due to drop in today.

A cylindrical shape appeared below the helicopter. Something didn't look right; Hayden ran. But, even at this distance, he heard and felt the sickening crunch as the object struck the lawn.

The helicopter rose in the sky and continued on its way. Hayden had his mobile in his hand in a second and sent the emergency call. Not to the emergency services in the city. The call alerted everyone on the Larcombe estate that a major incident had occurred.

As he reached the broken body that had been Les Biggar, Hayden saw a dozen people running across the lawn to join him.

Phil Hounsell left his office at one o'clock as planned. His escort followed him into Bath. Midday traffic in a city without a bypass made it impossible to keep close to his tail. Phil had to guard himself, but he never saw a dark saloon or a van that looked familiar.

He entered the busy road where they had lived for the past four years. There were vehicles parked everywhere, as usual. A hundred yards from home, he checked for cars with drivers still sitting in their vehicles. He saw none. Every car was empty.

Phil edged onto the driveway to park alongside a van. The vehicle carried the logo and details of a firm that purported to provide a comprehensive central heating service at competitive prices. It had to be the man sent by Olympus to increase their security.

Phil wondered how much longer it would take. He looked at his watch. Less than two hours before, he needed to leave again to pick up Shaun and Tracey from school.

"Hello there?" he called out as he entered the house.

He heard someone moving upstairs. As he stood at the foot of the stairs, Phil could see the loft hatch doorway open. This guy was conscientious and prepared to go the extra mile.

Phil carried on walking into the kitchen. An empty mug stood on the draining board. Erica must have given the man a hot drink before she left. That was hours ago. The poor chap must be thirsty by now. As he intended to get himself lunch, he thought he'd at least get the guy a coffee. He heard footsteps on the stairs.

"How's it going," he asked, "are you nearly finished?"

"Just one job left to do," came the reply.

Phil filled the kettle. The accent told him that even Olympus found it easier to use a Polish electrician in these changing times. When he left school, dozens of lads had been off to start apprenticeships as plumbers, bricklayers and electricians with local firms. On second thought, that accent was further east than Poland.

Phil sensed the man right behind him.

The noose fashioned from an electrical cord looped around his throat before he could move. The kettle fell onto the draining board and bounced onto the floor as his hands automatically transferred to his neck. Phil knew he had only seconds to act before lapsing into unconsciousness.

His police training kicked in, and he tried to smash his elbows into his assailant's face and kick back at his shins. Unfortunately, the confined space in the kitchen gave his attacker a vital advantage, and Phil found himself trapped against the floor unit as the pressure on his carotid arteries increased. He knew his brain was deprived of oxygen.

The pressure was relentless, resistance futile.

Phil Hounsell's last conscious thought was of Erica and the children.

His killer continued with the one task he had left to complete.

Afterwards, he wiped clean every surface he had touched, closed the front door behind him and walked one hundred yards up the road to his parked car.

Inside the van on the Hounsell family driveway lay the agent sent by Olympus. His work had been interrupted while he fetched a tool from the van. Someone delivering charity bags door-to-door dropped an envelope onto the doormat.

As he turned to watch him leave, something struck his head. He had slumped against the floor of the van. He was semi-conscious when the hard barrel of the gun touched the back of his head.

As events unfolded at Larcombe Manor, eight-year-old Shaun and six-year-old Tracey reached the end of the final school lesson. The other schoolchildren gathered in the playground, ready to make their way home. Some were collected by their parents and walked towards the nearby housing estates. Others stood in a queue as it inched towards the bus's door, waiting to ferry them further out of town.

Shaun and Tracey followed their usual routine. They watched the pantomime of the school run as flustered mothers stopped in the most inappropriate places to avoid their kids having to walk five yards more than necessary. Several were rushing to get home for that chilled glass of Prosecco that they moved off before their kids had closed the door behind them.

"I hope Dad's not late again today," sighed Tracey.

"At least he doesn't have to work weekends now he's not a policeman or running that security firm," said Shaun, "he can help me with my homework."

The bus moved away, and so did the pedestrians. They

were the only children waiting to be collected. A teacher called out from a classroom doorway.

"Why don't you come inside to wait?" she called. "It's wet and windy out there. Who's picking you up today?"

"My Daddy, Miss," said Tracey, "he's forgotten."

The teacher called the administration office. They found Mrs Hounsell's work phone number and made the call.

"Erica?" called one of her colleagues at the building society, "it's the school. Your children are still waiting for you to collect them."

"Damn," said Erica, thinking Phil must have been late finishing today. Why couldn't he have called her? "Tell them I'm on my way."

Traffic was lighter near the school, but it took Erica fifteen minutes to get out of the city centre. It was four o'clock by the time they arrived home. With Phil's car, plus the van on the driveway, she had to waste more time hunting for a parking space near their house.

Her mood did not improve as she reached the house to find it in darkness. Surely, these security issues didn't need them to be without lighting? How long was this going to take?

The kids crowded the doorstep as she slid her key into the lock.

"Hurry, Mummy," said Tracey, "I need a wee."

Erica opened the door and stepped into the hallway. The silence was deafening. She should hear power tools, conversations, and the television. The place felt deserted. Something wasn't right. She found the light switch for the hall and landing and strode towards the kitchen door.

The children's screams chilled her to the bone. She rushed back to the foot of the stairs.

Tracey had wet herself. She and Shaun stared at their

father's body hanging by the neck from the rafters inside the loft space. Erica dragged the shivering and shaking youngsters into the lounge and closed the door. She somehow kept hold of her phone to dial 999.

The paramedics arrived eight minutes later. There was no rush, thought Erica, as she heard the sirens approach.

She knew her husband was dead the second she saw him.

The first police officers arrived twelve minutes later. Erica and the children clung to one another on a settee. She could hear the paramedics whispering in the hallway. Erica thought they were discussing whether they should have cut down the body. Was it a crime scene? Finally, the senior paramedic tapped on the door and beckoned Erica to join them.

"We're very sorry, Mrs Hounsell," he said, "there was nothing we could do."

Erica nodded that she understood.

The front door opened, and a young female police officer entered.

"I'm the family liaison officer — my name's Charmaigne. I'm sorry for your loss," she said, "are your children through here? My colleague, James, is outside. A detective is right behind us."

Erica opened the door to the lounge. The young PC held her hands out to encourage Shaun and Tracey to join her in the dining room at the far end of the house.

Erica helped them on their way; they were in a daze.

She knew how they felt. Nothing seemed real.

"It's okay, kids. Mummy needs to talk to the policeman," she told them as they shuffled towards the young woman.

A familiar shape had followed the liaison officer through the lounge door.

It was Callum Wood.

Callum had been one of Phil's best friends when he worked at Manvers Street Police Station. He had been the best man at their wedding and was the children's godfather.

"Oh, Callum," cried Erica, "I can't believe this. There's no way it was suicide."

"Tell me what happened here today, Erica," said Callum.

"Phil drove to work this morning. I waited until the workman arrived and then took the kids to school. I was doing a shift at the building society today, so Phil picked them up for me. He finishes at lunchtime on a Friday, and he was due to come home, get himself a sandwich, and then drive to the school. Only he didn't."

"Where's the workman?" asked Callum.

"I've no idea," shrugged Erica, realising the implication. The workman wouldn't have attacked Phil, so who did?

"His van's still on the driveway," said Callum, "what were you having done? Did the boiler pack up or something?"

Erica saw this would be difficult to explain.

"It was nothing to do with the boiler. The guy was installing extra security. Phil thought someone was following him. I thought I saw the same car parked in the street every day this week. Somebody was watching the house. It sounds far-fetched, but that's why the man was here."

Callum ignored the discrepancy between the van's signage and the work carried out for the time being.

"Phil's the last bloke I can imagine taking his own life," said Callum, "and this was no freak accident. Even if this workman and Phil had a violent altercation that resulted in Phil dying, why go to the trouble of staging a suicide? Why not just jump in the van and drive?"

Callum got up and walked to the door.

"James," he shouted, and the young PC entered the hallway, "check the van outside for me. See if we can identify the driver."

Four minutes later, Callum rejoined Erica.

"I've called a forensic team out," said Callum. "I have no idea what Phil got himself into, but there's another dead body in the back of the van."

Erica let that news sink in for a moment, and then she said: -

"The killer disposed of the workman before Phil got home and surprised him while he was in the kitchen."

"What makes you think that?" asked Callum.

"My kettle is on the kitchen floor," said Erica. "It was the only thing I saw when I stepped inside before the kids screamed."

"That's something I wish they hadn't seen," said Callum, "it will be nigh on impossible to forget. For any of you."

"Have you examined the body yet?" asked Erica.

Callum could tell that living with a copper for many years had left its mark. But, unfortunately, he wouldn't get any peace to fathom this puzzle until Erica and the family were off the premises.

"Look, while I was outside with James, I called Debbie," he said, "she's driving here. I think the best thing for you is to return to ours tonight. I'll have people working here for hours. Debbie can go upstairs to fetch everything you and the kids need. I'll talk to you again tomorrow."

Debbie Wood was a PC who worked with Phil in Bath. She was Debbie Turner then, and she and Callum Wood were mad about one another. Not that either of them wanted to admit it. The evening Debbie was shot by Colin

Bailey changed everything. Their son Ronnie was two and a half now, and Debbie had hung up her handcuffs to become a stay-at-home Mum. She loved every second.

Erica knew the kids loved Auntie Debbie and would need all the tender, loving care available over the coming days and weeks. Debbie would be the perfect person to help Erica with that. Debbie would be her number one choice as a shoulder to cry on herself when the shock wore off, and the grief hit her later tonight or tomorrow.

Erica walked to the dining room to tell the kids what was happening.

The liaison officer followed Erica to the doorway when they heard Debbie's distinctive voice in the hallway.

"They haven't spoken a word since I arrived," whispered Charmaigne.

"Don't worry, it's not your fault," said Erica, "Debbie and I will look after them."

Debbie threw her arms around her friend as soon as they met in the hallway.

"Oh, I'm so sorry, darling," said Debbie, on the verge of tears, "let's get you out of here. Could you give me a list of what we need to take? Ronnie's asleep in the car seat at the minute. If this nice PC helps get your two tucked in the back with him and keep them occupied for two minutes, I can grab your things."

Police forensic vehicles pulled up outside the house, and screens were erected around the van as Debbie joined them in the car.

"What the heck's going on, Erica?" whispered Debbie as she drove off towards the other side of Bath.

"I wish I knew," sighed Erica.

Later that evening in London, Tyrone O'Riordan was itching to get out of his apartment. He was looking forward to a night on the town. All he needed was a phone call.

His mother hadn't surprised him with her reaction to his working with the Russians. He knew she disapproved; it was a risk worth taking. Vasiliev had a reputation to uphold. Failure wasn't a word in his vocabulary.

The man was in his late fifties now and had served time in the brutal Russian prison system. The men working with him here in the UK had the same experience. That brotherhood resulted in them becoming known as 'thieves in law'. These were men who adhered to a strict code of conduct.

Such criminals abandoned their families, and they never married. They shunned the establishment and everything it stood for and never cooperated with the authorities. Any money they earned came from crime.

Vasiliev explained to Tyrone that the UK police assumed that if they were Russians, they were the Russian mafia, and their presence threatened every UK institution. His fellow compatriots had been coming here since the break-up of the Soviet Union, and many didn't have documents. They congregate together, work in minimum wage jobs, and are soft targets.

Since he and his colleagues arrived in the past decade, they had been involved in low-level racketeering. They ran protection rackets and extorted money from those whose positions rendered them vulnerable. Over the last five years, they had added more strings to their bow. First, they produced copies of Visa and Mastercard to sell for a few hundred pounds. Then they used their fraudulent copies to go on extravagant spending sprees on luxury items.

"We cannot stop," Vasiliev told Tyrone, "we have to

make a living solely through crime. We lose face, and our power, if we don't keep going."

Tyrone had promised Vasiliev to offer him plenty of work in the future; if he didn't mind getting his hands dirty.

"How dirty?" Vasiliev asked him.

"I need people killed," said Tyrone.

"No problem," replied Vasiliev.

The ringtone on his mobile phone told Tyrone his caller was on the line.

"What news?" he asked.

"A three-for-two offer this week. The bonus one won't cost you a thing. If you get any more work you need doing, call me."

"That's great. Thanks," said Tyrone.

Time for fast-living and fast women. He knew just the place.

Chapter Five

Saturday, 10th January 2015

"I'm sure you understand why I called this meeting," said Athena.

Her senior team surrounded her in the meeting room. They were still coming to terms with the shock of three deaths connected to Olympus in the past eighteen hours.

"We witnessed Les Biggar's death early yesterday afternoon on the lawn outside these windows. The task of explaining the circumstances of his death to his family and the authorities is ongoing. We became suspicious when our agent didn't return from Orion's home. News broke in the evening of two unexplained deaths at a house in the city. The police have cordoned off the area around the property. They haven't released more than a basic statement at present. We're awaiting news on how both men died to be released later today."

Artemis sat with her head bowed. When she and Rusty

learned that her old boss had died, she burst into tears. She recalled their last conversation.

Phil had been surprised to see her as he had no clue where she'd gone after leaving Portishead. So he asked what she was doing.

"I can't tell you," she told him, "but if we meet again, call me Artemis."

"The Huntress, that's good for an ex-copper,"

"Well, you're Orion. We're well-matched."

"We were, weren't we?" said Phil.

"That was a long time ago, Orion," said Artemis, "I've moved on since then. Things are different now."

Now he was dead. The Grid targeted him because he agreed to work at Larcombe Manor. If he had continued to work in that office in the city, this would never have happened. All the other memories came flooding back.

You can leave the past behind in a physical sense and claim things were different, but the memories you shared are never truly buried.

That initial memory opened the floodgates, and she remembered the first day they met in Durham, the crazy drive south to Bath, when they received news of Erica's kidnapping. The night of passion with Phil that she'd always dreamed of in a Bristol hotel after the Kelly family trial ended in disaster.

Rusty had held her close last night as she sobbed her heart out. This morning they hadn't spoken. They were her memories. Since she'd been at Larcombe, there had been other deaths that had been hard to bear. The life she had chosen meant they both had more pain to endure.

Phoenix regretted the deaths of each of the three men. Biggles had been a great pilot, and although never on the payroll, whenever Olympus called him, he did whatever was needed, no questions asked. Phoenix never met the murdered agent, but he wore the uniform; therefore, whoever was responsible must pay.

As for Phil Hounsell, or Orion, there was so much history between them. It was hard to imagine life without him. Their stories had intertwined for twenty-five years.

Hounsell was the only copper to get close to catching him. He'd never know how they both survived that struggle in the River Avon. Before leaving the Gambia and returning to the UK five years ago, the cosmetic surgery had changed his features. Yet, his nemesis had realised who killed Neil Cartwright and so had no doubts who he chased along the towpath that evening.

Weeks later, Phoenix had changed his features again, thanks to the surgeon here at Larcombe. When he saw the policeman at Glastonbury three years later, he thought his time had come. Surely, he would recognise him? Somehow, Phoenix coped with the arrival of Hounsell's colleague, Zara, and the partnership forged with the security services firm Hounsell ran after leaving the police. They even devised a plan to absorb him into the set-up here at Olympus HQ. That move had cost him his life.

Were the three deaths his fault? Could he have handled things differently?

"As hard as we may find it to put yesterday's events aside," said Henry Case, "we must agree on a course of action. We know the helicopter had to land at a nearby airfield. Can we uncover the logged flight plan? How did the killers plan to make their onward journey from the destination point? Did they travel by plane or car? Which section of the Grid did they represent?"

"I can work on that, Henry," said Giles Burke.

"We'll know more of the other incident once we listen

to the police announcement," said Minos, "leave that to Alastor and myself."

"Yesterday morning, we talked of keeping a watch on our people who live off-site," said Rusty. "Things have accelerated. What do we do about your father, Athena?"

"My father will protest, but he's being brought back to Larcombe within the hour. Phoenix and I agreed it was the only way to keep him safe. So he stays here until we can remove the threat or confirm that he's not a target."

"Nothing will prevent us from completing the two missions we have planned for next week," said Phoenix. "As soon as we identify those responsible for yesterday's attacks, we will deal with them."

"Of course," said Artemis, "we mustn't allow the deaths of these three men to deflect us from our missions. Nor should we delay tracking their killers and taking revenge. However, we forget one important thing. How do we prevent the investigations into these deaths from uncovering the true purpose of the Olympus Project? Les Biggar fell out of his helicopter from over five hundred feet, trussed like a mummy in a sarcophagus. How do we stop the police from learning of his death? Is that even possible? We can't bury him in the pet cemetery and hope nobody asks where he's gone."

"The deaths of Orion and the electrician from our engineering section will be even more difficult," agreed Henry Case, "a police investigation is already underway. We can't control how that will proceed. We can only respond to situations as they arise."

"How will Orion's wife, Erica, react?" asked Phoenix.

"She'll be devastated," replied Artemis, "and so will the children. Her parents are both dead. I'm not sure about Phil's parents. Orion, I mean, sorry, it's too close to home. I lodged with Mary Trueman, Erica's mother, when I moved to Bath and took over her house for a while after she died. The kids called me Auntie."

"I think Phoenix meant, will she point the finger our way when the police ask why her husband died?" asked Henry.

"Could you get near to her again?" asked Athena. "It would be normal for someone who was a family friend to get in touch to pass on their condolences. You could discover how much she's told them so far and encourage her to be economical with the truth in future conversations with the police. Anything that got them to switch their attention elsewhere."

"It's a lot to ask," said Rusty.

Artemis looked at her husband. She would do whatever it took to protect him and the others in this room who had become her friends.

"I'll call her," she said.

"Is there anything more we can do this morning?" asked Athena.

"Sarah will go to and from Larcombe to carry out duties in her parish," said Henry, "I could travel with her without revealing why, perhaps? Oh, and Hugh Fraser drove somewhere early this morning."

"No, you should stay here," said Athena, "but put someone on surveillance. I guess the Grid targets people with a more active role in our organisation. That's why my father's staying here will only be temporary."

"Hugh Fraser is a vital asset," said Phoenix, "we should contact him en route to wherever he's gone and warn him. I hope he's armed."

"We both know where he's headed," said Athena, "he could be in the Leeds area if he left early. Hugh may have inadvertently exposed Ambrosia to scrutiny by the Grid. They might wonder how these two came into contact. The implications are too terrible to contemplate."

"Let's not jump too far ahead," said Phoenix. "Hugh Fraser is too experienced as an agent not to take precautions."

Rusty stifled a chuckle.

"Hugh Fraser will spot a tail a mile off, is what I meant," said Phoenix, "and will vary his route as much as possible. If he's arrived safe and sound, he needs to accept his weekend retreat will be under surveillance, and he will have an escort on his trip south."

"I'll ring him," said Giles.

"Let's call a halt to proceedings," said Athena, "we need to get to work. I suggest we meet again at four this afternoon to update matters."

Callum Wood had been in the office by eight this morning; he hadn't slept well last night. He doubted whether Erica had gotten any sleep. Tracey kept waking. Ronnie moved in with Debbie while he snatched the odd hour's rest on the sofa downstairs. Callum left before they gathered downstairs for breakfast. Debbie would handle the emotions better than he would. He didn't want Erica firing questions at him over his cereals and coffee.

The scenes-of-crime people worked late into the night. His boss issued a brief statement to tide them over until noon today. At least, that was what she hoped. Callum wasn't sure they had much to add to what the public learned last night. There were plenty of questions and very few answers.

An ex-copper, working for a charitable organisation, had

been found hanging in the stairwell of his house in Bath. If he'd been under stress at work or in financial difficulties, one might accept he'd taken his own life while the balance of his mind was disturbed — not a chance in Phil's case.

How do we explain the man in the van? No driving licence or identification was found on his person or inside the van. According to the logo, the firm he represented didn't exist as far as anyone could tell. So whoever he worked for needed to look for a new employee. He'd been shot in the back of the head execution-style. Two shots.

Did the workman ever meet the deceased? Erica suggested that he didn't. She let him in and left him working on upgrading security. Why did they need to improve their security? Who could be behind a threat that required such urgent work on their defences?

One thing Callum did know. It wasn't suicide. He believed that before he even arrived at the house. When he steeled himself to take his first look at his good friend's body, he knew he'd been right.

When he arrived earlier, the report on his desk confirmed his thoughts; Phil had been strangled with the electrical cord and then strung up in the loft space to make it appear that he had hanged himself.

Most people who commit suicide by hanging jump from a chair or a ladder. They slowly choke to death. Whether done with rope, belt, or electrical cord, hanging always leaves an inverted V bruise. The coroner found a straight-line injury which marked it as ligature strangulation. It was a murder, without a doubt.

The killer may have believed he could convince people otherwise because the face and neck are congested with blood and become dark red in either method. Callum could confirm it didn't make for pleasant viewing.

Ligature strangulations are almost always homicide. The coroner also noted that the murderer used more force than necessary to kill the victim, causing deep bruises and abrasions around the neck. The victim struggled, which resulted in damage to both the interior and exterior structures of the neck and throat.

"I wish you scarred the bastard, Phil," said Callum, "but there was nothing under the fingernails to give us a clue towards his identity."

James, the young PC on duty outside the crime scene last night, came into the office.

"Morning, sir," he said, "have we made any progress?"

Callum shook his head.

"The hit on the workman was professional, but the cover-up on the strangulation looked amateurish," said James. "Is there any chance the workman was the target and the homeowner disturbed the killer, making him panic?"

"Fancy a switch to CID, James?" asked Callum. "I wouldn't normally rule anything out this early in the game. Do me a favour. You reckon someone went to the trouble of putting the wind-up both the husband and wife to get them to find a firm to keep them safe. I wonder how he made sure the people they contracted to do the work employed that particular workman, let alone send him on that job? He died two hours earlier than the homeowner, too, by the way. Our killer then continued to wait in the house. Why bother? He'd done the deed. I think he would have pissed off, don't you?"

"When you put it like that...."

"Stick to what you're good at, directing traffic," said Callum.

"At the risk of getting my head bitten off," James continued, as he headed out of the office, "Bath doesn't have many contract killers. So, whatever sparked this rush to get tighter security started outside our area."

Callum watched the lad disappear into the corridor towards the canteen.

"Out of the mouths of babes and sucklings," mused Callum. "I need to follow up any connections between what Phil worked on with Hounsell Security Services and organised crime. The answer may lie there."

Callum called home. Debbie answered on the third ring.

"How are things?" asked Callum.

"Lots of tears," replied Debbie, "and lots of questions, as you would expect. Please tell me you've found something to explain this?"

"Nothing yet. Can you ask Erica if Phil kept the records from his HSS company at home? The offices they leased have been empty for a while, but when I drove past last week, I saw a notice on the window announcing a nail bar opening next month."

"Hold on. I'll give Erica a shout."

Callum waited. He looked out of his office window. Across the street lay the building where the new Bath Police HQ was to be situated. The University had snapped up this piece of prime real estate at the back end of last year. He wasn't keen to move. Most of his working life had been here. But maybe, it was time to look at getting out. He didn't sign up for the rubbish they got involved in of late. His time with Phil in the Nineties was his last enjoyable decade.

"Callum, are you there?" Debbie's voice interrupted his reverie.

"Sorry, love," he replied. "What did she say?"

"Boxes containing everything they worked on are in the

garage," said Debbie. "That's everything completed while he worked with Wayne Sangster. Wayne kept the cases open, plus new cases he worked on when he flew solo."

"I wonder where that Sangster Security Services paperwork is now? Wayne and his lady friend died in a fire on Halloween in London. When I saw Phil for a drink before Christmas, he told me he suspected murder. Now, twelve weeks later, he's gone the same way. Maybe there's a link? We've still got people at the house. I'll check the garage for clues. I'll call from there later. Can you ask Erica where Wayne lived in Bath? Let's hope that documentation is still there and not destroyed in the fire." Callum rang off and left the office. Fifteen minutes later, he was inside the garage at Phil's home. It was nothing like the state of their garage at home. Theirs was crammed from floor to ceiling with stuff he and Debbie had accumulated over the years. They had no use for ninety per cent of it but never got around to taking it to the dump. It was a fine art squeezing the car into the small vacant space that remained.

Phil and Erica parked their cars in the driveway. The garage was a workspace attached to the house; one wall held every tool and utensil known to man needed inside or outside the home. On the other wall stood the shelving that contained the items he sought.

Typical of his old friend, every box was stacked in neat piles on the shelving. They were secured with tape and labelled by date. The HSS boxes were at the end nearest the back wall. He opened the latest box. He hoped the clue would emerge from a case they both handled. Callum leaned against the workbench and began to read.

Inside the house, he heard the landline. One of the forensic teams answered. The internal door opened from the utility room, and a head appeared.

"DI Wood, there's a woman on the phone wanting to speak to Mrs Hounsell,"

"Did she give a name?"

"She said she used to live here. The name of Zara Wheeler?"

"Zara? There's a blast from the past. I'll speak to her."

Callum placed the open folder on the top of the box and followed the white-suited techie indoors.

"Callum Wood speaking. Good morning, Zara. It's been a long time."

"Hi, Callum. I wish we were catching up under better circumstances," said Zara. "I wanted to tell Erica how sorry we were to hear of Phil's death. It came as a terrible shock. I understand you can't say much, but do you know how they both died yet? How was this other man connected to Phil? It's so strange."

Callum didn't miss the 'we' in Zara's words. She was an ex-colleague who would be his superior now if she'd stayed in the job. She knew their protocol and understood the detailed forensic analysis around him as they spoke. He also knew he must be careful how much he revealed, despite the friendship they had shared while they worked together.

"Where are you these days?" asked Callum, "where did you move to after Portishead?"

"Not far," replied Zara. "I still live and work on the outskirts of Bath. I got married in November. I met my husband in Bristol weeks before resigning from the police service."

That explained matters, Callum thought. He was surprised he hadn't seen Zara around the city or read a report on the wedding in the paper if she still lived locally. Ah, well, some people like to keep things under the radar.

Zara was always the quiet one. Although Callum had

suspected something going on between her and Phil from the night they arrived in Bath. After they left Manvers Street for the 'big house' at Portishead, he only saw them now and again. If they had an affair, it never found its way back via the rumour mill to their old office.

"I'll tell you as much as I'm able, Zara," said Callum, "for old times' sake, but promise me it won't go any further."

"I promise," she replied, pulling a face at Rusty as he crossed his fingers.

"They were both unlawfully killed. We have no motive for either killing at present. My gut instinct tells me the workman was just in the wrong place at the wrong time. Phil was the target. We'll go through every relevant case he worked on during his police service and the cases he tackled at his security services firm. Someone from his past was following Phil, making him and Erica nervous. They were upgrading their security. The killer went ahead with the contract regardless of who he found in the home. Thank goodness Erica was at work yesterday, or the kids might have lost both parents."

"Where are they now?" asked Zara.

"At home with Debbie," said Callum, "did you know we had a son, Ronnie? He's two now."

"Yes, I heard. It's wonderful, Callum," replied Zara. "You could have four by now if you two hadn't ignored how you felt for so long. Is it alright to give me your home number so I can talk to Erica? You've got my mobile number now, so please ring me when you find out when the funeral is. I very much want to attend. I owe it to Phil, and if you can update me on how things are progressing without getting rapped over the knuckles, I'd appreciate it."

Callum gave her his home number and promised to

keep in touch. He understood the nosy nature of ex-coppers; they never gave you a moment's peace. It had been the same with Phil and Wayne. They never stopped asking for details that shouldn't concern them anymore. Maybe, somewhere in those boxes was evidence that they asked the wrong people for more information about something they shouldn't, which cost them their lives?

At Larcombe Manor, the phone call ended; Artemis sat opposite her husband, Rusty.

"You played that well," said Rusty.

"Easy to show concern for Phil and his family," she replied, "that was genuine. I've opened the door to allow us to keep in touch with the police investigation. Now, I need to talk to Erica."

"I'll leave you to it, darling," said Rusty. "Their search for a motive in his past offers our best chance of keeping Olympus out of the frame."

"It would help our cause if the fire destroyed those most recent records," said Artemis,

"The police might believe getting rid of the evidence in a fire, along with one of the investigators, was deliberate, you mean?

"Yes," said Artemis, "but it still feels wrong to be sidelining the official investigation. I feel responsible for discovering who killed Phil."

"Olympus will continue to search for who killed Orion and our other agent," said Rusty. "Does it matter who gets justice for them?"

Rusty left his wife alone in their apartment. He needed to find Phoenix; the weekend was slipping through their fingers. The time left to plan for next week's missions grew shorter by the hour. If they worked in the orangery for two hours before meeting with Athena again, at least they could make a start.

In the ice-house, Giles pieced together the last movements of Les Biggar and his helicopter.

Alastor and Minos awaited the scheduled news conference from the steps outside Manvers House police station in the administration offices.

At Burnham-on-Sea, Geoffrey Fox packed a suitcase. He was doing it under sufferance. This Project business was far more dangerous than a charitable organisation had any right to be. He had always suspected the charity was a façade for what happened at the Manor.

Geoffrey was no fool. His only daughter went to University, worked at Random House publishers, and then joined MI5. After experiencing life at the sharp end, she threw in her lot with a charity helping veterans. Every time he and Grace visited, a veil of secrecy was apparent. Nobody goes back to sparkling wine once you've tasted grand cru champagne.

On social occasions, there were one hundred people present. Geoffrey knew how many slept in the main building. He could hazard a guess at how many the stable block held. Why did they need extensive leisure facilities in the converted cottages at the far end of the estate for that number of people?

There must be accommodation somewhere else. Underground, perhaps? Whatever happened in the past forty-eight hours must have been serious. Annabelle was adamant he stayed at Larcombe until further notice. The goons hovering over him as he gathered his things were stone-faced. He was leaving his bungalow, whatever happened.

Geoffrey's only regret was that Grace was missing this excitement.

Meanwhile, two people were spending their day very much indoors over two hundred miles north of Burnham. Hugh Fraser had arrived at Piya Adani's home at ten o'clock. When she answered his knock, Ambrosia hid behind the door and pulled him inside. She was naked.

"I've been waiting for this since we talked yesterday," she said. She fetched the champagne bucket from the kitchen, and they went upstairs. Two bottles were now empty. Ambrosia's head rested on his chest. The steady rhythm of her breathing told him she was asleep. He should rest, too, because when she awoke, he would be required to satisfy her again. He sighed. If only she knew. Piya was upset by his news about a colleague's death, but she was unaware of what he'd experienced himself trying to get here today.

Hugh had followed his usual route north via the M5 and M1. He spotted the car in front and the one following him before travelling ten miles on the M5. The vehicles stayed with him until he joined the M1. Then, with his senses on high alert, Hugh searched for the next cars to pick up the baton.

His unwanted escort was an organised group. They were looking for more blood. Hugh had been among the first to reach Les Biggar's body yesterday afternoon. He had gone to bed early last night despite his death. Hugh was determined not to let the Grid thwart his plans.

It was easy to lose the lead car. He hadn't been followed on any of his earlier trips to see Ambrosia, so they couldn't know his exact destination. He stayed in the outside lane until the last possible second. Then, with the lead car committed to passing Junction 39 and the exit to Wakefield, Hugh swerved to the inside lane and onto the exit road.

The driver in the second car almost collided with a car

transporter as he followed suit. But, again, Hugh used his advanced driving skills to good effect. Rusty Scott would have approved of how Hugh led the pursuing car a merry dance through the side streets. Ten minutes later, he was off on the last ten miles of the journey to Leeds with nobody in his rear-view mirror.

Hugh parked the car a mile from Ambrosia's house and walked the rest, keeping watch the whole way. If his pursuers caught up with him again, he would phone Ambrosia to say he would be late. Then, he would use the silenced pistol he brought to eliminate whoever drove the car.

Ambrosia stirred.

"Getting your head down for five minutes, darling?" he asked, stroking her back.

"Your word is my command, master," purred Ambrosia.

Hugh groaned. He would have to tell her the Grid's agents were out to kill him earlier. He needed to protect Ambrosia's anonymity by leaving the house under cover of darkness. It would be wise to take an alternative route back to Larcombe. Hugh heard the 'ping' of a message arriving on his mobile phone, but it had to wait. It took her less than five minutes to get his attention.

Chapter Six

It was four o'clock in the afternoon. Athena was eager to begin the meeting. Phoenix and Rusty were on their way from the orangery. Alastor and Minos were in the room when she arrived. Voices on the stairs showed Giles, Henry, and Artemis were not far behind her.

Athena had tried to soothe her father when he arrived from Burnham an hour ago. Geoffrey couldn't have his old room back, but the guest room on the opposite side of the corridor from his daughter's apartment was acceptable. He was closer to his granddaughter.

"I'm sorry to uproot you so soon after you moved in, Daddy," she told him. "We need to keep you close until the danger's passed."

"If I learned why things could become dangerous around here, it would help me understand the haste to wrap me in cotton wool," he replied.

"The less you know, the better," she muttered.

Athena then ushered him through to their lounge, where Maria Elena looked after Hope. She left the three of them playing, so she could concentrate on Olympus' problems.

The meeting room filled. Everyone was ready.

"Giles?" Athena asked, "can you begin, please?"

"I located the flight plan logged by Les Biggar. He made for Old Sarum, near Salisbury, from his home base near Kemble. Images I sourced via the webcam at the Cotswold airport showed a large maroon limousine parked next to the helicopter before take-off. I've tried to enhance the images, but reading the registration is impossible. There was nothing useful from Old Sarum. I assumed the car travelled to collect the men who flew with Biggles in the helicopter. So, an agent in the ice-house is searching for the car on the roads between Kemble and Salisbury. If he can trace it, he can capture the number plate. His next task will be to see where it went after it left Old Sarum. Progress is slow but steady."

"Did the news conference produce anything new?" Athena asked Minos.

"The Assistant Chief Constable informed the media that one of the dead men was retired DCI Phil Hounsell, who had previously worked at Manvers Street. The ACC said he had many friends who still worked there and at the headquarters in Portishead. Mr Hounsell left a wife and two children. The identity of the second man was as yet unknown. He was white, six-foot-one-inches tall, weighed around thirteen stones, and aged between thirty and thirty-five. He had fair hair, cut short. No rings, tattoos or other distinguishing marks."

"That vague description won't help them much," said Giles. "Which gives us a window to erase his links to Olympus."

"One reporter asked whether they found photo ID,"

continued Minos, "a driving licence, a card for the homeowner to verify his identity. The ACC said there was nothing whatsoever. The reporters' follow-up questions caused a few people to turn green. Why didn't the police create an Identikit photo of the man to assist in the search for this man's relatives? The ACC merely said it wouldn't be possible in this instance."

"Did she give further details on how the men died?" asked Rusty. "Apart from giving a huge hint, our man had half his face blown away."

"The ACC skirted around those details. Instead, their focus centred on motive. Officers review cases handled by the former DCI involving organised crime to see whether that lay behind the killings."

"I've sown the seeds to lead them to the fire at the Wishing Well café," added Artemis. "The police will be encouraged to look closer at who might have wanted both Wayne Sangster and Phil Hounsell dead. Then, while they are following those wild geese, we can find the killers."

"Find and eliminate them," said Phoenix, "and continue to deflect attention from the connections between their targets and Larcombe."

"I'm waiting to learn when Orion's funeral is," said Artemis, "I wish to attend if that's acceptable."

"I'll come with you," said Athena, "to represent the charity. That would make sense to his widow and the police. Moreover, your presence is easily accounted for, which enables us to avoid the need to reveal that you work here at Olympus."

"Good thinking," said Phoenix. He paused as he thought of the other bodies that required burial.

"Our agent's body may not get released for days. Giles,

can you cobble together a plausible history for him? Good enough to satisfy the authorities?"

"I'll try, Phoenix," replied Giles.

"What about Les Biggar," asked Henry.

"Can we trace his family?" asked Athena.

"Les Biggar was a loner," said Phoenix, "it might take too long. Our time frame is narrow."

"Agreed, I suggest we retrieve the helicopter from Old Sarum today," said Henry. "If it's left unattended, the people there will become suspicious. They would have expected Biggar to fly straight back. Once it's in the hangar at Kemble, we can plan how to dispose of the helicopter and the body."

"The Irish Sea is plenty big enough to lose a chopper," said Rusty. "With the stormy winds we've been experiencing, it wouldn't be difficult to believe he could have suffered a tragic accident."

"That would need a lot of planning," said Phoenix, "but it could work. It sounds right up Hugh Fraser's street. Did you contact him, Giles?"

"I didn't talk to him, but GPS puts his mobile phone in the Leeds area. So we can assume he arrived safely. When I get back to the ice-house, I'll try him again. I'll persuade him to have an escort on his return journey."

"That covers everything until Monday morning," said Athena, "the missions will be underway before dawn. The events of the past twenty-four hours have been tragic, but they cannot prevent us from continuing to attack the Grid wherever possible."

"I cannot believe Sarah is a target," said Henry, "but I shall stick close by her during her good works on the parish today and tomorrow. Don't worry. I'll remember to wear loose-fitting clothing to hide my shoulder holster. I don't want to frighten the parishioners."

"Let's get back to the orangery then, Rusty," said Phoenix. "The sooner we finish these plans, the sooner we can get back to our loved ones."

Athena brought the emergency meeting to a close. Time to get back to Hope and her father.

"You understand I can't stay here indefinitely, Annabelle?" said her father. "I have made arrangements for next weekend."

Athena sighed. Why were parents so tricky sometimes?

"Alright, we'll get you home on Friday if nothing major has happened, but I reserve the right to come to stay if I think you need company."

"Agreed," said Geoffrey.

Callum Wood was hours away from getting back to his loved ones. He had spent several hours working through the boxes in Phil's garage. He found dozens of criminals Phil helped put away during his time at Portishead. Whether any of them were violent enough to kill him was another matter.

Those that threatened a revenge attack, or yelled abuse from the dock, were often career criminals whose offences were minor. Burglars, car thieves, and criminals who were nuisances kept re-offending. No matter how many times they got caught. None had the bottle required to kill the workman in that fashion. None seemed the type to strangle a man either.

The more he thought, Callum reckoned delving into decades of Phil's police history would be a waste of his time. He could get one of his young DCs out here tomorrow. It was better for them to do something futile than get under his feet in the office.

Callum drove across Bath to Wayne Sangster's last known address. He remembered Wayne as a PC. He was amiable enough, didn't push himself to get promoted, and never let anyone down. Callum tried to recall whether Wayne was ever married. When he reached the house, it looked respectable and smart. The garden looked tidy, and the bins weren't overflowing. The house stood out like a white swan in a pond full of grubby ducks.

"Hello, my lovely," said the old lady as she opened the door, "and what might you be after?"

"Are you Mrs Sangster, Wayne's mother?" asked Callum. He showed her his warrant card.

"That's right, Inspector Wood," she sighed, "but he died."

"Everyone was sorry to hear the news," said Callum. "Wayne was popular at the station. I understand he worked at Hounsell Security Services after he left the police, is that right?"

"Wayne loved that job," she replied, "come on inside, my lovely. It's too cold for me to stand on the doorstep."

Mrs Sangster wandered into her front room; Callum followed. The inside was as pristine as the outside. Many little ornaments that must take her hours to dust each week sat on every spare shelf or window sill.

"What a lovely home," said Callum. "Did Wayne have a place of his own, or did he still live with you?

"My boy came and went, Inspector. Wayne joined the RAF straight from school and came back here until he found another job. He moved to Bristol while he worked out at Cribb's Causeway. He rented a flat in Filton. Then, after his Dad passed, he returned to stay, so I wasn't alone."

"Wayne never married then?"

"I always thought him a confirmed bachelor until he came home from working in London last April. He met a lady up there and never stopped talking about her. Then, when Mr Hounsell closed the business, our Wayne went into security independently. He moved in with this Bridie Carragher soon after. I had high hopes of buying a hat for the wedding. But, in the end, I needed a new black coat for the funeral. It was so sad. The police said the fire was deliberate. Can you credit it?"

Callum could see the old lady was on the verge of tears.

"Shall I make us a cup of tea?" he asked, moving to the door to the kitchen. If he had a pound for the number of houses with this layout in the city, he could have retired by now. Hundreds got built when the Admiralty had a significant presence in Bath, but those days had gone, and the estates were on a downward spiral.

Callum found everything he needed within minutes. Then, as she heard the kettle boil, Mrs Sangster called out to him.

"There are Hobnobs in a tin in the cupboard, my lovely."

"Already found them," said Callum, "I am a detective, remember."

The old lady looked more composed when Callum returned with the loaded tray.

"You've done this before," she said with her first smile. "I suppose you're married? Do you have kids?"

"Just the one. We have a boy of two," replied Callum. "I found my soul mate when I was forty, similar to Wayne. When he worked for himself, I don't suppose he left any of his business correspondence here?"

"Oh no, dear," said Wayne's mother, shaking her head,

"I didn't want the place cluttered up with his rubbish. I told him if he moved to London, he should clear everything out. It would save time when I was dead and gone. Now there's nobody to have this when I go. What do you think, my lovely? Should I leave everything to the rescue centre at Claverton Down?"

Callum looked again at the ornaments. Figurines of cats and dogs. Fair enough, her house contents wouldn't fetch more than a few hundred pounds, but the money would go to a deserving home.

Time to leave; apart from a decent cuppa and three biscuits, he hadn't learned much from this visit. Any records that might have helped may have perished in the fire along with Wayne and Bridie.

Mrs Sangster saw him to the door. As he pulled away from the kerb, he saw her waving goodbye. Of course, he waved back. So few people did that when a policeman came to call. Callum wondered how many people ever called on Mrs Sangster nowadays. He thought he might ask Debbie whether she fancied a trip up here next Sunday afternoon with Ronnie. They could pop into a shop on the way over to buy a packet of Hobnobs.

In his penthouse apartment, Tyrone O'Riordan opened one eye. He wondered if he should risk the other eye yet. What a night last night. He had no idea what time he returned home. He vaguely recalled winning an awful lot of money in the casino. Thirty thousand? Or forty thousand?

Tyrone remembered he had attracted the attention of two blonde escorts, who did everything they could to convince him to quit while he was ahead. Finally, they promised him he'd get better value for money by inviting them back to his place.

Tyrone wavered between a night of debauchery and pursuing that winning streak. The gambler in him won. Not for the first time in recent months. As he lay there with a thumping headache, he wondered if he had a problem. Not a chance. He'd continued to win, hadn't he? He doubted they were blondes, anyway.

There was a noise from the bathroom. Tyrone opened both eyes and sat up in bed. God, that hurt. The bathroom door opened, and a young girl staggered out. She was still drunk. When did that happen? Tyrone couldn't remember her name. What was her name? He couldn't even remember ever laying eyes on her.

"What time is it?" she asked.

Tyrone thought her slurred speech was from the effects of drinks, drugs, or both. She wasn't English either. Tyrone looked at the clock on the wall above the girl's head. It was a few minutes after five o'clock in the evening. He groaned. The girl looked behind her.

"My father will kill me," she said and flopped on the bed beside him.

Tyrone could smell the vomit on his shirt. That explained the noise from the bathroom. How she came to be wearing the shirt he wore last night was something else altogether.

"I need the bathroom," he said, scrabbling on the floor for his Calvin Klein boxers.

The girl didn't move. Tyrone made it to the bathroom and locked the door. His brain wasn't in the mood to fathom out what he'd done. The top of the low-level cistern showed the tell-tale signs of where she'd snorted a line of cocaine. He lifted the toilet seat. The cow hadn't flushed away the contents of her stomach. Terrific. As he urinated, he tried to unscramble the events of the past twelve hours. Maybe a shower would help?

Tyrone stood under the ice-cold water for as long as he could stand. He was positive he'd left the casino before four o'clock. Where did he go next? Did an Uber cab take him to another club? He could check his phone. Tyrone had a dim memory of getting into the back of a car. Did someone he knew offer him a lift home? Why couldn't he remember?

He heard a knock on the bathroom door. Tyrone didn't want that girl puking on his bedroom carpet. He unlocked the door.

"Good afternoon," said Leonid Vasiliev.

The young girl lay on the bed naked. She no longer appeared wasted. She looked quite well.

Tyrone had a sinking feeling. What the hell was Vasiliev doing here? How did he get in? Was it the Russian's face that had been a dim memory from this morning?

"Don't worry, my friend," said Vasiliev, making himself at home, lounging on one of Tyrone's leather settees. "Your memory will return in time. Meet Tara, by the way."

"I never touched your daughter," said Tyrone. "I don't remember a thing after I left the casino."

"Don't be ridiculous," snorted Vasiliev, "Tara is not my daughter. We 'thieves in law' do not marry. We do not form relationships that would hinder our sole purpose in life - to separate people from their money. Tara is an actress. I waited outside the casino until you finished playing your silly games. You were very drunk. It was easy to get you to join me in my car. We drank vodka during the short trip back here. Well, I drank vodka. You drank vodka with a kick. You slept like a baby while we filmed Tara on top of you on the bed."

Tyrone searched the room for signs of a camera but found nothing. Finally, Tara retrieved a tablet from under a pillow, switched it on and showed Tyrone the video.

Tyrone wanted to wipe the smirk off the little cow's face.

"Do you see why Tara is in such demand?" asked Vasiliev, "she is nineteen years old next month, but she has a gift. She looks so much younger. Her fans believe Tara is fourteen, maybe fifteen years old, which excites them. The co-stars in the films she features in are wide awake, of course, and more energetic than you, but our cameraman is clever. He left no clue that this was anything but genuine, wouldn't you agree?"

"I thought we had an arrangement," snapped Tyrone, "you followed people and killed them when I asked. You got paid well for your work. Blackmailing me is not a good career move."

"My people followed the third man yesterday morning on a long journey. He was not like the others. They were easy targets. This one was a professional. He fooled our drivers and escaped. We don't know where he stayed last night, but we have found the car. I decided it was too risky. It was a quick way to earn one hundred thousand pounds. If we follow him and kill him before he reaches Bath, we only get twenty thousand. If he knew we followed him, we could be trapped. My men might get killed. No, this way is better."

Tyrone racked his brain, thinking of how to extricate himself from this mess. Did he have enough money in the safe?

Was Vasiliev armed? He hadn't seen a weapon yet.

"Tara found the money you won at the casino," smiled Vasiliev. "I can see the wheels of your brain turning. You need to find another sixty thousand to make this go away. It's only business, nothing personal. I thought if I joined your war, it would be fun, but it's boring for me now."

Vasiliev stood and pulled out a snub-nosed automatic. He waved it at Tyrone.

"Hurry, I must get Tara home soon. She will need her beauty sleep before a day's filming tomorrow. Open your wall safe. Tara found it while you slept off the effects of the drink and the drugs."

Tyrone approached the safe. He had to act casual. As Tyrone punched in the security code, he heard the lift return to the ground floor. He wondered if it signalled his salvation or the final nail in his coffin.

Vasiliev ordered Tara to run to the monitor by the lift door.

"Who is it?" he yelled.

Tyrone now had the safe door open. He picked up a stack of notes and threw them on the table beside him. "That's twenty thousand," he said.

"It's a woman," said Tara, "it could be his mother."

"Quicker," Vasiliev yelled at Tyrone, "just hand it over."

The gangster darted forward to grab the extra cash Tyrone dropped onto the table.

The lift door slid open. Tyrone's mother, Colleen, entered.

Tara ran back to the centre of the room in fright.

Colleen had that effect on people when she was angry.

Tyrone had both hands inside the safe now. His hands found what he sought — his trusty throwing knives.

"What the hell's going on?" shouted Colleen and stood with her hands on her hips.

Vasiliev raised the gun and pointed it at her.

Tyrone's aim was true; the first knife pierced the gangster's throat. The second buried itself in the heart of the young porn actress. Their bodies hit the floor within seconds of one another.

"I'm waiting," shouted Colleen.

"Calm yourself, mother," said Tyrone, "everything's under control."

"Bloody well looks like it. I told you not to trust these Russian bastards. Who's the naked tart, anyway? She doesn't look old enough to have left school. I thought you knew better than that, Tyrone. Tommy cheated on me more than once, but they were always legal."

Tyrone's headache returned with a vengeance. Earache from his mother was something he wouldn't miss. His breathing had slowed, though, and the cold sweat on his brow stopped dripping into his eyes. Finally, Tyrone slumped onto the settee.

"Vasiliev tried to blackmail me," he said as his mother stepped over the gangster's body to sit opposite him.

"With the girl?" asked Colleen. Tyrone nodded.

"Vasiliev gave me a lift home this morning. He spiked my drinks and then brought in the girl and a cameraman. She was older than she looked, but it would finish me if the film got onto the internet. He wanted a hundred grand. I played for time until I found my knives."

"This isn't the first time we've needed to have this place cleaned by professionals," said Colleen looking at the bloody mess, "people will talk. Why couldn't this Vasiliev stick to the tidying-up work we put his way? Didn't that pay well enough?"

"Vasiliev dealt with the helicopter pilot and the ex-copper," said Tyrone, "but things got harder when he followed one of the newer arrivals at Larcombe Manor. The bloke was too good not to spot the cars tailing him, so

Vasiliev backed out. He worried they might have spooked the people at Larcombe enough to have someone ride shotgun when he drove south."

"Leave the foreigners out of it. I told you they were trouble."

"Vasiliev reckoned he had the car under surveillance in Leeds. We could check his phone?"

"OK, find out where the car's parked. Put a bounty on this bloke's head. He's not to get back to Larcombe," said Colleen. "No matter how many people we lose. You wanted to send a message. His death will let them know we mean business."

Tyrone called for a crew to remove the dead bodies. Two more long-term visitors for Hackney Marshes.

Colleen checked Vasiliev's jacket for his mobile phone. She found the SMS message notifying him where their target parked the car.

"I'll put the money back in the safe, along with this phone," she told Tyrone. "You ought not to have so much cash lying around, son. It's too tempting for these petty criminals. I'll let you fetch your knives. I don't want to get blood over these Louboutin shoes. They cost me a bundle."

"Someone's on the way for the removals, Mum," Tyrone replied. "I'll get the cleaners here first thing in the morning for the rest. I'll sleep at yours tonight if that's okay?"

"I suppose it will have to be," shrugged Colleen. "Make sure you make the price on that agent's head attractive, won't you?"

"Yes, mother, don't worry," said Tyrone.

"I always worry, just as I did with your father. I had to clean up his mess too."

Sunday, 11th January 2018

Hugh Fraser showered and dressed by eight o'clock.

"Are you sure you have to drive back so soon," said Ambrosia.

"Better safe than sorry," replied Hugh.

He had read Giles's text message late last night. The news from Larcombe Manor was grim. The deaths of Orion and the other agent came as a great shock. He had been sleeping when that news broke and left before anyone in the stable block could speak to him. Hugh realised the seriousness of the situation.

"We must protect your identity," he said to Ambrosia. "I'll slip away over the back wall and follow a zig-zag route through the streets until I reach my car. The team was in position because they wanted to check the car hadn't been booby-trapped. If the coast is clear, my escort will drive back with me. Then, three cars, using the tactical pursuit and containment principle, will shepherd me along the motorway."

"Please, take care," pleaded Ambrosia.

"Don't worry. The team know what they're doing."

They kissed, and Hugh headed for the wall at the end of the garden. Ambrosia saw him clamber over the wall and drop from sight on the other side. Hugh was in the field that backed onto the property. It would be five minutes before he reached the road and a further fifteen minutes before setting eyes on his car. Ambrosia sat in her kitchen and waited for the news that Hugh had reached home without incident. Nothing could have persuaded her to do otherwise.

The escort lead driver was Andy Walters, the leading man in the team that shadowed the prison transport vehicle when Tommy O'Riordan launched his fatal prison break. It was a dangerous and challenging assignment, so Olympus chose their best operator.

The first task was complete; nobody had been near Hugh's car. It was as he'd left it. Andy was in contact with the drivers of the other two cars; they cruised the local streets hunting for potential pursuit vehicles. Street by street, they informed Andy there were no suspicious signs.

"Our passenger has arrived," said Andy as he spotted Hugh Fraser at the end of the street. Hugh made his way forward, looking around him until he got to the car. Andy Walters edged alongside and gave Hugh the thumbs-up. The agent was soon inside the car and pulled away from the kerb, ready to follow Andy.

Two team members joined them, and the convoy headed for the motorway.

The nervous wait for news in Leeds and at Larcombe had begun.

Chapter Seven

In the orangery, Phoenix and Rusty discussed the first of the week's missions. Their target was the chop shop operating out of Ilford that had employed Miguel Fernando. The proximity of the North Circular Road had proved a significant benefit in delivering their vehicles to the garage and transporting the parts to their clients.

Chop shops operate in the criminal underground all over the world. They made lots of money through the suffering of others. They stole any vehicle that could be disassembled and resold. That included cars, trucks, SUVs, and motorcycles. In a city the size of London, where commuting by bicycle was commonplace, even bicycle chop shops had appeared. The gang in Ilford favoured the higher end of the market. They did dismantle them, but occasionally, they rushed the whole package along the North Circular Road to a waiting container park. From there, they disappeared within days to Africa and the Far East.

"These thieves go after parts that have a high resale value and are easy to remove," said Phoenix, "wheels, entertainment systems, catalytic converters and airbags. To avoid detection, they disassemble a car within hours of stealing it. That way, the owner and the police never find it. Since they are running an illegal business, the people operating chop shops try to be as inconspicuous as possible. They hide them away in residential garages and small commercial spaces that do not draw attention. Chop shops rarely work independently. They are part of large criminal organisations."

"It makes sense," said Rusty, "a dismantled vehicle is much harder to identify than one still intact. Also, selling individual parts brings a much higher profit. That makes it a win-win for criminals who want to steal your car and make as much money from it as possible. Did you ever watch the film Gone in Sixty Seconds?"

Phoenix stared at his friend.

"I can't remember the last time I visited the cinema," he said.

"You don't need to go to the cinema. What about on TV?"

"If a programme lasts over thirty minutes, I fall asleep," said Phoenix, "I get bored. That's why I was never interested in sports. It took too long. What's this film got to do with this, anyway?"

"I'm reading this report from Alastor," said Rusty, sliding the folder across the table for Phoenix to study. "There's been a spate of thefts in London where criminals have driven cars away from homes without taking the owners' keys. Gangs exploit weaknesses in technology that allow a car to be opened without touching a key and started by a simple push of a button. They source gadgets online which amplify signals between the car and new-generation key fobs to trick the vehicle into thinking the owner is nearby. When the car receives the signal, it unlocks, even though the key fob may be inside the owner's home."

"Where there's a will, there's a way," said Phoenix. "These bits of kit cost thousands, which suggests organised criminals bought them and quickly recouped the cost. Your average car thief couldn't afford it."

"The technology for keyless entry was only for high-end vehicles," said Rusty. "But it will become more common as it spreads across different ranges and makes of vehicle."

"I wondered why they had a proportion shipped abroad," said Phoenix, "when they can make so much on the parts. The top-of-the-range models are difficult to restart once they're out of the owner's key fob range. I don't know what they do with them once they arrive at their destination. I don't care that much. It's just another example of how criminals adapt their methods to technological advances. As soon as the banks, the computer people, or the car manufacturers tell us they've designed an impregnable security system, the criminals find a way to beat it."

"It makes you wonder, doesn't it?" said Rusty. "Why don't they advertise for the criminals who can bypass the new levels of security to work for them? They could command a high enough salary to avoid choosing a life of crime then."

"If only life was that simple," said Phoenix. "Although it's given me an idea. We never target the low-level thugs who steal the cars or drive the transporters to the container ports. We always cut the head off the snake. In the future, we'll identify the hacker, forger, or technical wizard these gangs utilise. If we neutralise them, it will have a longer impact on the gang's operation. We might get a knock-on impact among these smart cookies you mentioned. If people in the same line of business are disappearing for good, they might think it's time to seek alternative employment."

"What time do we leave in the morning?" asked Rusty.

"Six o'clock," replied Phoenix. "I've added two teams from east London. One at the garage and the other on the North Circular Road."

"We had better get over to the meeting room," said Rusty. "Athena will be waiting. I look forward to a lie-in on Sunday mornings. This Grid nonsense is ruining my beauty sleep."

The two friends reached the main building to see the others already halfway up the stairs.

"Everything ready for tomorrow?" asked Henry Case.

"We don't anticipate any problems," said Rusty.

"What he means is, I've anticipated any problems we're likely to face," said Phoenix.

The third emergency meeting of the weekend was soon underway.

"We traced the maroon limousine on the A303 late on Friday afternoon," said Giles Burke. "it had left Old Sarum and headed east towards London. We identified the registration number. The vehicle belongs to Leonid Vasiliev, a Russian gangster who arrived in the UK ten years ago. He's dabbled with low-level racketeering, credit card fraud and extortion since he arrived on our shores. Most of the people he fleeced were fellow countrymen and women. He has a dozen known associates, but none have ever served time in jail."

"Was this Vasiliev known to be connected to the Grid?" asked Henry, "the name isn't familiar. If his activities focused on his people, I suppose he was under our radar?"

"Our paths hadn't crossed," said Phoenix. "I suspect this level of violence is common if we dig deeper into the murky world in which he operates. Many of his victims are here illegally, so the crimes never get reported. Any missing bodies don't attract attention from the authorities."

"Do we have an address for Vasiliev?" asked Athena. "Can we pinpoint the addresses of these twelve colleagues of his?"

"That's in hand, Athena," said Giles, "I'll pass the details to Phoenix. Then, he can take the appropriate action whenever he's ready."

"Anything else from the ice-house?" asked Athena.

"Hugh Fraser is on his way back from Leeds with Andy Walters as his escort," said Giles. "They should have reached the M5 by now."

"I didn't think we should delay formalising a plan to handle the helicopter issue," said Artemis, "nor Les Biggar's body. Time is short, and who knows what might happen."

"You're right," said Athena. "We can't be sure of anything at present. So, what's the plan?"

"The helicopter is being collected from Old Sarum this morning. It will return to the Cotswold Airfield. Fintan O'Sullivan is flying into Bristol later today. I found a qualified pilot among Hugh Fraser's Irregulars. Sandy Nesbitt was one of the five newbies you planned to use on the Northamptonshire mission, Phoenix. We should get her back to you within a day or two, so you can continue to include her in your plans."

"I like Fintan," said Phoenix, "he was great when we worked together in Dublin. An odd-looking bloke with one brown eye and one green eye. You wouldn't have said his face was ever his fortune, but women found him devilishly handsome. They fell at his feet."

"Perhaps his face wasn't his most attractive feature," said Artemis. "Let's hope this Sandy concentrates on her flying skills. The plan is for Fintan to collect Les Biggar's body from Larcombe, then drive to Kemble, where he'll meet up with Sandy Nesbitt. They then fly to Wexford, near Fintan's cottage. He's hired a fishing boat out of Kilmore Quay."

"Say no more," said Phoenix, "I've no concerns over that as a plan. Fintan used the same people to get me back from Ireland last Spring. I take it Biggles will be buried at sea?"

"Indeed," said Artemis. "The helicopter will suffer the same fate as the cars you're dealing with tomorrow. After it's dismantled, any valuable parts we can salvage will find their way across the Republic to be used by Olympus agents. The scrap materials will be recycled. Not at the same site, of course. Fintan has plenty of options. He guarantees it will disappear without a trace."

"What about the sudden departure of the flying business from the Cotswold Airfield?" asked Henry. "Will Fintan explain that to the people there?"

"I've sent them a letter from Les Biggar," said Giles, "confirming he had discontinued flights from the airfield due to the economic climate. He apologised for the short notice. It should be enough to keep them from making waves."

"Well done," said Athena, "but it's such a shame I'm congratulating you on a successful outcome to a tragic event. Biggles died because of the occasional flights he undertook for Olympus."

"This Vasiliev and his colleague will pay for their part in his death," said Phoenix.

"One final thing I can pass on this morning," added Artemis. "Erica Hounsell told me last evening that the funeral service will be at noon on Monday, the nineteenth, at Bath Abbey. There will be a significant police presence among the mourners. The family will then move to Haycombe crematorium for a private ceremony."

"Thank you, Artemis," said Athena, "we will travel to the Abbey separately as agreed."

"All roads lead to Ilford in the morning," said Rusty, "wish us luck."

"I know I need to take a break from this," said Athena. "I'm sure you could use a few hours of rest. I suggest we call it quits for today."

Nobody argued as they left the room. The past forty-eight hours had taken their toll. Nine o'clock tomorrow morning would come around soon enough. Another hectic week lay ahead.

"I'm off to church to meet up with Sarah as soon as I leave here," said Henry. "I'll offer a prayer for the success of your mission, Phoenix."

"Pray we don't get bad news from Andy Walters or Hugh Fraser," said Phoenix, "or we'll be back here with another headache to sort out."

The mood at Larcombe was dark. In the capital, Tyrone and Colleen O'Riordan waited in her penthouse. They, too, awaited news from Leeds.

Further north, Andy Walter's troubles had begun as soon as they joined the M1 a little over ten miles from the pickup point. He knew seventy-five miles of hard road lay ahead of them until they headed for Birmingham on the A42.

His car was at the head of the TPAC formation. Andy relied on his wingman in the middle lane to spot potential dangers. He and his colleague behind Hugh Fraser concentrated solely on maintaining their position. They mustn't lose contact.

"Roadworks up ahead, Andy."

It was Denzil Cornish, his wingman.

"I saw the signs," said Andy. "We've got a stretch where speed restrictions limit us to forty maximum. Congestion will soon bring us to a stop. That's when we need to keep close tabs on what's going on around us,"

Up in front, traffic slowed as if on cue. Andy watched as his speed dropped from fifty to thirty to fifteen. Traffic came to a halt. Three pairs of eyes watched everything that surrounded the cars. The convoy edged forward as the bottleneck caused by the roadworks eased for a few valuable seconds.

"Go,"

The order came from Mitchell 'Mitch' Blackstone. A Sheffield man who had spent his life on the wrong side of the law. Now in his mid-forties, he had seen the chance of a good payday. Tyrone's request for someone to take out an opponent of the Grid was too rewarding an opportunity to resist. Mitch enjoyed driving, and at weekends he took out his frustrations by smashing into other cars at the local stock car racing stadium.

He had called his mates late last night to ask if they fancied a drive. Mitch told them of his plan. First, they had to steal a vehicle. That part was simple. The site was in total darkness, and the overnight temperatures had dropped below zero. They didn't see a soul. It was too big to miss when the employees arrived for work this morning, but that wasn't his problem.

Mitch explained to his gang that timing was their primary issue. They had to post a lookout on a motorway bridge so they knew when the car they sought had passed that point. Mitch received the call ten minutes ago. He then began joining the motorway and reaching the closest works site to the first stretch of roadworks. He would hide in plain sight.

Success hinged on getting their four vehicles in the right spot. No different from on a race track. His own choice of transport was the key.

Two of his mates drove Range Rovers, cars with excellent visibility and capable of pursuit if their target attempted to escape at high speed. Mitch had seen the motorway warning signs about the roadworks for the past two weeks. Nobody went anywhere at high speed for months until this work was finished.

His mate in the overladen truck behind them was ready to prevent the police or pals of those cars in the little convoy from getting in on the act from the rear. The action lay ahead.

An alert tone on his Bluetooth headphone signalled a message from the driver of the lead Range Rover.

"I'm in position. Our guy is boxed in by three cars. Like Renzo said from the bridge, they are obviously riding shotgun."

"We'll hold back until everyone gets up to speed. Nobody will stick to the forty limit. Wait until I tell you I'm in position, then get in close and cut up the first car," said Mitch. "Make sure he slams on his anchors. I want the target to ram into his backside."

"Got it, Mitch,"

Mitch edged along the six hundred yards strip allocated to the works vehicles and Portaloos, moving closer to the target convoy of cars. He saw the tailback of traffic built up during the brief dead stop still slowed them down.

Mitch signalled right and waved a thank you to the lorry

driver, who let him back into the inside lane. He was right where he needed to be. It was time for the fun to begin.

"Now," he shouted.

Sixty yards ahead, the lead Range Rover veered across from the middle lane and almost rammed the car in front of Andy Walters. The Olympus team leader had no warning. There was no time to do anything but brake hard. He couldn't avoid hitting the Range Rover.

"What the blazes," shouted Andy, "you prick.

Hugh Fraser spotted the crazy manoeuvre and immediately sensed it wasn't random. He braked hard and turned the steering wheel hard right. He narrowly missed the rear end of Andy's car. Hugh's bonnet was now pointing towards the central reservation. Denzil Cornish had been shunted forward by a second Range Rover. They were under attack.

Denzil Cornish had only seen the grill of an SUV looming large in his rear-view mirror. The mayhem on his right could have distracted him, but Denzil didn't panic. He accelerated. The Range Rover had clipped his rear bumper, but he never lost control of the car. He grabbed his gun and prepared to leap out.

Hugh was relieved at what he saw behind him. The rear Olympus car had been far enough back to stop in time. The driver was getting out onto the hard shoulder. He held his gun close by his leg as he ran forward to check on him and Andy. Hugh saw Denzil Cornish nod to say he was okay.

Andy Walters had finally realised what was happening. He and Denzil Cornish had now both climbed out of their cars. Andy signalled to his colleagues to form a protective ring around Hugh Fraser.

The overladen truck that had been one hundred yards behind the convoy had moved into the outside lane. As everything ahead of him braked, the driver whipped his steering wheel viciously left and right. After they had stolen the truck from the stone quarry early this morning, he and Mitch had taken two hours stacking fridges, freezers, dishwashers and washing machines lifted from a local recycling centre. It looked perfect.

If he drove in a straight line, he was fine. To negotiate a bend in the city streets would have been tricky. On the motorway, the truck slewed across towards the middle lane and back again. The weight behind him had shifted so much that he was on two wheels. He braced for the inevitable impact. Mitch had been right. With several tonnes of white goods scattered across two lanes, the M1 would now remain closed for hours.

The first Range Rover moved forward. Andy wasn't concerned whether the attacker was leaving the scene of an accident. The priority was to protect his agent. Then, suddenly, there was the roar of an engine. Something deep and throaty. Andy thought it sounded industrial.

Andy realised the first car wasn't going forward anymore. The Range Rover slammed into Andy's car and kept reversing. His car shunted into the side of Hugh's car.

Mitch Blackstone revved the engine of the stone quarry earthmover.

"Get out, Hugh," shouted Andy.

In the middle lane sat the abandoned second Range Rover. Andy saw the driver darting between stationary cars and onto the hard shoulder. He was running back towards the last junction.

In the earthmover, Mitch continued to accelerate towards the car in front. He hit it hard and laughed as he heard screeching metal and breaking glass. He was almost up and over it. Unfortunately for the target car, it was right in front. He could see the driver panicking to get out. The giant front wheels of the earthmover reared up as the truck steamrollered over the flattened car.

The target Mitch aimed for disappeared from view for a few seconds, and then the truck's giant tyres crashed onto the car's roof. There was a satisfying crunch. Anybody still inside wouldn't survive once he'd driven over it. With his mate in the lead Range Rover completing the manoeuvre, they had the target car in a vice-like grip; this would be easy money.

Hugh Fraser jumped clear with a second to spare. As he rolled to the side, he pulled his gun from his holster. There was only one target left at the scene. The driver of the Range Rover who had caused the so-called accident had quit trying to crush him to death with Andy's car. He had now accelerated away and headed up the motorway as fast as the traffic allowed.

Andy Walters was already on the move towards the earthmover. Its driver continued to creep forward over wrecked cars, trying to reach a clear road ahead.

Andy couldn't let that happen. Hugh watched him clamber onto a wheel hub at the truck's rear and make his way towards the driver's cab.

"Sod that," thought Hugh, "this bastard tried to kill me,"

He raised his gun and emptied the magazine into the driver's cab.

Andy Walters hit the deck as soon as he realised Hugh's intentions. When the firing ceased, the truck stopped.

He checked the cab. Mitch Blackstone was dead.

"We need to get out of here," said Andy, "Denzil, is your car okay?"

"Yes, boss," shouted Denzil, "jump in. Let's make ourselves scarce."

"We've got a stretch of clear road behind and ahead," said Denzil. "Shall I leave the M1 at the next exit? Or do we cross over via the M42 and join the M5 as planned?"

"Stick to the fastest route for now," said Andy, "I'll contact Giles at Larcombe. We need additional security teams to get us home. That might only be the first attempt. We'll change our plans if Giles thinks we need to zig-zag our way across the country to reach Bath in one piece."

"That was hairy," said Graham Heath, the driver of the rear car, "it was a crude attempt, but it could have worked. What was happening behind us? I heard a crash."

"A lorry shed its load, but whether it was connected, I couldn't tell," said Andy. "It blocked the motorway, which is why things are so quiet. Until the next junction."

"I'll keep watch to see if any traffic joining the motorway poses a threat," said Denzil.

"Give me a shout if you see a tank," said Andy, "I don't fancy being rammed by one of those."

An hour later, they neared the A42 exit to Birmingham. Giles monitored traffic in the ice-house, looking for traffic jams, roadworks, and suspicious vehicles. The armed escort was outside Tamworth. They would pick up the convoy and take them south until Junction 15 and the M4 exit. A team from Larcombe would escort them home from there.

In London, Tyrone O'Riordan was still waiting for a phone call from Mitchell Blackstone, a call that would never come. Colleen stopped listening to music on her iPod and turned on the television.

"We should have heard by now," she moaned, "that's another team to disappoint you."

"Good help is so hard to find, isn't it, Mum," said Tyrone, "quit complaining. We're not finished."

Colleen flicked to the news channel.

"Someone is," she called. Tyrone joined her on the settee.

A reporter was standing in the middle lane of a closed section of the M1 south of Sheffield.

"This happens when you reduce police numbers and allow organised crime to ride roughshod over the law of the land. This road won't reopen until tomorrow morning at the earliest. The police are still trying to piece together what happened here this morning. A series of accidents occurred close to the stretch of roadworks you can see up ahead. Were they accidents, though, or were they orchestrated? This earthmover was stolen from a nearby stone quarry last night. It still carries its load of fifteen tonnes of stone. It flattened two cars; another was badly damaged. It was a miracle nobody died. What happened next shocked the drivers and passengers brought to a standstill by this mayhem. A man who had narrowly escaped death in this middle car fired eight shots into the driver's cab of the earthmover — a cold-blooded murder in broad daylight. The police refuse to comment on whether this was two rival gangs bringing their differences into the open in a horrific way. How much longer do we have to put up with this lawlessness? When will the Government act?"

"What do you make of that?" asked Colleen.

"Our target had protection," said Tyrone, "which suggests Vasiliev's thugs were spotted yesterday morning. Olympus knew we were gunning for them. They would have joined the dots on the other hits on Friday and laid the blame at our door. The police will identify the truck driver in time and link him to the criminal network in Sheffield. That will be no problem. What the police learn from the three cars under or in front of the earthmover interests me."

"They could trace them to Larcombe, you mean?"

asked Colleen. "If the Olympus Project comes under suspicion, the police might solve the problem for us."

"Dream on, mother," laughed Tyrone, "they can't find their arse in the dark. This organisation has avoided exposure for years. They've fooled the charity people all that time, and not one killing has ever been linked to a group working in secret. So, they have layers of security screening the identity of the people in those cars. Only one car might be traceable to the charity. That's the one driven by our target. The rest will lead to a dead end."

"Will they have reached their headquarters by now?" asked Colleen.

Tyrone checked his watch.

"We live in hope," he muttered.

Chapter Eight

The remaining Olympus car reached the Tamworth team over ninety minutes after leaving the attack scene. The Sunday morning drive had passed without incident, for which the four men were grateful.

Three cars moved into position around them.

"Do we stay on the motorway, lads," asked Andy, "or should we head into the country and find a decent pub for lunch?"

"Larcombe's orders are to get you back as fast as we can," the escort team leader replied.

"Any roadworks or accidents between here and the M4?" asked Andy.

"The road is clear at present."

"How long before we reach the next handover point?" asked Hugh.

"Two hours," replied Andy.

Hugh Fraser tried to relax. They had plenty of protection now. It would take a small army to prevent them from reaching Larcombe Manor. He thought about the first attack. They had to be thankful there were no cameras close enough to aid the authorities in identifying those involved.

The man he had killed would lead the police to his companions. No doubt, they came from the same criminal outfit. Ten minutes of scanning the known associate's list would throw up a few possible names.

His car posed a bigger problem. At least it didn't carry an Olympus logo. His name wasn't connected to it directly. It was a pool car that Henry, Rusty, Phoenix, and Athena could have driven.

"A penny for them," said Andy Waters.

"I was thinking of the evidence we left behind in those cars," said Hugh. "It's not Olympus practice to get caught in a shootout on a major highway. Nor to abandon our vehicles to leave clues for the police."

"Giles, are you listening to this?" asked Andy.

"I am Andy. It's not ideal, Hugh, but we take precautions. We valeted the car before you collected it yesterday morning. I take it you noticed?"

"It was spotless," said Hugh, "they always are."

"There are no documents inside the car. The only fingerprints will be yours. Andy and his crew are in the same boat. The police will trace the cars to dummy leasing companies. The smokescreen that surrounds those businesses will take them months to unravel."

"I get the picture," said Hugh. "On the rare occasion an agent gets caught in the open, Olympus is protected. The agent is the only one at risk. We have to hope the police don't match a name to the prints."

"Erebus believed it bought us time," said Giles. "In the past, where a mission has gone astray, the agent concerned got transferred abroad. Then, when the police asked questions, they were well out of reach in Timbuktu or Outer Mongolia."

Hugh didn't comment. He thought of Ambrosia. She would be unhappy if he had to disappear.

Denzil Cornish was enjoying the drive south. He felt more comfortable with the escort team. He could see the spire of Worcester Cathedral as it rose majestically above the River Severn. Cheltenham and Gloucester were less than an hour ahead. This ordeal was almost at an end.

Graham Heath had nodded off in the back seat. He woke when he heard the conversation with Giles that Andy shared with everyone. Graham Heath sat next to Hugh Fraser. He only knew Fraser by reputation. His work in Scotland had been exemplary, although the man's attention to detail marked his missions rather than his actions.

Heath was surprised by the agent's reactions when they came under attack. Fraser was angry with that guy who tried to kill him; two well-placed bullets would have done the job. But, on the other hand, Heath had heard a rumour he had a bloody good reason to stay alive and return to Leeds. Whoever she was, she must be worth it.

"Does the outlook stay sunny, Giles?" asked Andy.

"I've got two drones in the air," replied Giles, "one on the M5, one on the M4. The usual waves in traffic flow squeeze vehicles into small groups until the minor irritation that caused it to concertina clears. Nothing as bad as on a Monday morning or a Friday evening. Fingers crossed, no accidents."

"It's too bloody calm," muttered the escort team leader.

"Exactly," agreed Andy Waters, "the first attack seemed crude. As if it had been cobbled together at the last minute by amateurs."

"I spotted the cars tailing me as I drove north, and now

the Grid's leaders must have put a bounty on my head," said Hugh. "There could be more attempts lying in wait."

"Don't panic, Hugh," said Giles. "We've got you covered on the ground and in the air. There's nothing sinister on any camera Artemis, and I can access between you and Junction 15. If we spot a threat, we'll get you to leave the M5 early and reassess your route."

Hugh saw Junction 12 to Gloucester flash by the car window. He unzipped a side pocket on the bag he'd grabbed as he leapt from his stricken car — fresh ammunition for his weapon. Graham Heath watched him reloading. His hand inadvertently went to his gun in its shoulder holster. He hadn't fired it yet today. He was ready when the need arose.

At Michaelwood Services, a group of men ate lunch. They were members of a bikers group based in the Cotswolds; this was their first Sunday meet of the year. Around sixty bikers had scattered throughout the five food outlets available, munching on beef burgers, fried chicken, fish and chips or doughnuts. It takes all sorts. Not everyone wanted a Sunday roast with the trimmings these days.

Their bikes were parked nearby, with every manner of brand visible. Yamaha, Ducati and Suzuki dominated, but Harley Davidson and BMW drew the most attention from any members of the public passing.

As the Olympus car and its escort passed Junction 13 for Stroud, the bikers gathered to prepare for the next leg of their journey.

"Time to head out on the highway, then?" said Boz Mellon, the group's leader.

"Looking for adventure... or whatever comes our way," chorused a dozen bikers surrounding him.

The genuine laughter that followed was a sure sign Boz

made that same comment every meet. Several of the group had been riding when Steppenwolf was in the charts. As had Boz Mellon, but for the majority, it was before their time.

The peaceful Cotswold countryside shattered as the powerful motorcycles roared into life, one by one. Boz had plotted today's route with care. The service station was a decent rendezvous point for friends who travelled from South Wales, Bristol, Somerset and Wiltshire. He preferred not to spend the next four hours on a motorway. As soon as they reached Junction 15, they could strike out via the M32 to North Somerset. Boz knew some beautiful spots in that area, even at this time of year. Before returning via Clevedon and Portishead, the group would visit Chew Magna, Brean and Weston super Mare.

The echelon of riders strung out along the M5. High speed wasn't their aim, unlike the boy racers who gave bikers a bad name. Instead, they wanted to enjoy the views and ensure they reached their destination in one piece. Many machines in the group were capable of over a ton, but Boz banned anyone if they took the piss.

The rear escort car saw a bike in his wing mirror soon after they passed the service station. His team leader stuck to the same formation as Andy Walters used. If traffic wanted to speed overtake them in the outside lane, go ahead. They maintained a steady sixty miles per hour. A second bike appeared, then another. They closed on the escort. He assessed their speed at between seventy and seventy-five. Could this be the next threat?

"We've got company coming up fast in the outside lane,"

"Thanks, Cameron, I've got them. Giles, can you see how many?"

In the ice-house, Giles checked images from cameras on the motorway and his drone.

"There are dozens," he said, "it feels more like an organised group than a hit squad. They are re-joining the motorway from the service station."

Andy Walters relaxed. This group would be by them in minutes. They had twenty minutes more driving to reach the point where they parted company with this escort.

Bike after bike roared by; Junction 14 lay four hundred yards ahead.

Sat behind him, Graham Heath became agitated.

"Pull off! Pull off! They've got guns," he yelled.

The escort team leader was confused. He saw nothing threatening as the bikes roared past. In Hugh Fraser's car, Denzil Cornish's nerves got shredded earlier, and he panicked. He swerved up the exit road and tried to remember where he should go to find the best route to Bath.

Hugh Fraser looked behind him. None of the bikes was chasing them. The rear escort car had been far enough back to copy their manoeuvre. They had lost contact with the rest of the team but weren't alone.

"You must have been mistaken, Graham," said Andy.

"I know what I saw," the man beside Hugh said. "We should stop and liaise with the guy behind. Then you can get Larcombe to plot a route for us to meet up with their escort team."

"There's a truck lay-by a mile ahead," said Denzil. "We'll regroup there."

The Tamworth escort team leader watched the miles tick away as they neared Junction 15. That was the end of their involvement. He couldn't fathom why Andy's car thought it necessary to veer off the motorway.

"Can your cameras pick up Andy and Cameron's cars, Giles?"

"We're searching now," said Giles, "the drone is our best bet. I'm moving it into position."

In the truck lay-by, Cameron drove past Andy Walters. All four men still sat inside. A thirty-eight-tonne lorry had already parked in front. Cameron eased into a gap beyond.

"Busy little spot isn't it, Freddie?" said Cameron.

His partner grunted. Freddie was eager to get home. Today had turned out to be a waste of time.

Cameron saw someone walking towards their car.

"Here we go, Freddie. I wonder why they couldn't just use the comms to pass the message?"

Cameron pressed the button to lower his window.

"So, what's the plan?" he asked.

Freddie and Cameron never found out. The gunman's silenced weapon spat a lethal bullet into each man's brain.

Behind the lorry, Andy Walters was getting annoyed.

"Do you want to wander back, so we can sort out where we're going?" he called for the second time.

Andy wondered why the escort driver didn't respond to his comms.

"Have you got your drone re-located yet, Giles?" Andy asked. "Is there any reason for losing comms out here in the sticks? We can't raise our colleagues."

Giles watched the screen; the drone was now closing on the truck stop. They were too far away yet to get a clear picture.

"Nothing wrong with comms at our end," confirmed Giles. "The others are driving to Junction 15 and heading home to Tamworth. You can tell Cameron in the other car he can make his way home any way he chooses. My team from Larcombe are coming to you. Stay where you are until they arrive. Fifteen to twenty minutes tops."

Artemis sat beside Giles. She jabbed him in the ribs,

"That doesn't look right," she said.

The driver's window on the escort car was open. The driver slumped over the steering wheel. His passenger hadn't moved either.

"You have company, Andy," shouted Giles. "Someone has eliminated the agents in the escort car ahead of you."

Graham Heath drew his weapon as soon as he heard the woman's voice in the background. Hugh reached for his gun, but Heath's weapon pressed against his chest.

"Sorry about this," he said.

The gunman appeared from the near side of the truck in front. He fired through the windscreen, and Andy Walters and Denzil Cornish died before they moved.

"The money was too good to refuse," said Heath, pulling the trigger.

Hugh Fraser's last thought was of Ambrosia.

Heath got out of the car and joined the gunman.

"Let's get out of here, Paul," he said, "the cavalry is on its way."

Paul Heath, his twin brother, turned and returned to his cab.

"Spotting that biker group outing scheduled for today was genius," said Graham as he swung himself up into the passenger seat beside Paul. "After that, it was pure timing."

"A short drive to the M48 services at Aust, and we can lose this truck," laughed Paul. "I've got us both a change of clothes in the back. We'll park the truck, change clothes in the toilets and make our way to the bike one at a time. With full-face helmets and leathers, we'll throw them off the scent. We'll be miles away when the Larcombe teams search the truck and the Moto services."

"I love it when a plan comes together," said Graham.

"Twins who followed two different paths in life," said Paul, "that helped. You were always the one wearing the white hat. I preferred to wear black. So when they put the word out about the money on offer for this hit, it was a no-brainer. You were the only bloke who could help me do it. A man on the inside; what more did I need?"

"A man totally in synch with your way of thinking," said Graham. "You may be eight minutes older than me, but we get an equal share of the cash for this job."

"I've got no problem with that, bruv," grinned Paul. "You'll be looking for a new job now. Do you want me to put a good word in with my boss?"

"I'll be a marked man after this," Graham said, shaking his head, "no, I'm off to Spain and the Costa del Crime. You should join me as we look so alike. Olympus might kill you, thinking you were me."

"It's a thought," agreed Paul, "what would we do, though? I'm not sure I'm ready to retire yet."

"How about a tribute act, a duo like Bros?" suggested Graham.

"Can you sing?" asked Paul, who thought what he'd said and added, "OK, point taken, it never stopped them."

Giles and Artemis were powerless in the ice-house; they had watched the images from the drone grow closer and sharper. Olympus had been betrayed by one of its own once more.

The second gunman had worn a hoodie with a bandana covering the bottom half of his face. Apart from noting a similarity in height and build between the two killers, they had no other clues. Giles wanted to send the drone in pursuit of the truck, but Artemis pointed to the clock. They had run out of time.

"We'll land it as close to the escort team as possible," said Giles, "they can bring it home. I've turned the M4 drone around already. Hugh Fraser won't need its help now."

"I'll advise our team leader it's become a clean-up mission," said Artemis. "I take it we'll bring the bodies here?"

"Without a doubt," said Giles. "The police will arrive at the truck stop soon. If our people have time, they should set the cars alight. The car from Andy Walters's team could still match the crime scene in Yorkshire. Luckily, the police assume they were both involved, and the criminals abandoned them before escaping in another vehicle."

"Is there anything we've overlooked?" asked Artemis.

Giles paused for a moment, sighed, and said: -

"We can't do much more for now. I must inform Athena and the others of the tragedy. She will have the unenviable task of notifying Zeus and the others."

"Heaven knows how Ambrosia will react," said Artemis.

"Phoenix has lost his logistics man too, which loads extra pressure on his shoulders."

"As if he didn't have enough to cope with this week," said Artemis.

"The Grid is winning every battle at present," said Giles. "We've been outthought and outnumbered at every stage this weekend."

In Kilburn, Callum Wood had spent the morning with Dinesh Parvati, the Acting Sergeant at the local Metropolitan police station. The setup reminded Callum of

Larcombe Manor

his first posting in a small town near Bath. A handful of uniformed officers in a building on High Street. Plenty to cope with the low level of crime they experienced.

Fast forward twenty-five years, Kilburn had two thousand reported crimes in a year. Of course, the patch he served back then had a bad year if they hit two hundred. But Dinesh knew the borough he covered and the people in it. He knew the numbers to call when the shit hit the fan, when the detectives, the forensics, and the top brass needed a ring.

"How often do you make those calls, Dinesh?" he asked.

"Only every day, detective," he grinned.

The two officers had walked from the station to where the Wishing Well café once stood. Charred stonework and scaffolding showed work continued on repairs to the buildings on either side. The last skips of rubble that remained after they demolished the café were on the High Road.

"Two people died, Dinesh," said Callum.

"Bridie was a lovely lady," said Dinesh, "she baked delicious cakes. Look at my waistline. I couldn't resist. Now she's gone. I've lost half a stone since early November."

"Did you meet the man she lived with?" asked Callum.

"Only once," said Dinesh. "He was a former policeman, among other things, I believe? Bridie was fond of him."

"Did they salvage much from here after the fire?"

Dinesh shook his head.

"The people who started the fire didn't want survivors," he said. "I hoped to repay Bridie by finding her killers, but it was hopeless."

"Do you find it difficult to find witnesses prepared to give statements around here?" asked Callum. "Even though Bridie was so well respected?"

"People would have spoken out in this case," said

Dinesh, "but my gut tells me the killers were long gone. Not just from the borough. They returned to Europe."

"What makes you think they were foreigners?" asked Callum, wondering if he'd stumbled on a lead.

"A piece of jewellery was offered around by an Albanian fellow only days after that Hatton Garden robbery. His fellow countrymen were involved in that case and with the cash stolen from the compound."

"I hadn't realised the two crimes were linked," said Callum.

Dinesh gave a wry smile.

"Your bosses didn't think so either," said Callum.

"What is it, you say? Horses for courses. If you enjoy a good curry as I do, you visit an Indian restaurant. You get the Albanians to do it if you want a bank or jewel heist done to perfection. If that piece of bling came from Hatton Garden, it explains the fire here. The ex-policeman saw something."

Dinesh spread his hands.

"They had to silence Wayne," said Callum.

"I'm sorry," said Dinesh.

"No, you've helped me," said Callum. "I thought my case connected to Wayne Sangster's death. It didn't. That means I need to look elsewhere, closer to home, for the killer of my former DI."

"It hurts more when it's someone you know, doesn't it?"

"It does when you've been friends for twenty years. So I need to investigate what he did in the last few months that got him killed."

"Good luck with your quest," said Dinesh, "let's walk back to the station. Did you spot the bakery on the corner? I'll treat you to lunch. We both need cheering up."

Less than five miles from where the two policemen

stood, Tyrone and Colleen O'Riordan celebrated the news from Paul Heath. They were jubilant. The contrast in emotions couldn't have been starker.

"I knew the offer of a small fortune would bring the desired result," crowed Tyrone.

"Perhaps you were lucky Leeds to Bath is a long journey by road," said his mother. "If that man had visited someone in Cardiff, you would have been stuffed."

Tyrone knew his mother found it hard to be positive. Years of being downtrodden when his father was alive had left their mark. He joined her on the settee and put an arm around her shoulder.

"We planned to eliminate three key people associated with the Olympus Project this weekend. Vasiliev got greedy and tried to screw us over. He paid for that misjudgement, but his men did kill two of the targets. We will pay the twins who called just now to finish the job. So, it was a success, wasn't it?"

"How can you be sure these three were key people?" asked Colleen. "They might have been bit players in the organisation."

"Think of it this way. Every time we take one of their people out of the game, it's like that party game, Jenga. It doesn't matter how unimportant the first few blocks are; the overall structure is weakened. In time, it only takes one block to bring the rest crashing to the floor. The helicopter pilot flew people to and from Larcombe. He may have been part of the Project; maybe he was hired to help. It doesn't matter. These people have emotions; we see that in everything they do. They will grieve the loss of their friends. That makes them weak. While that weakness is exposed, we could strike again."

"How do you plan to do that?" asked Colleen.

"I said we *could*," said Tyrone, "but we need to watch. The police have two significant crime scenes to investigate. The incident on the M1, where Olympus had to abandon three cars on the motorway, will yield valuable clues. In Gloucestershire, two cars and five bodies are waiting for the police to arrive. That will need explaining. When they find our third target's body in one of the cars, it will create all kinds of problems for Olympus."

"Earlier, you said Olympus would have such elaborate smokescreens it would take forever for the police to find their way to Larcombe Manor. Why will this be any different?"

"It probably won't," shrugged Tyrone, "but it's time-consuming. While covering your tracks and burying your dead, you can't concentrate on what your enemy is doing."

Tyrone's mobile phone rang.

"They've finished cleaning my place," he told Colleen after he'd listened to the message.

"I can cook for us tonight if you wish," offered Colleen, "then I'll drive you home."

"We can treat ourselves to a night out, can't we?" said Tyrone. "We've had a good weekend."

Tyrone kissed his mother on the forehead.

"Get your glad rags on. We're going up west to an expensive restaurant,"

"You'll have a sore head in the morning," said Colleen.

Monday, 12th January 2015

"I can't remember such a terrible weekend for Olympus," said Athena as she began the morning meeting at nine o'clock. Minos and Alastor were there, and so too Henry Case and Artemis. "You can appreciate that my phone conversation with Zeus last night was one which neither of us wishes to repeat. The loss of lives was horrendous."

"Giles has remained in the ice-house," said Artemis. "The clean-up near Thornbury was completed before the emergency services arrived. Events in the North and the West will need his close attention over the coming days."

"To bring the rest of you up to speed," said Athena, "Phoenix and Rusty had notified me of their plans for the scheduled actions this week minutes before Giles told us the dreadful news. The Grid's assassins had caught up with Hugh Fraser and his escorts."

"We planned our way out of the mess from the failed attempt near Sheffield," said Artemis. "Andy Walters had almost reached the final handover point. He had been allocated a three-car escort team from Tamworth."

"Two men from the Tamworth team were slaughtered within minutes of them leaving the motorway," Athena continued, "The reason for that was not clear. Andy Walters and one of his closest friends, Denzil Cornish, died in the same car as Hugh Fraser."

"There were four people in the car driven by Cornish," said Artemis. "Giles and I watched events from a distance via a drone we had deployed to watch for any attack. Nothing suspicious happened until a gunman appeared from a thirty-eight-tonne truck in the lay-by. We believed that was a convenient spot to regroup after we dismissed whatever spooked them as a threat. Everything up to that point suggested Hugh was one handover from returning to Larcombe safe and sound."

"We didn't count on a second gunman," said Athena, "Hugh Fraser was killed by one of our own."

This news was greeted with stunned silence by the senior agents.

"After our escort crews raced to the scene, they removed the murdered agents, and both cars were set alight," said Artemis. "When police and paramedics reached the lay-by, there was nothing to see except two burnt-out wrecks. We now know the missing agent was Graham Heath. He's been with Olympus for three years. His record was spotless, and there was no clue he might switch his allegiance. So Giles looked into his family background, and Graham has a twin brother."

"The second gunman?" asked Henry.

"Without a doubt," said Artemis. "The Heath brothers share many things in common. They are the same height, build, blond hair and blue eyes. Where we believed they differed was their chosen career path. Graham came to Olympus via the Royal Marines. There were no red flags. Paul, on the other hand, has been associated with a criminal gang based in the Midlands for a decade. There was no sign the two brothers had been in contact since Graham joined us."

"Money is a powerful motivator," said Alastor. "The Grid must have offered a huge sum for a successful outcome. That goes some way to excuse the shambles yesterday morning. That attack smacked of having been thrown together in five minutes. With a big pay-day on offer, they attracted criminals who would try anything to get their hands on the cash."

"Giles must continue to cover our tracks as much as possible," said Athena. "Phoenix and Rusty will make their strike on the car gang in Ilford by ten o'clock. They wanted to pursue the Heath twins, but I persuaded them these missions should go ahead as planned. I authorised one amendment. Only three key personnel were due to be targeted this morning. I suggested that anyone connected to the gang was now fair game."

"Did we trace the twins' whereabouts after they escaped from the lay-by?" asked Minos.

"The lorry went to the old Aust services complex near the first Severn Crossing," said Artemis, "it's still there this morning. When we searched the buildings, the brothers weren't inside, but a high-speed motorcycle left the area. Giles is trawling through CCTV images from the motorway network to locate it. They both lived in the Midlands. Graham had a place in Sutton Coldfield, and Paul lived in Burton upon Trent. They'll turn up."

"When they do, we'll deal with them," said Athena. "There's a queue of teams standing by to take the mission. Andy Walters was very popular."

"Hugh was a valued member of the Larcombe team, too," said Henry. "I was impressed by his work in the few months we shared in the stable block. I can't imagine how Ambrosia took the news of his death."

Athena sighed.

"I'm afraid I passed that responsibility onto Zeus and Hera. Hera and Ambrosia were close; there was always tension between Ambrosia, myself, and Phoenix. She was ambitious. From her first visit here, we felt she considered us opponents rather than allies."

The sombre meeting ended before ten. Artemis was needed in the ice-house to help Giles. Phoenix and Rusty would be on the move. Athena returned to the apartment. She wished to spend time alone before tackling the pile of paperwork that awaited her.

Maria Elena tended to Hope in the nursery, so Athena went to the bedroom to gaze out the window. In time, she thought, I hope we can heal the rift between us. It was plain to see that Ambrosia and Hugh were very much in love. Hugh had been married before, but it was possibly Ambrosia's only chance of true happiness. To spend last night alone in her house in Leeds after hearing the heartbreaking news must have been awful. She had to have known of the close call only hours before near Sheffield. What a rollercoaster day for the poor woman's emotions.

Athena's tears rolled down her cheeks. Where was this going to end?

Chapter Nine

"All set?" asked Phoenix.

Rusty and the three team leaders replied in the affirmative.

He and Rusty had been stunned by the news of the death of so many agents yesterday afternoon. When it transpired that an Olympus agent had been responsible for killing Hugh Fraser, it stirred memories of the betrayal of Thanatos.

Thanatos had been one of the Three Amigos that Phoenix made fun of while Erebus was alive. There was something ugly in the hearts of those who betrayed their friends. Phoenix had only made real friends since his arrival at Larcombe Manor. He valued them above anything else and would never betray them.

The drive to the Chiswick safe house this morning had been sobering. Rusty wasn't in the mood to talk; Phoenix didn't want to listen to his favourite music channel. There was a job to do. Athena's words yesterday still rang crystal clear.

Nobody walked away unscathed, no matter what they found in the garage workshop today.

Collen O'Riordan was right. Tyrone had a sore head this morning. But not entirely due to the excellent red wine they shared with their meal last night. It had been months since the two of them had spent an evening together. In truth, she preferred her own company these days.

Tyrone preferred younger women. The type he could guarantee he took to bed after spending lots of money on them. It seemed odd to be dropped at their respective homes by a taxi driver. It was so bloody typical. Perhaps, she should give that Tinder a try?

It was the news he'd received this morning that annoyed Tyrone. She had only surfaced ten minutes earlier. Her first strong cup of coffee was going down a treat. Her phone had rung. She didn't care who it was; it was too loud and far too early.

"What?" she asked.

"They only set the bloody cars on fire, didn't they?" Tyrone spat into the phone. Colleen held the device away from her ear. She knew it was impossible, but she felt something, despite a check with her finger telling her different.

Tyrone was still shouting.

"They got the bodies out and away, doused the interiors with petrol and torched them," he yelled. "Not a bloody thing for the police to find when they waltzed up, late as usual."

"What? You're telling me the police don't know who died or even how many?" said Colleen. "Nothing? Can't they identify the cars, even though they burnt? What about the motorway cameras? Surely they can help?"

"Would you believe they were out of action? No, nor do I. Olympus must have hacked into the systems and erased any incriminating footage. They've not said as much on the news yet this morning, but my informant fed me this half an hour ago. Those bastards are as slippery as an eel."

"Take the positives, son," said Colleen, trying to reach the coffee percolator. It would take another cup to get over this. Heaven knows what Tyrone needed.

"Yeah, you're right, mum. We put eight into coffins, didn't we? So it wasn't a total loss. I thought we had a great chance of opening the lid on what goes on at that bleeding headquarters of theirs. I'm going to think. There has to be another way."

In his office in Bath, Callum Wood had half a dozen new cases to tackle. His trip to London yesterday had been on his own time. Although crimes in the Roman city were fewer than in the capital, villains didn't take the weekend off, despite their beautiful surroundings.

He saw the news last night when he got home. Ronnie was in bed. Callum and Debbie had been shocked at the violence and total disregard for members of the public.

"It makes you wonder who's running this country," said Debbie. "These gangs have no boundaries they won't cross."

"Warfare between rival gangs has been going on for decades," Callum replied, "but it never used to be carried out in public. Their chances of getting caught are low. When they are, the sentences are often a joke. It's no surprise they think they're untouchable. We've brought it on ourselves."

His mind drifted as he read through reports on a spate

of burglaries on a rundown estate in Twerton. It was old news; even the road's name concerned conjured images of old freezers and sofas cluttering the estate's car parks rather than the properties themselves.

He tossed the report aside. It was a job for one of the kids. He spotted the newest recruit to the squad of detectives he supervised.

"Damien," he called, "this one's got your number on it."

The laughter from poor Damien's colleagues in the outer open-plan office convinced the young DC his parents did him no favours when selecting first names.

Callum watched Damien strolling back to his desk with the report. The slumped shoulders told their own story. As soon as he'd read the location, Damien knew he had handed him a shit job. We all had to do our fair share, thought Callum.

Before he picked the next report from the top of the pile, he thought of Erica. The funeral was still a week away. Shaun and Tracey were due back at school this morning, but Callum imagined they were home with their mother. Compassionate leave, or whatever schools call it these days. Something bothered him from his conversation with Dinesh yesterday, but he couldn't get a fix on it. Time to switch focus. He should call Erica to remind everyone at Manvers Street was thinking of her.

The phone rang half a dozen times before Erica answered.

"Hello,"

"Erica, it's me, Callum. How are you? How are the children?"

"Hello, Callum," replied Erica, "as well as can be expected, I suppose. The neighbours have popped around with offers of help. The vicar is due tomorrow morning to go through the order of service. I've got so many sympathy cards to open; it's unreal. The postman hasn't even delivered yet. Cars pull up outside, and the letter-box opens and closes."

Callum let her ramble. None of that stuff mattered, but while it occupied your mind, you avoided facing reality. The man you loved, the father of your children, had been murdered. He was never coming back.

Erica was in limbo. She had dealt with the shock of discovering Phil's body hanging in the hallway. There was no point denying it happened. People dealt with grief in different ways. Callum decided that because of Phil's police background, Erica believed she could rely on people such as him to provide answers. Why was he killed? Who did it? Will they ever leave prison?

"Have you got any leads in the case, Callum?" asked Erica.

"We're pursuing several lines of enquiry," he replied.

"Nothing then," said Erica, "there's no point kidding me. I've heard Phil trot out that excuse a hundred times."

"How was he getting on at Larcombe Manor," asked Callum, "did he enjoy the work? What did he do? Can you tell me?"

"He was busy. I can tell you that. He didn't go into detail. It was great to have him home at a reasonable time in the evenings, and the kids loved having him here at the weekends."

Callum didn't think this was leading anywhere.

"It made a change from his security services firm, I guess? Phil travelled a fair bit with that business, I remember."

"Phil only had one job that took him away from home," said Erica. "Out of the blue, they sent him up to Edinburgh. He was searching for a missing person. Phil reckoned she was dead."

"When was that?" asked Callum. "Did he have any luck?"

"The last week in October," said Erica, "well, it wasn't lucky for the woman. Phil said he'd been proved right."

Callum made a note. A dead body was discovered near Edinburgh. Female. Late October. How did that relate to what he had imagined the charity handled? It didn't gel, somehow.

"I suppose he made new friends, even in the short time he worked there," Callum continued to probe. "Phil got on with most people."

"You-know-who worked there, of course," said Erica, "but apart from that, Phil said he was on a short leash. A man called Hayden was his supervisor. The chap in the next office, Hugh, was friendly. Other than that, he was isolated from everyone else who worked there. There was a strict timetable for when he should arrive and leave."

"Who do I know that works there?" asked Callum, caught unawares by the comment.

"Zara Wheeler," said Erica, "didn't you know? She's not Wheeler now; I don't know her husband's name. She went to Larcombe straight from Portishead. Phil was shocked when he bumped into her on his first day."

"I'll bet," said Callum. "Look, I'll keep in touch. Give them a call if you want Debbie and Ronnie to drop in."

"Thanks, Callum, you're a good friend. We need to keep busy. It's the long hours in between that are the worst. Especially at night."

Callum sat at his desk, staring at the notes he scribbled. What was behind that Scotland trip? Why didn't Zara tell him she and Phil worked at the same place? They had been so close. Lovers, if the rumours out of Portishead were correct. Why was Phil denied access to parts of Larcombe Manor? His copper's nose twitched. He was onto something; he knew it.

"I wonder why other businesses on this street haven't reported what's going on here?" asked Rusty.

"Afraid of having their place torched?" suggested Phoenix.

The targeted garage workshop stood on a street corner on the trading estate. Its external workspace was surrounded by high fencing and razor wire.

Teams closed in on the garage workshop. Scaling the fences would have been tricky. Phoenix had decided to burst in through the front doors. Olympus wasn't after the car thieves who kept providing a steady supply of high-performance cars for these villains. They wanted to shut down this part of the organisation for good.

The teams entered through the side door, next to the roller door, running the premises' width. A steel enforcer separated the door from its hinges. Phoenix, Rusty, and twelve Olympus agents ran through the gap.

Twelve vehicles lay in varying states of disassembly in the centre. Multiple vehicle parts, such as engines, transmissions, fuel tanks, seats, doors, wheels, and tyres, were stacked against the outside walls. There was heavy lift equipment, such as hoists, in several spots. So Rusty wasn't surprised it took several seconds for the men inside to realise they had visitors.

The noise inside the workshop was loud and constant. Music blared from speakers in the roof space. Many of the mechanics in the centre wore ear defenders. Those using the acetylene cutting torches wore masks. It was a slick operation, which Rusty knew went on twenty-four hours a day, seven days a week. It must pay well. These guys weren't skimping on Health and Safety.

Phoenix reckoned the men inside the main building thought the authorities were raiding them. The Olympus uniform confused them long enough that they offered no resistance. Some even carried on working.

He kept running through the workshop; as a team of four agents followed him. They headed for the offices in the Portacabin in the car park at the rear. That's where their documentation lay—the vital links from the initial theft to the eventual destination of the car.

Behind him, Phoenix heard the shouts and screams as punishments were delivered. None of the men would die, but they wouldn't be much use in this line of work for months.

As the agents ran out of the rear entrance, they saw the rest of the gang emerging from the Portacabin. There were five men. Three carried baseball bats, and one had a machete. The man bringing up the rear looked like he thought he didn't need a weapon. He was a giant of a man.

"The Grid's killers showed no mercy to your colleagues," Phoenix reminded his team.

The chop shop gang leaders stopped in their tracks and raised their weapons. A series of staccato bursts from the automatic weapons of the Olympus agents cut them down. Even the man mountain crashed to the ground. The sound echoed around the enclosure, and then there was silence.

"Rusty must have turned off that music," said Phoenix.

The team leader by his side grinned.

"Good job too. I can't stand that electronic UK garage stuff, can you?"

Phoenix led the team into the Portacabin.

"Everything in here needs to go, files, laptops, and mobile phones; it will give you leads to pursue in both directions. You can follow the trail along the supply chain to the thieves that lifted them off the streets. Then you can follow the cars on their onward journey to Africa and the Far East or trace who's in the market for these spare parts. It will keep you guys busy for a while. With luck, Larcombe will reward you for your efforts, and you will get the nod to take direct action against the rogues you identify. Good hunting."

"Cheers, Phoenix," said the team leader. "Not a bad morning's work. A few scores settled."

The other teams rounded up the crew in the workshop when they arrived.

"Take them outside and lock them in the Portacabin," said Phoenix. He watched as the men hobbled and stumbled towards the roller door. They wouldn't get any sympathy from him. After the agents returned, the door closed.

"We'll leave the rest to you," he said. "Every bit of kit in here needs to be put out of action, whether it's hand-held or on wheels. The Grid will get another team to keep this trade going, but this site must need a fortune spent on it to get it up and running again."

"Understood, Phoenix," said a team leader. "Come on, lads, let's do some damage."

Phoenix and Rusty returned to their van. Time to head back to the Chiswick safe house.

"We should be there in an hour," said Rusty. "Do we have time for a bite to eat, or do you want to drive straight on to Kettering."

Phoenix checked his watch.

"We do not need to rush," he said. "I vote for a visit to that takeaway we've used before. You never know when we'll get the chance of a decent meal again. The next mission won't be as easy as this."

Rusty smiled at his mate's idea of a decent meal, but he was hungry, and a large pizza would satisfy that hunger just as well as a slap-up meal.

"A trading estate that size would have security, don't you reckon?" he asked.

"I saw a kiosk on the corner when we drove onto the estate," said Phoenix. "No more than a token presence. I know what you're thinking. Loud noises of people using machinery at inappropriate hours. Vehicles that enter a location but never leave. All those high-valued cars at the rear of the garage and big cargo vans or trucks coming and going throughout the week."

"Yeah, security here leaks like a sieve," said Rusty. "We drove four vans onto the estate, and nobody took a blind bit of notice."

Phoenix called the team leader that he had left ransacking the Portacabin.

"When you finish there, visit the security guy in the kiosk on the way out. Lose any record he may have of our van registrations."

Rusty heard the guy on the other end ask a question.

"Don't hurt him too much, just enough to convince him he shouldn't mention having seen anything unusual today. He's used to it."

Rusty parked the van outside the row of shops that housed a string of fast-food outlets.

"What topping do you want?" he asked as he got out.

"We've got to start eating healthier foods if we want to reach fifty," said Phoenix. He pointed to a new place two doors up from the pizzeria that had opened since they were last in Chiswick. "I'll have a grilled chicken Caesar salad wrap, please. There are plenty of options on the menu, I'm sure. Don't bring back any rubbish for yourself."

Rusty swallowed hard and walked inside. He searched the menu. Phoenix's choice was on offer, and there were vegetarian options. No thanks. He wondered what a Vietnamese BLT wrap was when it was at home. Nothing ventured, he thought. If only they did a bacon roll.

The Heath twins made it home to the Midlands without mishap. Paul dropped his brother off in Sutton Coldfield before riding on to Burton. The town straddled the River Trent and had a reputation for its breweries. That was its charm as far as Paul Heath was concerned. He found it as useful as any to lay his head while waiting for the next job to appear. Paul wasn't attached to the place so much he couldn't grab his gear and up sticks. A spell in warmer climes seemed just the ticket, especially on a cold day such as today.

"Are you ready?" he asked when his brother answered the phone. It was now mid-afternoon.

"Leaving now, mate," replied Graham. "I'll see you at the airport. Did you get the money?"

"It's in my account," said Paul. "I'll transfer fifty grand to you when we get out there. Got to give the bank a few days to clear the funds."

Graham ended the call and slipped his mobile phone into his flight bag. He checked his passport and boarding card for the fourth time and then took a last look at the flat he had rented for the past three years.

Outside, the taxi waited to take him to Birmingham

Airport, a twenty-minute drive away. Paul's trip from Burton took an hour. The flight to Malaga left in three hours. Before the end of the day, they would start a new life in the sun.

Graham was relaxed as soon as he took his seat in the back of the taxi. He had always been someone for whom the holiday began when they left home. This trip was more than a holiday, but he still had that familiar buzz as a kid. Paul was just the same.

Birmingham International had a free drop-off point for taxis less than a quarter of an hour's walk from the terminal. Graham paid the driver, grabbed his bag and set off across the car park. Not the place to be in the cold and dark alone, but it was well-lit, and he could see other passengers a hundred yards ahead of him. He skirted around a dark van that had pulled into a parking bay.

"Excuse me, it's Graham, isn't it?" a voice called.

Graham Heath was surprised and turned back.

Two dark shapes were on him in seconds; strong hands bundled him into the van through the side door. He heard the door slam and felt the needle prick in his neck. As he slipped into unconsciousness, he put a face to the voice. It reminded him of Hayden Vincent, one of the agents in the group he trained with when he joined Olympus.

"Will his brother be coming to this car park, too?" asked Henry Case.

"Giles suggested we cover the premium taxi drop-off site, just in case. Graham didn't mind a short walk. Paul always was a lazy sod, according to his brother. Are you glad you came along, Henry?"

"It's different. I'll say that. Of course, a lot of hanging around, but with Phoenix and Rusty otherwise engaged,

Athena wanted to give us a chance to avenge Hugh's death."

"Wherever he arrives, Paul Heath won't make the Malaga flight. If we miss him here, or he avoids our other team at the premium drop-off, we've got it covered. Our man inside the airport is poised to get a call out over the tannoy for Paul Heath to meet his brother."

Henry and Hayden sat in the front of the Olympus van and kept watch. Their two colleagues in the dark interior monitored Graham Heath.

"It can't be long now," said Henry.

"Patience is something you learn on stakeouts, Henry," said Hayden. "No offence, but I miss not having Kelly beside me. Today is the first time we haven't teamed up for a job."

"She appears to be handling her condition better these days," said Henry, "that morning sickness must have depressed her?"

"It was a nuisance, but the result is what matters. We can't wait to be a family of three."

Henry wondered what that might be like for him and Sarah. It was early days, but Athena gave birth to Hope in her late thirties. She and Sarah were of the same age; there was still hope. Time will tell.

"This could be him. It's a taxi firm from Burton," said Henry. "Are we ready?"

They were. Paul Heath's cab stopped three rows across from where they parked. The van's side door slid open behind them as Henry and Hayden watched their target. The agents crossed the car park at an angle, bringing them to the terminal pathway and cutting off Paul Heath's access to the airport. Henry and Hayden stepped out of the van. They walked towards the second twin.

Paul Heath looked around him. Graham said they'd meet here. Where was he? Had he been delayed in traffic? Paul called his twin brother. Inside the dark van forty yards away, Graham Heath's phone rang.

"I can't take your call at the moment. Please leave a message after the tone, and I'll get back to you."

Paul was confused. He made for the terminal building and the check-in desk; Graham couldn't be far away. As Paul walked towards the pathway, he sensed company. There was someone behind him; he saw two men heading his way. Paul was unarmed. His only hope was to run into the car park and hope to force a driver out of their car. He looked in desperation for new arrivals. He tried to hail a taxi, but the driver ignored his flailing arms.

Paul hit the tarmac. The flailing arms were not him trying to attract attention. He had been thumped hard in the back by two burly men who now had him pinned to the ground. Hayden ran to the van and moved it closer to Henry and their colleagues. Paul was soon inside the van beside his brother.

A small group of businesspeople and holidaymakers stopped to watch events unfold. Mobile phones snapped several photos that would find their way onto social media sites later that night. They would be picked up by national newspapers and TV stations in the morning. The dark blue van left the car park at high speed.

"A pity about that," said Hayden, "but we snatched Graham without witnesses. The media will report the kidnap of only one man, which might help Giles cover our tracks."

"Home to Larcombe then," said Henry. "I know I shouldn't, but I'm looking forward to teaching these two that crime doesn't pay."

Tuesday, 13th January 2015

In Northamptonshire, a group of people started a new day. Phoenix and Rusty were awake by seven; they spent the night in a safe house in Kettering. They weren't alone; four Irregulars arrived late in the evening. Sandy Nesbitt, the helicopter pilot, was on her way back to the UK from Ireland. Giles informed Phoenix that she was due in Kettering by lunchtime.

One of Hugh Fraser's last tasks was fast-tracking five ex-homeless veterans to help with this county-wide direct action. He made the initial contact, but when he failed to return from his weekend away, Artemis took control. Along with the other duties she performed in the ice-house yesterday, she ensured Phoenix had the support he needed.

Phoenix had chosen a range of crime hot spots where the Irregulars could pass valuable information back to him and Rusty. He delayed taking them through the plans for the next few days until they finished breakfast.

While they ate, he called his wife at Larcombe Manor.

"Good morning, darling," said Athena, "congratulations on yesterday. Everything went to plan."

"What did you expect?" he replied, pretending to take umbrage at his wife's comment.

"You weren't the only team to have a good day," she said, ignoring his remark, "Hayden and Henry picked up the Heath twins at Birmingham International last evening. Their escape to the Costa del Crime is on indefinite hold."

"Good work by those two," said Phoenix, "and Giles. He needed to find them fast; otherwise, they would have slipped through our fingers. How does Henry plan to deal with them?"

"Did you have something in mind?" asked Athena.

"I wondered whether we could deliver them to the O'Riordans?" he replied.

"I'm not sure it's practical to drop two bodies into the Glencairn Bank. Parking in Gresham Street is a nightmare."

"I want the Grid to know we've found them, and they've paid for what they did. When we trace those responsible for killing Biggles and Orion, they will suffer the same fate."

"I'll discuss it with Henry," said Athena. "We will send a message. You have my word. Good hunting."

Phoenix called Giles in the ice-house.

"Do we have any further news on the people involved in Friday's murders? Where are we with that Vasiliev character?"

"I passed you the details of his address and his known associates late Sunday evening," said Giles. "With everything else going on, you may have missed it. You left for London early in the morning."

"Have we got someone watching the place?" asked Phoenix.

"We have, but there's been no sign of him. He's disappeared. A thug named Alexeev called at his house yesterday evening. He was in the helicopter with Les Biggar. I've checked the images from Kemble. There's no doubt."

"Have him disposed of," said Phoenix. "Can we link any of Vasiliev's men with the helicopter or the home invasion in Bath?"

"Vladimir Mikhailov flew the helicopter. The evidence is overwhelming. Two gang members match our vague description of the assassin at the house," Giles replied, "but it's inconclusive."

"I don't have a problem with that, do you?" said

Phoenix. "They wanted a war; they can have it. Alexeev will have three companions in the afterlife."

"I hadn't realised the Russians believed in that type of thing," said Giles.

"Thank Minos for that gem of knowledge," said Phoenix. "I do read his reports now and again. Since the demise of communism, many Russians have returned to religion. It's estimated forty per cent believe life does not end with death."

"That's good to know," said Giles, "I suppose."

"It comes to us all in the end, Giles," said Phoenix.

Chapter Ten

Rusty was ready to get on with his real job of work. He had cooked six fried breakfasts for the team and loaded the dishwasher. His domestic duties were over for the day. He waited until Phoenix returned to the lounge and allocated tasks to the group.

"Ben Anderson and Ross Summers? You served in the Royal Regiment of Fusiliers. Is that correct?"

The two youngest Irregulars raised a hand in confirmation. They both received shrapnel wounds from an IED in Helmand in 2008. They had flown home to Queen Alexandra Hospital in Birmingham for a series of operations. As with many others, although the body healed, the mind was reluctant to move on. A too-familiar spiral into drink and drugs left them living on the streets before the end of 2011.

As comrades, they stayed together and fought their way back to something approaching normality when Olympus came knocking.

"Your youth lends itself to the role we need you to play,"

said Rusty, "you're to become students again. We want you to mix with the student population at the University. Uncover as much as possible of the intimidation used by the dealers frequenting the campus. Give us the names of the major players and identify the sites where a large percentage of the deals get made. Remember, we're not interested in the users, only in the scum terrorising the students with these aggressive tactics."

"One whiff of a rumour you've slipped back into your old ways, and you're out," said Phoenix. "Out of this mission, out of the Irregulars. Are we clear?"

"We're clear," said Ross Summers.

"Cliff Barclay? You served in the Welsh Regiment, based at Tidworth?"

"Yes, chief," said Barclay, "I moved there in 2005."

His accent placed him from the North, possibly the Colwyn Bay area. Rusty had a good ear.

"We shipped out to Iraq for Operation Telic 6," Barclay continued, "I was air-evacced to the UK six months later. Seven of the past eight years was a dream from which I never awoke. It took a long time to get the right help. I can't wait to pay those people back for persevering."

"I see from your notes; you were married with two young daughters?"

"The wife left me and took Delyth and Jenna with her. I wasn't the same bloke she married, that's fair enough, but I wanted to keep seeing the kids. We're rebuilding our relationship, it will take time, but I'd do anything for them."

"That's why we selected you for this case. We have a nasty pair of individuals in Corby. A bloke and his partner are plying their victims with crack cocaine and encouraging them to engage in depraved sexual activity."

"How old are these girls?" asked Barclay.

"Between ten and twelve," said Rusty.

Barclay nodded.

"I'm your man, chief," he said.

"That leaves me," said Don Donovan, "ex-Coldstream Guards, two tours in Northern Ireland, followed by two decades of decline."

"You're partnered with Sandy Nesbitt when she joins us," said Rusty. "The two of you will be on the streets of Northampton. There has been a spate of gang-related shootings in the area. You will listen for names of potential victims. I'm afraid much of your day will be in and around Castle Ward and St Crispin. In the evening I suggest you stay in well-lit areas. The parks and gardens tend to be full of drunks, druggies, and Eastern Europeans intent on stabbing someone. Pretty much anyone."

"Charming," said Don. "Is this a job for a woman?"

"Sandy will cope," muttered Rusty.

"Some people have loose lips when they think it's only a woman listening," said Barclay. "Which shows how stupid they are,"

"Quite," said Phoenix. "Right, Rusty, hand out their information packs and get them on their way. Don, you wait with us until Sandy arrives. We can drop you in the Castle Ward after lunch."

"What will you two be doing while we're gathering information?" asked Donovan.

"We'll be removing the risk of another violent sexual assault in Wellingborough," said Rusty.

"That won't take us too long," added Phoenix, "so get moving. Find the men responsible for the shootings so we have something else to do."

Phoenix left Donovan with his information pack to read.

The guy wouldn't have been on his list of Irregulars. Hugh Fraser would have weeded him out, for sure. He didn't want to chew Rusty's ear off, but Artemis needed a sharper red pen when scrutinising the backgrounds of these veterans.

Rusty returned to the safe house. The first three Irregulars were in position — comms were in place to liaise with the ice-house, Phoenix, and himself. The game was afoot.

"Any sign of our fifth wheel?" asked Donovan.

Rusty gave him a stare.

Phoenix shook his head.

"He's not worth the effort,"

It was noon. Sandy Nesbitt was due any minute. Phoenix wanted to get her and Donovan on the ground, listening for information. Anywhere that took Donovan miles away.

Back at Larcombe, Athena neared the end of the morning meeting. Minos and Alastor covered most items, with Phoenix and Rusty on the other side of the country. They worked tirelessly, digging out data valuable to agents in the field. Now and then, they saw the first green shoots of an issue that became a national crisis.

"In the early days of Olympus, Erebus and I passed many evenings discussing our earlier lives," Minos said. "Court cases I sat on where we made far-reaching judgements, his memories of the war in the Falklands. Alastor and I have noticed speeches in the House of Commons, articles in respected journals, and online interviews where important people have expressed opinions that surprised their interviewer. Individually, they didn't raise too much comment. When taken together, the Government has taken note of the mood in the country. The Grid's arrogant flouting of the law and the frequent terror attacks have provoked a groundswell of anger that could bring down the Government."

"They scraped by that vote of no-confidence by a narrow margin," said Athena. "The clever money is on a General Election in the summer, isn't it?"

"Those conversations with Erebus concerning events thirty years ago brought these different rumblings into focus. Last year we saw sickening footage of the beheadings of journalists. They were reporting on conflict without the restrictions in place three decades ago. Satellites and the internet allow journalists the freedom to report what they want, how they want. Their safety gets compromised, and we've seen the penalty. ISIS has access to the same technology and uses it to spread their message of hate."

"That's gone quiet in the past month," said Henry. "Thank goodness. They contained the threat."

"Which begs the question of why there were references to them in these speeches, Henry asked Alastor. "With everything else the Government needs to tackle, why would they foster interest in something no longer headline news? What if factions exist that don't want that situation to continue?"

"Before the Falklands War, the Government weren't in a favourable position with many in the country," continued Minos. "There was high unemployment, high inflation, plus cuts in public expenditure. The Tories were unpopular. After the war, the Falklands Factor helped them win the 1983 Election. The reality of a fractured nation got lost in the hysterical headlines of British heroism. In the decade that followed, the conflict played a significant role in Cool Britannia emerging."

"Are you suggesting the Government has orchestrated these rumblings to prepare the public for military action against ISIS?" asked Giles Burke.

"What better way to deflect the public's attention from what's happening at home where they are losing the battle with organised crime?" asked Minos. "Imagine the positive spin they could put on showing ISIS they can't bully us; we've had enough of standing by waiting for them to strike at us on our shores. We're confident enough to bloody their noses in their backyard."

Athena was dumbstruck.

"They hope to transform the fortunes of the Government before the Election by taking us into a war in the Middle East. That would be madness."

"That is our interpretation of the articles, unguarded comments and opinions expressed by respected politicians," said Minos. "In the coming weeks, we expect an escalation in the warmongering."

"What evidence do you have for that?" asked Henry.

"You are aware of the role of the BBC Monitoring Service?" asked Alastor.

"I know it started in WWII," replied Henry, "to give the British Government access to foreign media and propaganda. It provided valuable information in places where foreign journalists were banned."

"That role has continued," said Minos. "The Monitoring Service played an important role in helping observers keep track of developments during the Cold War and the eventual collapse of the Soviet Union. It's a part of the BBC which monitors and reports on mass media worldwide, based at Caversham Park, Reading. It has overseas bureaux in cities such as Moscow, Cairo, Nairobi and Delhi. They select and translate information from radio, television, press, news agencies and the internet from one hundred and fifty countries in over seventy languages. Reports produced by the service are used as open-source intelligence by elements of the Government and commercial customers."

"I understand their role," said Henry, "but what have they gleaned that has got the Government so agitated?"

"A series of messages on the web emanating from ISIS-held territory within Syria and Iraq speak of the escalation of sustained attacks within Europe," replied Minos. "They're designed to create havoc and panic. They also hope to encourage thousands of young men and women to return from Europe to join them."

"How can the public expect the presentation and interpretation of the material they have gathered to be impartial?" asked Giles. "Given that the BBC is neither impartial nor neutral."

"It has a liberal bias, but not so much a party-political bias," added Henry. "How could these warmongers guarantee they avoid mixed messages from the BBC?"

The Two Amigos had stumbled upon something that divided opinions around the table. Athena wished Phoenix and Rusty were here to contribute. Artemis was in the icehouse, ensuring they received up-to-the-minute data on the Northamptonshire mission. Her counsel was always valuable.

"Athena, should we continue to log voices in favour of conflict?" asked Minos, exasperated at the impasse, "or do you think we see something that isn't there?"

Athena considered for a moment.

"Please continue, Minos. We would be foolish to ignore any data you gather on our behalf. It may not get used in the short term, but little since Olympus began has been of no use."

"I agree," admitted Henry Case, "this could be significant. The more I consider what Alastor said, the more intriguing it becomes. How could the Government guarantee they received data from the Monitoring Service to support their 'sabre-rattling'? It would be far more likely the BBC took a polar-opposite stance. These days it's an urban-based organisation whose numbers are dominated by youth and diversity. Has that mix ever aligned with any idea the Establishment favours?"

"Never in a million years," said Giles, "but for the messages to be consistent across the board, we need to be talking about the 'c' word."

That brought a smile to everyone around the table. Not uttering the actual word conspiracy was a legacy from Erebus, their founder.

"Olympus has always avoided describing anything like a secret plan by a group to do something unlawful or harmful," said Athena. "Erebus hated ascribing a simple explanation to an event that defied instant explanation. He was a great believer in playing a long game. Watch and wait. The truth will reveal itself; he used to tell me. So, if your suspicions are correct, Henry, we must continue to watch and wait. If there's a hidden hand guiding this, we will discover it. It may not even come from within the Government."

Sandy Nesbitt arrived at the Kettering safe house at last. She looked tired and dishevelled.

"Apologies for the delay, Phoenix," she began.

"I hope it was worth it,"

Don Donovan couldn't resist chipping in. Phoenix watched the colour in Sandy's face spread from her throat to the top of her head. Donovan had hit a nerve.

"Not to worry," he said, "you're here now. Better late than never. Get your gear stowed away. The only bedroom that doesn't look like a bomb's hit it. That's yours. Report back when you've showered, changed, and are ready to talk. Are you hungry?"

Sandy nodded as she headed upstairs.

"After Sandy and I have finished, we'll eat lunch together. Can you and Don nip into town to pick up something, Rusty?"

"Come on, Rusty," grinned Donovan, "we'll go shopping. Give the boss alone time with the little woman,"

When they got outside and into the van, Rusty asked: -

"Were you born a tosser, or have you had to work at it?"

"What were you? SAS? Did you work undercover much?" asked Donovan, ignoring the barbed comment.

Rusty nodded. "Yes, to both," he replied.

"I never had the intensity of training you had," Donovan went on. "I didn't enlist until my late twenties. I'd studied linguistics at Oxford. My early career was in the same field. Circumstances on the ground in Iraq forced me into hiding behind enemy lines. I got separated from my two companions in a dust storm. I thought if I kept my wits about me, I could survive. I was fluent in the local language, so I went on that patrol. The Iraqis mistreat people with disabilities. But I preferred suffering intolerance as I played the role of a deaf-mute to that of being exposed as a British soldier."

"How long did you have to keep up the pretence?" asked Rusty.

"Forty-seven days," Donovan replied. "The longest

forty-seven days of my life. An armoured patrol came into the village before dawn. I had to sleep outside on the outskirts. When they stopped close by, I heard voices in an accent I recognised for the first time in six and a half weeks. I whistled the theme tune from 'When The Boat Comes In', and a squaddie from Tyneside joined in the chorus. He was suspicious. Thought I might lure him into a trap. I stood up and walked towards him with my hands in the air. He looked at my rags, scraggly beard and long hair. Guess what he said?"

"Go on," said Rusty.

"Fuck me, Donovan; we thought you were dead, man."

"Did it take long to get over that?" asked Rusty.

"Who says I did?" replied Donovan. "My smart-mouth remarks are a way of hiding what's scratching away inside my head."

Rusty knew Phoenix would never appreciate what this guy went through. He did, and he must tell his friend to give Donovan slack.

"Right, let's get that food," he said, driving the van towards the town centre.

Sandy came downstairs in the safe house and found Phoenix in the lounge. She looked a good deal fresher. Her brushed hair and the chunky sweater looked good on her. He wasn't sure the scarf was necessary indoors. The central heating was in good working order. What did he know? Maybe it was the fashion these days for thirty-something females?

"I've paired you with Don Donovan," he said, "though not by choice. If he gives you any trouble, let me know. He'll be off the mission and out of his new accommodation pronto."

Phoenix showed her the background file and explained

what was required of the pair once they arrived in Northampton.

"Anything else you need, just ask," he said.

"Can I explain why I was late?" said Sandy, that redness in her face Phoenix had noticed earlier climbed again.

"Did you get delayed in Wexford?" he asked.

"The flight over to Ireland went fine. It wasn't the first time I'd carried dead or dying passengers. I saw enough of that in Helmand. Fintan arranged to get the chopper collected from the field where we landed. Nothing official, just a large open patch of heathland a mile from his house. We called into his place for a spell while we waited for the tide to turn."

"Don't tell me," said Phoenix. "He cooked for you, and you washed it down with a glass of Jameson's?"

Sandy Nesbitt still blushed.

"How did you know?"

"Fintan entertained me too, but I'm guessing he had an ulterior motive in your case?"

"I was due to be driven to Waterford to get a flight home," said Sandy. "Fintan suggested I crossed to South Wales on the fishing boat. He offered to travel onboard to keep me company and be there when they buried Les Biggar at sea. He thought it only right someone Biggles knew was there."

"Fintan always planned to be on that boat," said Phoenix with a grin. "He wanted an excuse to be with you on a long sea journey."

"Well, you know what a charmer he is," said Sandy. "It's ages since anyone paid me so many compliments. I couldn't resist that animal magnetism."

"You needn't join the dots," said Phoenix, "and it explains the scarf."

Her bright red face filled in the dots, regardless.

"Two people, one bunk, on a boat gently rocking on a calm sea. I thought I might never see him again. What the hell?"

"Then, when you reached the Welsh coast, you had the problem of getting from the back of beyond to civilisation," said Phoenix. "I can sympathise. It took me longer to negotiate that stretch than to get from there to Bath."

"I got a train to Cardiff from Haverford West, found a park bench to sleep on, and caught a train here this morning. Six hours of agony. I was knackered, ached from head to foot and needed a shower."

"I can confirm you needed a shower when you arrived," said Phoenix. "As for being tired and weary, much of that was self-inflicted."

"Mmm," said Sandy; the distant look in her eye told Phoenix that, self-inflicted or not, there were no regrets.

Outside the house, they both heard the van return. Rusty and Don Donovan walked indoors. The food smelled delicious.

Sandy's stomach rumbled.

"I take it you didn't get breakfast at this park bench hotel?" asked Phoenix.

"No, I didn't, and I'd worked up such an appetite. Still, I can put that right now."

"Sorry, Phoenix," said Rusty. "We couldn't find a store with a healthy option today. You'll have to suffer a burger."

"I could eat a horse," said Phoenix.

"There are several racecourses in the area," said Donovan, "it's not beyond the realm of possibility."

Sandy laughed.

"If they dish up horse meat, it won't be on the plate fur long," she cried.

"We're going to have trouble with these two," groaned Rusty as he brought plates through from the kitchen. "Tuck in, you need to be in Castle Ward, and we have a date with someone in Wellingborough this evening."

After they had eaten, Rusty drove the odd couple off to the county town. Don and Sandy had dressed down for the occasion. Their clothes, hair and features were now more appropriate for the homeless people they portrayed. It wasn't difficult to get the look right. They both had experience.

"They'll blend into the scenery within minutes," said Rusty on his return. "Have we heard from the others yet?"

"Nothing since the check-in message via our comms when you delivered them to their patch. It's early days."

"Have you talked to Larcombe?"

"I spoke to both Athena and Giles first thing. Artemis was on duty this morning while Giles attended the meeting. I'm hoping for news on that from Giles later.

"When you're ready, it's only a twenty-minute drive from here," said Rusty.

"He won't get there until six," said Phoenix.

"It will be dark before then; why wait? He doesn't deserve the extra hours."

The two agents changed into dark clothing, checked their weapons and left the safe house. The sooner this was over, the better.

Glenn Cornell was thirty-eight years old. He had worked as a personal trainer for twelve years and had spent the past four years in Wellingborough. Although it fitted its description as a market town in the last century, it now had a population of fifty thousand. Wellingborough was part of a sprawling borough that increased the number of residents to seventy thousand.

What had attracted Cornell to the area was the borough intended to grow even more extensive as it spread towards Milton Keynes. It looked like an ideal place to set up his business. Cornell hunted female victims who wanted to keep fit. Young ones who tried to look their best to attract a mate; the young married women who wanted to lose the extra pounds they put on after having kids. The elderly who desperately tried to recapture their youth; they were fair game to Glenn Cornell. As Wellingborough grew, so did his number of potential victims.

Cornell was meeting a new client at six, outside the local library. She had called him and insisted on meeting on neutral territory. Glenn Cornell tried to put her mind at rest over the phone. He assured her his premises over an estate agency were perfectly safe. He had group sessions there three evenings a week. She could attend those until she felt comfortable enough to make a solo booking.

Women could book individual sessions on the other two evenings. Each session lasted an hour. Cornell could accommodate any client who wanted a home visit during the day. He kept his weekends free, officially, but he'd made exceptions for several clients in the past four years.

Artemis had listened to Cornell's voice as he coaxed and cajoled her into attending a taster session. He had a way with words. She wasn't fooled but understood how other women succumbed to the flattery. As instructed by Phoenix, she insisted on setting the ground rules for this first meeting. Rusty had thought there was a risk he wouldn't accept, but Artemis reckoned his record suggested he would see her as a challenge. With his macho image, she was a challenge he couldn't resist.

Artemis had been right. Cornell was fascinated by her voice over the phone. It told him she wasn't a teenager or an old biddy. He imagined her to be a few years younger than himself. He always hoped they were attractive, but it didn't matter; he needed to persuade them to book an individual session.

Cornell kept himself in excellent physical shape and ensured his clients got a good view while they trained. He watched for the signs. He made his move once he realised he had sparked their interest in something other than keeping fit. The secret cameras on the premises gave him ammunition for blackmail.

On home visits, the holdall he carried his gear in contained another recording device. Cornell was a devious predator. He never attacked someone at random. What aroused him were the game's various stages; the initial spark at a group training session — a negotiation over where they met. Cornell tried to guess whether the client would make the first move or if he had to force the pace.

It was better if they came on to him. That gave him the edge when he revealed what he'd recorded. Not that it was money he was after. He wanted to fix the date and time when they met again. That was where Glenn Cornell uncovered his darker side. The sex became much more physical and often violent. He got off on almost strangling them and beating them around the body. He left bruises they could hide from boyfriends, partners, or husbands. Cornell took great care not to mark them anywhere visible.

Cornell had an overriding need to dominate. It didn't work for him otherwise. If a client enjoyed the rough sex, even encouraged it, it spurred him to a physical assault. They had to be submissive. There could be no equals in this relationship. If they then complained, he shrugged and reminded them of the filmed evidence he held. He could produce that at any time and prove their sex had been consensual.

A handful of women had dared come forward with their story. Giles and Artemis discovered messages on a social media site. When they trawled deeper on the web, they found evidence of Cornell carrying on the same sordid routine at premises he leased before moving to Wellingborough. Not all his victims would ever surface, but the trail led back to North London, Aldershot and Torquay.

The predator moved on when the number of victims grew too large in any location. As soon as Cornell sensed a client was about to go to the police, he closed his business and moved on to explore new fields. He was adept at covering his tracks. He left his reputation behind; it was baggage he didn't need. Cornell had played this game for years.

Phoenix parked the van opposite the library, thirty yards from the nearest street light. They saw everything they needed to see, but Cornell wouldn't know they watched him.

"There he is," said Rusty, "hooded jacket, beanie and shorts. Even in January. A typical sporting jock. Can't resist showing off the gastrocnemius and the soleus muscles."

"If you say so, Rusty," said Phoenix.

They watched Cornell pacing the pavement outside the library. He looked impatient. The personal trainer took his mobile phone from his jacket pocket and made a call. In the ice-house back at Larcombe Manor, Artemis let it ring for a while before answering: -

"I'm running late," she said, sounding breathless, "please wait. Just two minutes. Look for a red Mini Cooper."

Cornell moved to the edge of the pavement, looking left and right.

"Which direction are you coming from?" he asked.

Phoenix heard the passenger door close behind Rusty. He switched on the engine.

"I don't know the area well," said Artemis. "I must be close."

"Excuse me, mate?" Cornell heard a voice behind him. "Have you seen a red Mini Cooper?"

Glenn Cornell turned to see who was behind him. A van pulled up by the pavement. The client still spoke to him on the phone.

"I think I need to find a different personal trainer," she said. "I reckon you're going out of business."

Rusty shoved Cornell towards the open van door. Phoenix grabbed his arms; the mobile phone flew into the air. Rusty caught it, helped Phoenix subdue Cornell and then closed the door. The streets of Wellingborough were safer now. All done and dusted in less than twenty seconds.

"Thanks for your help," Rusty said to his wife. "I wish we could chat, but I must dash. Talk to you soon."

"Remind Cornell of Maisie Reynolds, from Aldershot," said Artemis, "the lonely widow he attacked in her own home. She was so traumatised she took her own life. Maisie would have been sixty today."

"If we kept searching, we might find other victims out there," said Rusty.

"Perhaps, and if we allowed him to keep offending, there might be more deaths. My conscience is clear."

"Mine, too," replied Rusty.

"Good luck with the rest of the mission," she said. "Tell Phoenix to check in with Giles tomorrow. He's off duty this evening."

Phoenix drove away from the library once Rusty got back in the van.

They would deal with the low-life when they returned to the safe house in Kettering. A clean-up crew could dispose of the body tomorrow.

"Nobody will miss him," said Rusty.

"It's just a shame those unknown victims can't watch him suffer," said Phoenix.

Chapter Eleven

Wednesday, 14th January 2015

"What time were our crew arriving?" asked Rusty as Phoenix pulled into a parking space near the town centre.

"Fifteen minutes after we left the safe house,"

"Good," said Rusty, "our guest wasn't alone for too long then."

Phoenix had moved on to focus on today's mission.

"Ben, can you hear me?"

"Yes, Phoenix, loud and clear. I can see the van. I'm making my way over to you."

"Don't approach the van. We don't want it associated with you. We'll meet you in that cafe two doors further on from the bank."

Ben Anderson crossed the busy road and headed inside the warm café. He ordered a drink and grabbed the only free table. He saw the two Olympus agents follow him a minute later; they joined him.

"How's student life?" asked Rusty.

"I've seen little of Ross," said Ben, keeping his voice low, "he's been hanging out in Abington. A lot of students live there. It's two miles from here. He's due to arrive in the centre by noon. I'll go by then. So, nobody will connect us."

"I'm meeting Ross alone to put any nosy parkers off the scent," said Phoenix, "we can't be too careful. OK, what have you learned?"

"Dealers from Manchester and Liverpool are targeting the students," said Ben, "they've established county lines and are big on intimidation all over the campuses."

"That's what we understood," said Rusty, "the county lines are phone lines used for the buying and selling drugs. Those drugs come from larger metropolitan cities for distribution in smaller market towns. In a university town, there's a ready market in a concentrated spot."

"There's drug-related anti-social behaviour at the St John's hall of residence," added Ben Anderson, "The police were there last week executing search warrants. They arrested a student on suspicion of being in possession with intent to supply."

"Have you heard of any addresses taken over in the town or student accommodation in the halls?" asked Rusty.

"They're not on the campus yet, but Ross has seen evidence in Abington. He will fill you in on that later."

"Any names that have cropped up yet? I know you've not been there long, but…" asked Phoenix.

"There are two names associated with the intimidation," Ben answered, "Brantly Mason and Demarai Scott. They're mid-twenties, from Manchester. Hard as nails, I reckon they've been in a gang since they were ten or eleven. I've seen them at work, but I've kept away. They're evil bastards."

"Great work, Ben. That's what we need. I'll get

Larcombe to dig out their backgrounds. It gives us someone on which to focus. Drink up, and get back on the streets. The longer you're here, the more suspicious people will get."

"Yeah," grinned Ben, "why would a student be hanging around with two wrinklies like you?"

Ben finished his latte and left.

"Do you think they do any of those wraps here?" asked Phoenix.

"I'll ask," said Rusty, "but this café feels more old school."

It was eleven when the two agents left. The second mug of coffee and the bacon roll filled them up and kept them away from the chilly wind.

"Another hour before we meet Ross Summers," said Phoenix, "where shall we head?"

"The Grosvenor Centre is undercover. It will be warmer than standing on this street," said Rusty.

Phoenix tried the comms at noon to see if Ross was in range.

"Ross, have you got into town yet?"

"Hi, Phoenix. I've just got off the bus. Where are you?"

"On the first floor of the Grosvenor Centre. Get up here as soon as you can."

Ross appeared ten minutes later. He waved a greeting from twenty yards away.

"Crikey, he looks even younger dressed liked that," said Rusty.

"Ross fits in with the modern student," said Phoenix, "but I'm not sure we should be outside this kid's toys store. It's bound to look creepy if they catch us on CCTV. Let's keep on the move."

"Ben said you had seen evidence of vulnerable people

intimidated by the dealers, Ross. Is that right?" asked Phoenix.

"There was one poor guy with mental health issues whose house was being used by drug dealers, prostitutes and alcoholics. He thought they were friendly when it started but couldn't prevent the escalation. The dealers weren't local. They had moved in from Sheffield."

"Is that the only case you've seen so far?" asked Rusty.

"The only one I've witnessed, but chatting with students and other locals in the pubs, I've heard it's spreading over the town. The signs are obvious. Increased anti-social behaviour is typified by increased comings and goings from a property. Litter increases, noise becomes intrusive, and disturbances spill onto the street. These don't always get a response from the police, but neighbours are pissed. Often, the gang takes over several properties and moves between them. Or they use one property for the odd day before moving on to keep one step ahead of the police."

"Keep trawling for names that crop up," said Phoenix, "I want to have more than the two we've identified so far. If they don't materialise soon, we'll consider another way to close these operations."

"Will do," said Ross, "when do you want to meet us again?"

"This needs to happen by Friday," said Rusty, "if we don't hear from you and Ben before then, we'll switch to Plan Two. On Friday evening, we'll remove you both. Someone will ask questions when you are parachuted into an area like you were. Once that becomes a gang member, instead of the students and locals you've pressed for information, it means trouble."

"Understood," said Ross, "we're as careful as we can be, but thanks for the warning."

Ross left them and made his way to the ground floor via the escalator. The two agents headed for an exit at the opposite end of the shopping centre — time to get the van and return to the safe house.

Tyrone O'Riordan had been in the Glencairn Bank for less than an hour. He arrived at noon, and if he was still there at four o'clock, it was because he'd had a hectic day. At least, that's what he told himself. There were thousands of others doing the hard work for him.

Tyrone had to ensure the dirty money they moved through his private bank was clean when it arrived in their High Street bank accounts. His commission reduced the amount, but it was clean.

Tyrone had checked the financial indicators he used to ensure the money the Grid invested worked as profitably as possible; that had been Hugo Hanigan's legacy. He had developed a great strategy, one Tyrone followed in many markets. The Glencairn had earned a reputation for performing well above the rest of its competitors. Tyrone took more risks than Hugo, especially with the commission he had collected. The figures he had looked at this lunchtime still showed a positive trend. Tyrone was content.

There was a knock on the office door.

"This was just delivered by courier, Mr O'Riordan."

It was Philomena, his assistant. She handed him the jiffy bag and closed the door behind her. Tyrone caught a whiff of her perfume; it was intoxicating.

The twenty-three-year-old graduate had been working for him for three months now. The chemistry between them was evident from the day she attended the interview.

Why hadn't he slept with her yet? Tyrone made a note to rectify that.

The Grid's operations and its enemies occupied his mind for far too much of his time. Tyrone was aware he over-indulged in his few hours of leisure time. If it continued, he could damage his health and his bank balance. Was it time to take things at a slower pace?

Tyrone knew it would please his mother if he moved in with a woman. If he introduced her to a fine-looking, intelligent Irish girl such as Philomena, she wouldn't be able to contain herself. Tyrone forced himself to put thoughts of a long-term relationship to one side until work was finished. He left the jiffy bag until last.

"Right, let's see what this was," he said, opening the padded envelope.

Tyrone slid out a photograph and looked at it in horror. The twins, Graham and Paul Heath were united in death. Side by side as they had been in their first photo in the hospital at birth. This final image showed them with a bullet hole in the forehead. He grabbed the jiffy bag and looked inside to see if there was a note.

Two thumbs fell onto the highly polished desktop as he tipped it up.

Tyrone called his mother. He told her what he had on the desk in front of him.

"It's a shame you were so quick to pay those boys for their work," she said, "you could have saved yourself a bundle. Olympus didn't take long to find them, did they?"

"Olympus know about the Glencairn and that I run things from here. They don't have either of our addresses yet, but we've waited long enough. It's time to raise our game."

"You can't blame them for retaliating, Tyrone. You killed eight of their people last weekend."

"I never told you what happened at Ilford, did I?" said Tyrone, "we had to dump five bodies on the Marshes after Olympus hit one of our garages on Monday. The local Accident and Emergency hospitals, ten miles in every direction, were at crisis levels with broken bones from the punishments they dished out to the crew; nobody walked away unscathed. That place is out of action for a month. It will cost us two million quid, easy. They're hitting us hard, mother. I haven't got a clue where's next for treatment."

"What can you do?" asked Colleen.

"Hit them where it hurts," Tyrone replied. He dropped the thumbs back into the jiffy bag and took one last look at the photo before shredding it. Time to get home. Time to rally the troops.

In the Kettering safe house, Phoenix was talking to Giles.

"We still need to follow up on Cliff Barclay's progress on his case this afternoon," said Phoenix. "As for the shootings, unless Donovan and Nesbitt uncover something fast, we will have to go with the names we've uncovered so far. We have neither the time nor the resources to stay anywhere for an extended period. Security at Larcombe is uppermost in my mind."

"The Grid received the message at lunchtime," said Giles, "they will know we are balancing the books from the weekend. The Grid has two ways to go. Either they carry on their crooked business and ignore the occasional dent we make in their armour, or they go on the offensive."

"They have escalated their response on each occasion since this O'Riordan seized control," said Phoenix. "My gut tells me he will choose the latter. That's why Rusty and I must get back to Larcombe by Friday evening at the latest."

"I'll pass that on to Henry. I know he has stepped up the patrols, but is it enough? Maybe we need to establish our defensive lines. If those are visible from the lane or the air, the Grid will know we are ready for an attack. The element of surprise won't be available."

"Keep Athena in the loop," said Phoenix, "and discuss whatever Henry proposes with Rusty. If he's unreachable because we're in the middle of direct action, consult Thommo and Bazza. They will know what's required. They've got the battle scars to prove it."

"It feels inevitable, doesn't it?" said Giles.

"Armageddon, a final battle between good and evil? Yes, that's inevitable," said Phoenix. "Erebus prepared me for that day in those late-night meetings."

"We'll never defeat them without help from the authorities," said Giles. "They outnumber us."

"Numbers don't always count," said Phoenix, "I never professed to understand the analogy Erebus used. He said when a side has a man sent off in football, the ten men often prevail, even when playing a far superior side. They perform better as a team than they did when they had their full complement. They find reserves of strength they didn't know they had."

"I've seen that happen," said Giles. "It often means a change of tactics. Is there something we could do to even up the score?"

"Erebus was a strong believer in targeting the most significant gang members in the actions we undertake. When the attack comes, we must defend Larcombe for as long as possible to enable us to attack the heads of the Grid. If it were possible to remove O'Riordan and his mother and close the Glencairn Bank, it would paralyse the network protecting the organisation. It would create a vacuum if they didn't have easy access to a bank to launder their money. While they fought amongst themselves over who would take control and the money situation festered, those who survived that final battle could come out of hiding. We would be able to hand over the information the authorities need to reverse the trend. They would never end crime altogether, but whichever party is in Government would be forced to recognise public opinion is with them. We can already see how fed up they are with the Grid's influence on their daily lives from the demonstrations across the country."

"So, either way, the Olympus Project would face massive change," said Giles. "If we fail to create that vacuum, then we perish. If we succeed, we risk removing the veil of secrecy and giving the authorities additional intelligence to break the organised crime network and its stranglehold over the UK. Do they have the resources to make it happen?"

"I'll leave you to ponder that, Giles."

As the call ended, Giles turned to Artemis.

"Did you catch any of that?" he asked.

"Only snatches," she replied.

Giles nodded. He feared Artemis had heard more than that.

Danger lurked around every corner for Phoenix and Rusty when they were in the field. It was a chilling thought that the same might soon apply to everyone working here in the ice-house.

"Whatever we learn here has to be kept from anyone other than our superiors," he reminded her. Maria Elena was innocent in this. It might soon be time to suggest she visited her parents back in Estepona.

In Kettering, while Phoenix was talking to Giles, Rusty had contacted Cliff Barclay. The Irregular arrived back from Corby thirty minutes later for a debrief with him and Phoenix.

"Do we have their names?" asked Phoenix.

"Rick Francis, the bloke involved," said Cliff, "is one sick, depraved individual. His partner, Leigh-Anne Dyson, is complicit in everything that's happening. She's the manipulative one in the team. She persuades the youngsters to start on the drink and drugs. She's not afraid to use violence to get what she wants, either. Francis is a dangerous bastard, but the pair of them are evil. Their victims are traumatised beyond belief. Who knows if they'll ever find their way back?"

"Thanks, Cliff. Sorry you had to go through that ordeal, mate," said Rusty.

"Make them suffer, Rusty. That's all I ask."

"Take a break, Cliff," said Phoenix. "We'll sort them out tonight. The sooner those kids get help, the better."

Cliff went upstairs to his room. Phoenix and Rusty prepared for their evening's mission. As night fell, they left the safe house. Two hours later, Rick Francis and Leigh-Anne Dyson were parked outside the safe house in the back of the Olympus van.

Cliff Barclay asked if he could drive the prisoners to Larcombe Manor. He wanted to hand them over to Henry Case in person.

"I know he won't let me watch," said Cliff, "but I want to tell them what will happen to them on the way to Bath."

Phoenix sent him on his way. He called Giles to let Henry know to expect an angry Welshman.

Phoenix asked for one of the nearby Olympus teams to send a car they could use until they returned to Larcombe on Friday.

Rusty could travel back on the train with him to Bath Spa. He had often let the train take the strain when Erebus was in charge.

"After three hours with Cliff, those two will check into Hotel California without a murmur," said Rusty.

Thursday, 15th January 2015

"Any news on the children?" asked Artemis.

"We had to quieten them to get them to come with us," replied Rusty. "Francis and Dyson were high as kites when we broke into the flat. The kids were asleep, locked in the spare bedroom. We busted open the door as soon as we'd taken out the two so-called adults. You don't want to know the state of their living conditions. It would turn your stomach. The kids cowered in their beds; the stench of urine was overpowering. We tried to calm them without using the needle, but it was hopeless."

"Where did you take them?" asked Artemis.

"To the police station on London Road. We did our usual drop-off with a message — no big surprise. Nobody came outside to see what we had done. Giles put the CCTV camera on the fritz for one minute. Enough time for our visit to be undetected. Pray those kids receive the help they need."

"Weren't this bloke Francis and his accomplice ever on the radar from social services?"

"I think so, years back, but they didn't have the

resources to pursue the case. One of the staff went on long-term sick, and the others couldn't handle the extra workload."

"A familiar story," sighed Artemis.

"I love you," said Rusty.

"I know you do; come back safe," said Artemis.

"You OK, mate?" said Phoenix, overhearing the last exchange.

"We both want kids," said Rusty, "and there's no way we could ever treat a child as those two did. It's the uncertainty that's the problem. With trouble brewing, is it the wrong time to even be thinking of it?"

"Don't wait," said Phoenix. "It was the best thing that ever happened, both times. Enjoy every day while you can."

Phoenix stood up and headed for the door.

"That sounds like our car, Time to stop being morbid. Let's find Don and Sandy. I want to get the guy responsible for these gangland shootings."

Rusty drove them into Northampton. It felt better not having the van. They had used that when they were meeting up with Ben and Ross. They entered Castle Ward at ten o'clock and used the comms to set up a meet.

"Sandy can you and Don get across to Victoria Park?" asked Phoenix.

"We're on our way," replied Sandy.

Rusty parked the car, and the two agents walked through the park. It was far from deserted despite the wintry day.

"There's the Irregular couple," said Rusty, spotting them ahead.

"Or the odd couple," said Phoenix. "They look scary, don't they?"

"Right, you two," said Phoenix, calling them on his

mike. "Sit on the bench twenty yards in front of you. We'll stop here on the opposite side of the path, looking across to the stream. If anyone approaches, keep talking amongst yourselves. We'll pick it up once they've gone."

"Understood," said Don Donovan, "we've got a name for you."

"Kieran Freeman, a twenty-eight-year-old gang member," said Sandy Nesbitt. "He's been the enforcer for the main gang in the town for the past two years."

"Freeman has three confirmed kills, two possible and two kneecappings," added Donovan. "I half expected him to have emblems on the side door of his flash car, the same as fighter pilots in WWII."

Sandy had a fit of giggles.

"Is that for real, or is she still playing a role?" asked Rusty, with his hand over his mike.

Phoenix shrugged.

"I'm not that worried. We have a name now. We can take care of business and move on to the next job."

"You've got a plan, haven't you?" said Rusty.

"I do. What's Freeman's MO, Don?"

"Every killing has been a drive-by, Phoenix," replied Don.

"Happy days. You two can follow us back to where we parked. Your work here is over."

Chapter Twelve

Once they had arrived in Kettering, the Irregulars showered and changed into regular street clothes. Four Olympus personnel then gathered in the kitchen.

Rusty prepared for an early lunch.

"Can you explain the plan to us now, Phoenix?" asked Rusty.

"You and Sandy will take Freeman off the streets for an hour. Then, don and I will take his car into Northampton for a drive. I need you two Irregulars to come up with a timeline for where Brantly Mason and Demarai Scott will be in the next thirty-six hours."

Ten minutes later, they handed Phoenix a schedule the pair of thugs had followed since they were on the ground.

"This is only a brief snapshot, Phoenix," Sandy cautioned. "We weren't there long enough to gauge whether these few sightings were habitual or random."

"How did it feel to you, Don?" asked Rusty.

"Most criminals are creatures of habit," said Don Donovan, "especially if their stock-in-trade is violence.

They're thick by nature, so I'd bet these regular outings each day passes for normal in their world."

"I'd take a gamble too on this occasion," said Phoenix, "time isn't on our side. Which of these three sightings do you think gives us the optimum window?"

The two Irregulars studied the options, and both pointed at the same one.

"When they leave this Caribbean restaurant at lunchtime," said Don, "it's always between one-forty-five and two-fifteen. A car picks them up and takes them to their next place of business. That varies…"

"We're not worried about their destination," said Phoenix, "only how long they spend walking from that doorway to the car."

"A minimum of twenty seconds," said Sandy. "But, if the car has to wait to pick them up because the traffic lights ahead are against them, it could be up to a minute."

"We need an extra pair of legs," said Phoenix. "Rusty, call Ben and Ross. Get one of them on this street at one-thirty today. We'll explain why closer to the time. Whatever Freeman plans to do between those times must change. Is that clear?"

"Got it."

After they had eaten lunch, Phoenix called Giles. It was time for another update.

"Bring me up to speed on events at the morning meeting, Giles,"

"The three Russians have been disposed of with no problems to report."

"Good. Has the Grid learned of those deaths yet?"

"We may have another twelve to twenty-four hours on that score," replied Giles. "Still no sightings of Vasiliev. If he's overseas, O'Riordan might not be on top of what thugs on the low-hanging branches of the Russian gang are doing."

"See if you can trace Vasiliev. It's a low priority, though. What do we know about the funerals for those agents that died at the weekend?"

"Athena has talked with Zeus. He and Hera will attend Hugh Fraser's funeral in Scotland. They agreed to collect Ambrosia on their way north. That's on Wednesday of next week. Athena is going to Bath Abbey for Orion's funeral. Henry Case has agreed to attend the service on Friday next for the Larcombe-based agent who died at Orion's home. The families of the agents who died in the same attack as Hugh learned of their deaths the same day. As is usual in these circumstances, the local teams will send representatives. Funerals will be low-key. With everything going on with the Grid, Zeus advised Athena not to make more public appearances than was necessary. That same message went to each of the senior Olympians."

"That's good, we must tread warily, but we owe it to our agents to have someone from the organisation at their funeral wherever possible. Have we received anything further from the Monitoring Service?"

"There was another message intercepted last night," said Giles. "I'll send it through to you."

"Thanks, Giles. We'll be back tonight if everything goes to plan. Oh, one last thing, did Henry have something to report this morning?"

"His two guests checked out," said Giles, "and Cliff Barclay is on a train heading for home. It doesn't sound like you need him anymore on this mission, am I right?"

"Yes, did Henry keep Cliff away from the action?"

"He did, but he relented early this morning. He added him to the duty roster for the trip to the pet cemetery.

Henry said he'd never seen anyone so happy when told to dig a hole in the rock-hard ground in the dead of winter."

"You can't beat job satisfaction," said Phoenix. "Cheers, Giles. I'll see you in the morning."

"Ross Anderson is moving into position for our mission," said Rusty, "it will be good to get him away from the area. He said the dealers became increasingly suspicious of him being around the halls of residence. One made a half-hearted attempt to run him over last night."

"OK," said Phoenix. He fired up his laptop and searched for the new message the BBC service had thought worthy of being forwarded to its audience.

The four agents watched the transcript on the screen as they listened to the message.

"Further confirmation that ISIS is on a major recruiting drive, and Europe can expect ten terror attacks for each one we've suffered in the past," said Rusty.

"Can you access the other messages your man at Larcombe accessed?" asked Don Donovan.

"I can get them, Don," said Phoenix, "why do you ask?"

"If I can listen to the others, I can confirm my suspicions," Don replied.

After they had listened to each of the messages, Donovan shook his head.

"There's something fishy here," he said. "Dozens of regional dialects exist, which hamper translators who want to get a precise interpretation. I studied several at university but became attuned to the more delicate nuances when I got stranded in bandit country. Someone distorted those messages. ISIS threatens to continue attacks in Europe, and they are asking young Muslims to join them, but that's it. It's just the same twisted rhetoric we've heard for ages. There's no talk of escalation."

"Are you sure?" asked Phoenix.

"Positive," said Donovan.

"The people behind the hostile propaganda Minos and Alastor collated must have someone on the inside at Caversham," said Rusty. "These messages have been manipulated to suit their purpose."

"Only a handful of people in the country could unscramble those messages," said Donovan. "A news bulletin wouldn't relay it in full without a commentary over the top to mask the true meaning."

"Are you saying it's a conspiracy," asked Sandy Nesbitt.

"We avoid the word," said Rusty, "but it smells like it, doesn't it, Phoenix?"

"I'll call Athena at once. We need to act on this before they get enough ammunition to commit this country to a conflict it can ill afford and struggle to win."

"What time do we leave?" asked Rusty.

"Freeman is at home," said Sandy Nesbitt, "his car is out front. He hasn't surfaced yet today. When he's not working, he's a night owl."

"How do you know?" asked Phoenix.

"He lives in a first-floor flat on a street with two CCTV cameras. I'm watching his pad now on my tablet. We can get over there now. Rusty and I will look after him."

"Right, let's load up the car and get on with it," said Phoenix.

Thirty minutes later, they were in the lane behind the row of shops. It was a quarter to one. Sandy moved onto the street to ring the doorbell for the first-floor flat. She relayed her movements to Rusty. He was in the rubbish-strewn space behind the newsagents and had clambered onto the outbuilding's pitched roof. When Freeman answered the door, he prepared to enter through the window.

Rusty heard the bell; Sandy kept pressing it. He heard Freeman cursing and stomping across the floor. Rusty levered open the wooden window and slipped inside the flat. Downstairs, Freeman was cursing Sandy. What the hell did he care if her cat was on the roof? The voices grew louder as Freeman realised the only way this woman was leaving was if he leaned out of his window to rescue her bloody cat.

He stepped through his flat door, and Rusty whacked him with a cosh. Freeman kissed the floorboards and was unconscious.

"Car keys?" asked Sandy.

"On the table by the door," said Rusty, "let's get those to Don."

Sandy went to the open window, whistled, and Don Donovan peered over the fence.

"Can you throw straight?" he asked.

Sandy lobbed the keys at him. He caught them in one hand. "Not bad for a girl," Sandy grinned and disappeared out of sight. He and Phoenix needed to be elsewhere.

"Put your feet up," said Rusty, "we've got to babysit for a while."

"Do you mind if I keep this window open? Maybe open a few more?" asked Sandy. "Freeman must love his weed; if I stay in here too long, I'll be off my head."

"Chill," said Rusty, relaxing on the leather sofa.

Sandy sat by the window, hoping Freeman stirred.

Don Donovan was driving into town, heading for the restaurant.

"We can park just along here," he said. "I spotted it when we were on surveillance."

"Are you in position yet, Ross?" asked Phoenix.

"I'm on the opposite side of the street to the restaurant. It's one forty-three by my watch."

"Agreed. Don and I have parked on that side of the road. We have a visual on the doorway."

"Me too," said Ross. "I know what to do."

The early afternoon traffic kept moving steadily. Shoppers crossed the street at random places. Sometimes they even resorted to using light-controlled crossing. Phoenix kept an eye on the door.

"Two o'clock," said Don Donovan.

"Any sign of their ride?" asked Ross.

A stretch limousine eased into the street. As it rounded the corner, it brought traffic in the opposite lane to a standstill due to its length. Donovan switched on the engine of the Mercedes. He edged out of the parking space and inserted himself into the nearside lane forcing a car to brake; he raised a hand in apology. Donovan moved into the far lane. They were right in front of the limo. The limo's need for space to negotiate the corner had created a gap which played into their hands.

The door to the restaurant opened, and Mason and Scott strolled onto the pavement. Arrogance in every step. They stopped and waited for the limo to travel the next thirty yards. Ross Summers stood at the crossing and pressed the button. The limo was now yards from the restaurant door.

Don Donovan and the Mercedes were preventing them from reaching it.

The lights turned red. Pedestrians got the green light to walk; Ross raised his phone to his ear and walked.

Don had slowed for the lights, but there was room for him to allow the limo to park. He stopped. Mason gave the Mercedes a disdainful sneer; Scott raised the middle finger.

"Get out of the way, fool," he shouted.

Ross Summers had crossed onto the pavement and aimed his phone up the street.

Rusty lowered the passenger window. Mason and Scott's eyes widened as a man inside the car opened fire with the Skorpion machine pistol.

Ross Summers started to film with his camera.

The lights changed. Don Donovan accelerated away.

"Drive straight to Freeman's place," ordered Phoenix. "Ross, send that film to Giles Burke at Larcombe Manor. He'll post it on social media and make sure the police know it's there; it won't be traced back to you. They'll be flooding this street in the next few minutes. You get back to the halls of residence. Lie low for the next twenty-four hours, and then you and Ben can return to your digs. Olympus will contact you when we need you again. Good job."

"Thanks, Phoenix. I won't be sorry to get out of this town. Those dealers scare me rigid."

Rusty and Sandy still babysat Kieran Freeman when they reached the killer's flat. He was awake now and not happy.

"I take it that everything went like clockwork?" asked Rusty.

Phoenix nodded.

"What now?" asked Sandy Nesbitt.

"Don's valeting the car, free of charge. As soon as he's finished, we'll be on our way. Mr Freeman can then get on with his day. We need to disable him for an hour."

Sandy opened her bag and removed a zipped wallet; inside was a needle and an ampoule. Rusty held Freeman as she injected the drug.

"Night, night," she said.

The thug was in a deep sleep within fifteen seconds.

Rusty removed the restraints from his hands and feet and ripped the duct tape from his mouth. Phoenix and Rusty lifted him onto the bed.

Don Donovan appeared at the door.

"Did I miss the fun? Everything's finished downstairs. Where were the keys when you found them?"

"On the table there, by the door," said Rusty.

"Do you want me to tidy up that window?" asked Donovan. "If we nail it shut, the police will dismiss it as a security measure. They'll not look too closely at what's up here, considering the evidence they've seen with their own eyes. But it's one less worry."

"I may have underestimated you, Don," said Phoenix. "Don't take too long. We need to be on our way."

It was after four when they reached the safe house in Kettering.

"I'll call the local team leader and tell him he can have his car back," said Rusty. "How far is the station from here?"

"A ten-minute walk, Rusty," said Donovan. "Do we have much to carry?"

"Nothing to stop us from blending in with the other travellers," said Phoenix.

"If we get short of space, Sandy can fit it into that voluminous bag of hers," said Don.

Sandy giggled and dug him in the ribs.

Phoenix gave up trying to understand women.

"A walk to the station then," said Phoenix. "We'll be in Bath by ten at the latest. Do you two have far to go to get back to your digs?"

Sandy looked at Don.

"My place is in Corby," she said.

"I'm in the opposite direction, Rugby," replied Don.

"Not far then," said Phoenix.

"Manageable," the two Irregulars replied at once.

"We'll be in touch when another job comes up," said Phoenix. "You two can stay here and use the facilities until they collect the car. Safe journey home."

"What did you mean by that?" asked Rusty as they strode out towards the station.

Phoenix left Rusty in the dark.

Friday, 16th January 2015

The morning meeting contained a mixture of light and shade. Athena was pleased to have her husband home safe from the Northamptonshire mission. Rusty and the others contributed to a successful outcome. Two depraved individuals would never harm another child. Two drug dealers were dead, and the only person who could have been responsible was another suspected killer, Kieran Freeman.

The police had wanted enough evidence to arrest Freeman for months. They couldn't believe their luck. They had a film of his car at the scene of a gangland killing, and then he calmly drove home and went to sleep. He protested his innocence and blamed a group of people who broke into his flat and held him hostage. It was the daftest alibi the detectives had ever heard. They even had a Skorpion machine pistol with his fingerprints as the confirmed murder weapon. Open and shut case sprang to mind.

Giles confirmed both Ross Summers and Ben Anderson had returned home without incident. Another team would replace Brantly Mason and Demarai Scott in time, but their deaths opened several police lines of inquiry. Giles would spread as much information as he could to aid in reducing and eventually removing the levels of intimidation suffered by the University's students.

There were darker moments, too, as they discussed the subsequent rash of funerals. It reminded the senior agents around the table that the successes were almost as frequent as the losses Olympus suffered.

"The distortion of those Monitoring Service messages was a surprise, Phoenix," Minos remarked. "It puts a different light on the subversive attempts to justify engaging in a war against ISIS."

"These people mean business," said Alastor, "but how do we respond?"

"It's plain to see the most vociferous people on this matter are only puppets," said Athena. "The faces of those holding the strings will never reveal themselves."

"Do we have the time and resources to fight on a second front?" asked Phoenix.

"What do you suggest?" asked Henry. "We can't stand by and watch the country fooled into believing the rubbish these people are broadcasting,"

"I propose Giles and Artemis become whistle-blowers. They can uncover the distorted messages intercepted at Caversham. That will sow seeds of doubt in the public's mind. For now, we can offer little else."

"I agree," said Athena. "Henry, what progress have we made on establishing our defensive lines?"

"Eighty per cent complete, Athena," replied Henry, "we'll finish on Sunday. Our available personnel will fetch weapons and ammunition from the armoury. Larcombe will be on alert twenty-four-seven. We won't get caught unawares."

"Fingers crossed, we don't get a snap inspection visit

from the Charity Commission," said Rusty. "It might be difficult for the gardeners to explain why they need Glocks while digging up our vegetables."

Light and shade, with Rusty providing a final lighter moment, Athena closed the meeting and prayed nothing dramatic happened in the next forty-eight hours. Her father was going home today. She was tired and feeling queasy.

Monday, 19th January 2015

At Larcombe Manor, the phoney war had begun. Every veteran who lived in the grounds of the Georgian mansion knew their role if the worst happened. They patrolled the boundaries day and night. Ice-house security systems watched for intruders who might appear overhead.

Athena had awoken early; there was a familiar feeling in her stomach. It was not the right time. Athena planned for a brother or sister for Hope before she reached forty and knew the longer she waited, the more difficult the pregnancy might become. Should she tell Phoenix of her suspicions or wait until the doctor confirms it?

Today, another matter to confront was Orion's funeral service in the Abbey.

The morning meeting would be brief today. There were briefings and training sessions for personnel in the ice-house. Several had served in one of the armed forces, but Artemis, for instance, brought layman's skills to the command centre.

They had to know what to do if an evacuation was necessary.

When the senior agents gathered at nine o'clock, Athena asked Giles for an update.

"The misinterpretation of the ISIS messages has been made public," said Giles. "Serious questions are being asked of the people who started this concerted campaign. It may not have derailed it altogether, but it's no longer on the main line. We've got enough momentum to see this matter side-lined until after the General Election. One good shove will see it finished."

"Terrific, Giles," said Athena. "Minos, will you and Alastor give that final shove, please?"

Minos nodded. He knew they would find a way if he and Alastor dug deep enough.

"Henry, what do you have to report?" asked Athena.

"Kelly Dexter is six months pregnant now. Hayden doesn't think she should serve on our defensive line. Kelly planned to keep working for as long as possible, but the possible escalation of the Grid's attacks has made Hayden think twice."

"If Kelly wishes to take a step back into a pure training role, that's acceptable," said Athena. "We will have agents going through retraining and recruits coming to Larcombe until that becomes impossible. Olympus must not alter the public perception of what we do by bowing to pressure from the Grid."

"Business as usual," said Phoenix.

"Next Sunday, at midnight," said Tyrone O'Riordan.

"What's that?" asked Colleen.

"D-Day. The destruction of the Olympus Project."

"How many men did you find prepared to risk their lives?" asked Colleen.

"More than enough," said Tyrone. "I told them to expect a picnic."

"The gangs and their leaders won't thank you if it goes pear-shaped," said his mother. "How many is more than enough?"

"Three hundred," Tyrone replied. "We have an unlimited supply of automatic weapons and ammunition. Loads have come into the country from Eastern Europe. They won't know what hit them."

"Do you know what they have at Larcombe Manor?" Colleen asked. "What if they have heavy artillery, rocket launchers, grenades? Won't the neighbours raise the alarm once your men start the attack?"

"We'll overrun them by sheer weight of numbers, mother. Don't be so weak. Remember, they've got women and children to protect, so if we walloped them with that first strike, they'd crumble."

"I don't want us killing women and children, Tyrone," said Colleen, "your Dad never stooped that low."

"Don't worry, mother. No women and children, but we can't afford to let this organisation recover. You understand that, don't you?"

There wasn't a spare seat in Bath Abbey as Phil Hounsell's coffin arrived. His Portishead colleagues stood shoulder to shoulder with the Manvers Street contingent. There were high-ranking police officers from across the country; Phil Hounsell was one of their own. He was a man who had moved on to a different career, but he was respected.

The manner of his death shocked the local community. Artemis recognised members of many of the families that had lived on the street near Mary Trueman's old home.

They had been her neighbours when she worked in Bath and Portishead.

Artemis was a few rows behind Erica. Shaun and Tracey stood on either side of her; heads bowed throughout the service. Artemis wanted to hug them as she had done when she had first met them. They had driven south as the news of Erica's kidnapping had broken. When he went into the station to help in the hunt, she had worked with Erica's mother, Mary, to comfort the young children.

Artemis spotted Callum and Debbie Wood in the congregation. He caught her eye. It was clear he wanted to talk when the opportunity arose.

Athena was alone in a pew filled with people she had no connection with. She found herself crying at poignant parts of the service. It was only a few months since they had attended her mother's funeral. Her emotions were all over the place. Her father had returned to Larcombe this morning; he was moaning already. He had plans for next weekend, as if she didn't have enough on her mind.

Callum Wood wasn't one hundred per cent sure if he had spotted the CEO of the Olympus Project. He would ask Artemis when they talked.

When the service ended, the family left the Abbey, walking behind the coffin. The midday traffic didn't let them travel over five miles per hour on the short journey to Haycombe crematorium.

Row upon row of uniformed police marched outside into the bitter wind. Nobody stood around chatting for long. Within minutes, the Abbey courtyard was deserted as the rest of the congregation slipped away to find a warm place to remember a colleague or friend.

"Zara," it was Debbie Wood who called her name.

The two women hugged. They had always been on good terms.

"Hello, Debbie. It was lovely to hear that you and Callum had a son. Ronnie, is it?"

"Yeah, my mum's got him today. I'm picking him up now. Callum wants a word, and then he's going back to work. Nice to see you again; shame about the circumstances. You know where we are if you ever want to chat."

Debbie scuttled off, wrapping her coat tighter against her.

"Let's get out of this wind," said Callum. They found a table in All Bar One around the corner from the Abbey. It was warm and welcoming.

"Hot chocolate?" asked Callum.

"Bugger that, I need a drink," said Artemis.

Callum fetched two large whiskies and a bottle of dry ginger.

"Right, it's time to put our cards on the table," he said after taking their first sip. "I've followed up on the dates Erica gave me for the only trip Phil made for Olympus. He was near Musselburgh at the end of October. At that time, police arrested Sir James Grant-Nicholls and charged him with the murder of his wife, Fiona, who had been missing for years. They found her remains on his estate. What possible connection could that have with the charity? Did Phil find the body?"

Artemis took another sip of her drink. She might need to get another whisky. She didn't say a word.

"The CEO was there today, wasn't she?" asked Callum. "A tall, dark-haired woman sat near the back at the end of a row. She was there representing the Olympus Project, I imagine? Erica told me you work at Larcombe too. Why didn't you sit together? Why didn't you tell me you worked with Phil? What have you got to hide?"

"Callum, I've never lied to you. It doesn't do to lie to the police. I told you what I thought you needed to know. I want to find who was responsible for his death as much as you."

"We haven't made much progress on that front," he sighed. "We keep confirming who it wasn't."

Artemis knew it was dangerous to say more. Phil's killer belonged to the Vasiliev gang. He had disappeared, and those who murdered Phil and Les Biggar were no longer breathing. She wished she could tell Callum, but it was impossible. As for Phil's trip to Scotland, that was even more dangerous to discuss.

"I work in one department at Larcombe. Phil worked in another," she said. "We never encountered one another at work. What he was involved in on that trip, I've no idea. The case you referred to can't have concerned Phil, surely? It must have been a coincidence. He was looking for the family of an ex-serviceman, I expect. We don't get requests to search for dead bodies."

Callum remained unconvinced. He was sure Zara knew more than she was admitting. His copper's nose told him so, and it was rarely wrong. They had finished their drinks.

"Same again?" he asked.

"Not for me, thanks," Artemis replied. "I promised my husband I wouldn't be late."

She got up to leave.

"Don't forget what Debbie said. Give us a ring if you want to talk," said Callum. "I might have more questions for you. Are you planning to go anywhere?"

"I won't be moving far away from Larcombe," she replied. "As for questions, I don't think there's any more I can add to what I've told you, Callum."

Artemis left the bar in the city centre and walked to the station. As she walked, she called Rusty.

"Can you send a car to fetch me from Bath Spa, please? I've had a drink. I'd better not drive."

"Don't worry, I'll come into Bath," he replied.

"Thanks. Did Athena get back yet?"

"She drove back from the Abbey," said Rusty. "The only person I've seen her talking with since was the doctor. They were chatting in the corridor outside Athena's apartment."

"You don't think…?"

"Another baby? No, Phoenix would have mentioned it."

Artemis wasn't so sure. Athena might hide her pregnancy from Phoenix with the imminent threat of action from the Grid.

She wouldn't want him to worry.

If Athena was pregnant, it changed everything.

Chapter Thirteen

Tuesday, 20th - Friday, 23rd January 2015

The grounds of the manor house had lost a little of their beauty. As Athena looked over the lawns from the guest bedroom windows, the vehicles from the transport section felt an ugly intrusion. She had persuaded Henry not to dig trenches. That would have been too much; Erebus would turn in his grave.

When the Grid's thugs attacked, Larcombe's defenders had cover. Athena couldn't imagine those moments. She prayed they were brief. When someone stood toe to toe with bullies, they chose flight over fight. After she met with the doctor yesterday, she wished that was the case more than ever.

Athena watched a car leaving Larcombe as it drove along the elegant driveway and rattled over the cattle grid. She waved a hand even though she knew the driver wouldn't look back.

Nine o'clock. Time to get to the morning meeting.

Phoenix was heading to the Midlands. Despite her opposition, he insisted on attending Andy Walter's funeral in West Bromwich.

Phoenix elected to stay on the A46 for most of the journey. A short stretch of unfamiliar roads brought him to the part of West Bromwich where Andy was born and raised. He had time for the scenic route — time to remember working with Andy and the others buried or cremated this week.

The responsibility of leadership weighed heavy on his shoulders of late He never set out to be a leader. He preferred to work alone. Erebus and Rusty taught him to be part of a team. A team that had become his family' it hurt when a family member died.

Phoenix had first met Andy Walters when they needed a shadow team of drivers to follow the transport vehicle from Belmarsh prison. There had been plenty of action in those few days last June, ending in Tommy O'Riordan's killing. Andy had been a driver for senior military personnel in Iraq and Afghanistan. He left the Army in 2011 and freelanced as an armed chauffeur for Arab Royalty when they visited London.

Phoenix recalled that he referred to him and Rusty as Batman and Robin. You never saw one without the other.

After a three-hour drive, Phoenix pulled into the Sandwell Valley Crematorium. He had thirty minutes to wait. The car park was only half-full. Whoever was inside, making their final journey, didn't have a big family. Several cars arrived as he waited.

Erebus insisted any funerals should be low-key, with family and close friends only, to protect the organisation's security. Phoenix expected to see a handful of Andy's former colleagues but not so many as to attract unwanted attention.

The funeral cortege entered the crematorium gates with seven minutes to go. The hearse bearing the coffin stopped at the door. Two funeral cars drew up behind. Andy's widow and three children got out of the first car; two elderly couples emerged from the second. His parents and in-laws, Phoenix assumed. Andy had been fifty-one. He was lucky to have the complete set.

The other mourners gathered on the pathway leading to the main door. Phoenix got out and walked across to join the queue. Nobody spoke. They filed inside. The service followed a traditional format; forty minutes later, they were outside again.

Phoenix made his way to his car; he was not alone. He counted five men altogether. Agents he had never met. Olympus personnel didn't stand in line to offer condolences to their colleague's family. Andy knew that when he joined. The Olympus pension fund would look after his family's financial well-being.

"When the family is grieving," Erebus told him, "they need reassurance that everything is taken care of, not platitudes."

Phoenix waited as, one by one, the cars left. He followed them at a distance through the gates. He needed time to reflect, to rest for a while, before facing that drive back to Larcombe. Phoenix drove into West Bromwich for a late lunch.

Phoenix parked near a shopping centre and strolled around the nearby streets to clear his head. A new-looking police station stood on the opposite side of the road. Maybe there was a café closer to where he parked. He turned and headed back the way he came. Inside the shopping centre, he found just what he needed. He ordered a healthy snack and a coffee. Rusty wasn't around to get him into bad habits.

"Hello, stranger," said a voice, "mind if I join you?"

The man who sat opposite Phoenix was a policeman.

"Mick, how are you? What brings you to West Bromwich? Are you working undercover again?"

"You know I can't tell you that, Frankie, or whatever you're calling yourself this week," said Mick, the barman from Newcastle who Phoenix met during the Dwyer case.

"Something tells me you didn't find me here in this café by chance," said Phoenix, "have you been following me?"

"You would have spotted me," grinned Mick, "no, it was just my good luck. I was leaving the station when I saw you pause on the pavement. I wondered why anyone would turn around and head in the opposite direction unless they had an aversion to police stations. Then the face and the way you walked brought it back."

"I'll wear a wig and a false moustache next time," said Phoenix.

"There may not be a next time," said Mick. "Look, the people you work for helped put away those criminals on Tyneside last year. My bosses were very grateful, but it didn't stop the top brass from starting a covert operation trying to track you."

"One more worry," said Phoenix.

"You're getting flak from organised crime, aren't you?" asked Mick. "No big surprise. Police around the country continued to receive unexpected help in cases where they've struggled to find sufficient evidence to break these gangs and put people away."

"We do our bit," said Phoenix, "without attracting too much attention."

"Several big names disappeared too, with no clues who was responsible," Mick continued. "The team investigating your outfit put these disappearances at their door. My input early on convinced them you were good people using methods outside the law to get results. The trouble is there's another bunch of people to concern us both."

"Are you implying police areas are giving us unofficial permission to continue our work because of its positive effects?"

"You didn't hear that from me," said Mick. "In London, top-brass, intent on pursuing the PC culture that has neutered the police force, want you hunted like dogs."

"So, these are the people you meant?" asked Phoenix.

Mick leaned closer and dropped his voice to a whisper.

"It goes far deeper than that," he said. "The establishment in this country is a collection of powerful groups with a permanent need to protect their position. They will do whatever it takes to influence the democratic process, so it doesn't threaten their interests. I'm aware in my job that the law favours the powerful. Look who controls the media. The unemployed, those on benefits, and immigrants are forever under the microscope. It's all done to switch focus from those who wield the real power."

"Hang on," said Phoenix, "are you referring to this concerted effort to embroil us in an unwinnable war in the Middle East?"

"Why am I not surprised you worked that one out," said Mick. "The public doesn't have a clue."

"What is their ultimate aim?" asked Phoenix. "We can't believe they think an all-out war against ISIS is the way forward."

"To understand that, you need to identify which power

group is behind this campaign," whispered Mick. "Are they on the extreme right or extreme left?"

"I've no idea," answered Phoenix truthfully. "I don't profess to understand the difference anymore,"

"This crowd are as far-right as you can get. You might describe the group as an elitist faction with racist tendencies. They've expanded in the past five years but have never shown their hand in any local or bye-elections. They may have councillors and even MPs in high positions, but they never adopted a party name to identify them to the electorate. That will happen at the June General Election. They plan for us to be at war with ISIS by that time. Can you imagine what this country would be like if they ever got into power?"

"Are there any connections with the Grid? That's what we call the network of organised crime."

"No confirmed links, but it's entirely possible," said Mick. "The Grid? That's good. We had our eye on an Irish banker called Hugo Hanigan last year, but he's disappeared. My superiors gave you credit for that."

"Cheeky beggars," said Phoenix. "No, we had nothing to do with that. It must have been an inside job."

"The O'Riordans' had to be responsible then. Mother and son live in penthouse apartments in the City. Tyrone has a place from which he could throw a coin into his private bank in Gresham Street. Mother lives closer to St Paul's Cathedral."

"Write those addresses for me," said Phoenix, "we've been after them for a while."

"I couldn't possibly sanction any action you might take," said Mick with a wink.

"I'm guessing you don't know where we're based?"

Mick shook his head.

"Not exactly. Our guess is you have teams across the UK."

"We're expecting visitors from the Grid soon. The outcome of that will determine whether we'll be able to help in the fight against these conspirators. Just be aware, we don't have the resources to fight on both fronts."

"If we can work with you, allowing you to continue your vigilante activities, then resources won't be such an issue."

"There are no guarantees we'll get over this first hurdle."

"Good luck," said Mick, handing Phoenix a note of the two addresses, "and be careful. If you think this Grid lot is an evil bunch, they're pussycats compared to the men behind this conspiracy. They will do anything to stay in power."

Mick left the café. Phoenix glanced at the note. Two addresses and Mick had added his mobile number, with 'keep in touch' scribbled underneath.

Phoenix returned to his car. He could be back to Larcombe by six.

As he left the car park, he saw a man on the opposite side of the road snap a photograph on his phone. Someone was watching him. Had they followed Mick to the café? Were they checking on who he had met?

Phoenix changed his route home and drove straight to the M5. He raced back to Bath using the motorway system all the way. He parked in the transport section garage and left instructions to change the number plates on this car.

It was still only five-thirty.

Wednesday, 21st January 2015

Hugh Fraser's funeral took place in Bishopbriggs, a town four miles from Glasgow. Zeus, Hera and Ambrosia represented Olympus, but Hugh's ex-wife didn't attend. Several of Hugh's colleagues from the Scot's Guards were there, resplendent in their uniforms. It was as Erebus wished. A low-key affair. Zeus and Hera did their best, but Ambrosia remained inconsolable.

Athena and the others continued with the day's business at Larcombe Manor. The news from the policeman Phoenix knew as Mick interested Minos and Alastor. They would use every method to identify the hidden power behind the men who had spoken out and written to date. Somewhere, lay a link connecting them.

The addresses Mick had provided intrigued Athena. She asked Giles to access CCTV in the area to keep watch on the O'Riordans' comings and goings.

"Any news from the ice-house, Giles?" Athena asked.

"Nothing new," Giles replied, "by the way, Maria Elena is returning to Estepona on Friday. I think she needs to be with her family."

"Understood," said Athena. "I may visit my father this weekend. Hope will be with me so that Maria Elena would be at a loose end with you on duty."

Giles looked at Henry Case. Henry raised an eyebrow, which was as demonstrative as he got. While the Grid's threat was real, neither would get much rest.

Friday, 23rd January 2015

The agent killed at Orion's house in Bath was buried at Haycombe cemetery. Henry attended the ceremony in the little chapel. Eight family members sat beside him. Outside on the hillside, the wind cut them in half when they watched the coffin lowered into the ground. The temperature never rose above zero throughout the day.

Maria Elena flew to Malaga from Bristol airport. Giles waved her off and hoped he would see her again soon.

Athena called her father after lunch. Geoffrey was over the moon to have his daughter and granddaughter join him to stay this weekend. He was even more excited to learn that Athena had something to tell him. Geoffrey hoped to persuade her to stay in Burnham until Monday. He wanted to attend a Burn's Night supper on Sunday evening.

Phoenix helped his daughter get ready for her trip to the coast. Athene wrapped Hope in warm clothes and piled additional items into a bag.

"It will be too cold to go to the beach tomorrow, Hope," said Phoenix. "You'll have to play indoor games with Grandad by the fire."

Hope gave her father a sympathetic look.

Silly, Daddy. Granddad has central heating in his new house. It's not an old building like our home, she thought.

Hope watched as her mother and father kissed and cuddled.

"Are you sure you'll be alright?" asked Athena.

"I'm happier knowing you're both safe," said Phoenix.

"Take care," she said.

He carried Hope to the car and gave her another kiss.

We're only going for a while, Daddy, thought Hope. *It's no big deal.*

Phoenix watched as Athena drove out through the gates and into the lane. When the car disappeared, he walked back indoors with a heavy heart.

Later that evening, he called Mick. Not because there

were matters to discuss but because he was on edge. His gut told him this weekend would be significant. How important, he wasn't sure. He wanted to check Mick was okay, in case his gut feeling concerned him, instead of those here at Larcombe.

He let it ring. There was no reply, and it went to voicemail.

Phoenix had no message to leave, so he ended the call.

He called Athena as he got ready for bed. The trip to the coast was lovely. Hope was fast asleep, and she and Geoffrey had enjoyed a late-night drink.

As he lay his head on the pillow, Phoenix wondered if he should try Mick again. He decided it would wait until morning.

Saturday, 24th January 2015

Phoenix was alone in the apartment. It felt strange. He made his breakfast and took it through to the lounge. Time to kick back, have a lazy breakfast and watch TV.

Nothing is ever forever.

The headline story on the nine o'clock news was of the death of an undercover policeman. Detective Sergeant Mitchell Ferguson carried out various operations across the North and the Midlands in the past three years. The Police couldn't divulge the substance of his current assignment. A group of walkers found his body on Cannock Chase yesterday afternoon. He was shot in the head. DS Mitch Ferguson was thirty-eight-year-old and single.

Phoenix forgot about his breakfast. He called Rusty.

"Are you free?" he asked.

"I can be," said Rusty. "Artemis isn't needed in the icehouse until two this afternoon."

Phoenix heard Artemis in the background.

"He wouldn't call you unless it was important. Get going."

"On my way," said Rusty.

A minute later, he tapped on the door and entered.

"Coffee?" asked Phoenix, finishing the last of his breakfast, "I'm running late."

"Sure, what's up?" asked Rusty.

"Mick, or Mitch Ferguson, I mentioned the other day, has been murdered. The people watching me when I left West Bromwich must have been responsible. The police haven't said what he was working on or who they suspect. This far-right group were who he was investigating. Mitch told me they hadn't found a connection with the Grid and these elitist maniacs, but O'Riordan has access to dozens of killers in the Midlands. Giles and Artemis might find a name if we could learn more about the hit."

"What do you propose we do?" asked Rusty.

"Giles is working throughout the weekend, isn't he? I've got a mobile number I need him to trace. It's still switched on. If he can get a location, it could help."

"Leave that with me," said Rusty. "You finish that food and get in the shower. I'll catch up with you in an hour in the orangery."

Meanwhile, in Burnham-on-Sea, Geoffrey Fox had a smile on his face. It was bitterly cold outside, but the news Athena brought him last night would keep him warm inside for weeks. She was fourteen weeks into her pregnancy. The doctor had said a scan could confirm whether it was a boy or a girl in four to six weeks.

While he and his daughter had a late breakfast, Hope went from room to room in the bungalow.

"What *is* she doing?" asked Geoffrey.

"If I didn't know better, I'd say she's checking everything's secure. She's making sure you haven't left a window open anywhere. Who knows what goes on in that head of hers?"

"Have there been problems at home to cause her to be anxious?" asked Geoffrey.

"More than usual," said Athena with a sigh. "To be honest, that was the reason behind our visit this weekend. Phoenix believes we may have unwelcome visitors."

"You've got vermin? Well, Larcombe is an old building," said Geoffrey.

Athena laughed.

"Vermin? I can't think of a better description."

By half-past ten, Giles had tracked Mitch Ferguson's mobile phone using its GPS. Rusty stood looking over his shoulder as the triangulation technique arrowed in on the location.

"It's in West Bromwich," said Giles.

"The building closest to that dot is what?" asked Rusty.

"The West Midlands police station in New Road," replied Giles.

"Call Phoenix and tell him I'll be with him in five minutes."

Rusty headed for the lift to take him to the surface. He entered the orangery to find Phoenix deep in thought.

"This is where that phone is," said Rusty, showing Phoenix the details Giles had printed.

"I'll call straight away and ask to speak with the senior detective working on the case," said Phoenix.

Rusty sat across the table from his friend. It was something neither of them had anticipated. He wondered what Erebus would have thought.

"Good morning," said Phoenix. "I met with DS Mitch Ferguson on Tuesday last. He asked me to keep in touch. However, after watching this morning's news report, I will need another contact. Can you find someone there who wishes to speak with me?"

The officer on the other end of the line asked who was calling. Phoenix told him to tell his superiors he had met Mitch working as a barman in Newcastle. They knew who he represented.

There was a brief wait. Then Phoenix gave Rusty a thumbs-up.

Phoenix was waiting to connect with the Assistant Chief Constable.

"Good morning,"

"Good morning," said Phoenix. "Don't waste time tracing this call. I just heard of Mitch's death. Maybe we can help you find the man who carried out the hit?"

"What do you need?" asked the ACC.

Phoenix sensed he was talking with a man in his fifties, someone a few years older than himself, who had been born in the Black Country. It was a relief. This guy had come up through the ranks and knew every blade of his patch. Mitch had suggested the people he worked with were 'old school' coppers. He hadn't realised there were many of them, judging by the muppets he saw on TV.

"The MO of the hit, type of bullet used, a possible weapon. Was Cannock Chase the murder scene, or was the body moved?"

"The body was moved. Someone shot DS Ferguson at close range on the driveway of his house. He was leaving to start a surveillance shift. I can give you everything we have so far. How do I reach you?"

"You don't," said Phoenix. "A courier will collect the data from your front desk in an hour. There will be no point in following them. They will fax the data to us on a secure line while they return to their base. We'll be on the case before you can start the car."

"What next?" asked the bewildered police chief.

"We need to handle a minor dispute in the next few days. Can our people meet with you and your colleagues in your office next Friday?"

"To be clear, what's on the agenda?"

"Mitch Ferguson suggested we might continue our covert work. The major beneficiaries would be the public. The police and ourselves also have opportunities to gain from the partnership."

"It promises to be an interesting discussion," said the ACC, "and you can come here safely. This meeting could create a new beginning for law enforcement. Secrecy is of the utmost importance."

"I won't say a thing if you don't," said Phoenix.

The two agents sat in silence after the call ended.

"Wow," said Rusty, "did that just happen?"

"I've leapt into the unknown," said Phoenix. "As each day passes, the threat from the Grid has become greater. The police will never overcome them on their own. We have helped where we could for eight years. Olympus has been fortunate not to have had its true purpose uncovered by the authorities. Either by the police or the secret services. Even by a zealous reporter."

"You have put your trust in this group of police

personnel who are unhappy with how the service they joined has changed," said Rusty. "Let's hope that trust isn't misplaced. What will Athena's view be? How will Zeus and the others react to your proposition.?"

"The talks will be the key," Phoenix replied. "Whoever attends from Larcombe Manor must gain agreement to our continued anonymity. If we don't have that, we walk away. The financing and the top-level operation of the Project must remain unchanged. The police can realign their depleted resources to cover areas of major public concern. We will continue to eliminate the hardened criminals, the recidivists and the terrorists. The prisons will no longer be full of criminals who can never persuade to change."

"Can you sell that to Athena and the others?" asked Rusty.

"Can I sell it to you?"

"I'd follow you to Hell and back. You know that."

"That's a trip I hope we can delay until after this weekend," said Phoenix.

"You reckon they'll attack soon?" asked Rusty.

"My gut tells me it's close," said Phoenix.

Chapter Fourteen

Sunday, 25th January 2015

"I've got something, Phoenix," said Giles Burke.

Phoenix ran to the ice-house and descended to Level One.

"What did you find?" he asked.

"Analysis of the data sent by the West Midlands Police threw up three potential hitmen. The modus operandi is a match. The bullet recovered came from a Glock 19. I narrowed it further by looking for cars belonging to our three suspects driving between Ferguson's home and Cannock Chase. The only one on the road at the right time was Steve Nash, a thirty-three-year-old gang member from Smethwick."

"That was quick. You've done well," said Phoenix.

"I had help," admitted Giles, "Artemis has been with me since six this morning. She couldn't sleep."

"I'll call the ACC with the good news," said Phoenix.

Ten minutes after passing the killer's name to a grateful

senior police officer, Phoenix drove towards Burnham-on-Sea. He had delayed this too long. Athena must learn what he had done.

"Daddy," cried Hope as she stood by the window.

"Don't be daft, darling," said Athena, "Daddy's busy at work."

The doorbell rang. Geoffrey answered.

"Phoenix, this is a surprise."

"I need to talk to Annabelle. It's urgent," he said.

His wife stood by the lounge door.

"Is something wrong?" she asked.

"Let's take a drive. I'll fill you in on everything that's happened since Friday."

They returned to the bungalow as the last few slivers of daylight remained. Geoffrey and Hope looked up as they entered the lounge together.

"Everything okay?" Geoffrey asked.

"The whole world has tipped on its head," said his daughter. "But things might become clearer if we can get through the next few days."

"I need to get back to Larcombe," said Phoenix. "Come and give Daddy a kiss, poppet."

Hope trotted towards her father. Mummy wore a serious face, so there must be trouble ahead. She kissed her father and clung to him, trying not to let him go.

"I'll brief Minos and Alastor when I get back, and I'll see you both tomorrow," said Phoenix. "I'll call as soon as I get the chance."

Athena held him close.

"Please, be careful," she said, "Friday's miles away."

Phoenix left his family in the warm bungalow and headed back to Larcombe Manor.

Athena prepared to call Zeus. But, first, they had to

inform the others of this audacious plan. She knew Phoenix had made the right choice. Alone, they were vulnerable to exposure and arrest by the police and the secret services. Worse still, at the hands of the Grid.

The constant need for new Gods to provide funds to keep the Project afloat could ease, if not cease altogether.

When Phoenix told them about the far-right group Mitch Ferguson had been tracking, she recognised the threat they posed to every individual in the country. The link to the Grid might be tenuous, but she didn't doubt they would confirm it in due course. Organised crime in alliance with an influential faction of the establishment could produce a nightmare scenario. They must stop them. Phoenix's plan might be the only way.

She picked up the phone and called Zeus.

Later that evening, Geoffrey took her and Hope to a local club for the traditional Burn's supper. Hope was half-asleep. Geoffrey drank several large whiskies. Athena's mind was on events at Larcombe Manor.

Across the Roman city, sporadic firework displays lit the sky as people celebrated Burn's night.

The attack began one minute past midnight.

A patrol on the perimeter came under fire first. The three men fell to the ground, and neither moved again. Finally, the alarms sounded as cars and vans stormed across the cattle grid and spread across the lawns. Henry Case ordered the ice-house staff to initiate a lockdown. A skeleton crew was to remain underground until the battle was over.

In the main building, the noise woke Minos and his wife,

Claudia. Alastor, too, was out of bed and looking through his curtains. Sarah Case huddled in the corner of their room and prayed. The doors were locked and barred. The Grid's gunmen had to break through four defensive lines to reach the house.

Armed personnel guarded each door and window. Henry wanted to contain this fight within the grounds at the front of the estate. If that failed, the battle would be lost.

Phoenix and Rusty stood side by side near the stable block and the transport section. There were others alongside them whose duty was to prevent the attackers from reaching the rear of the house. Beyond the lawns lay the ice-house and the workers' cottages.

The two friends had an unhampered view of the approaching threat.

"This is only the first wave," said Rusty, "look, headlights in the lane. Sixty men have joined the attack so far. How many more do you think they have?"

The sound of automatic fire filled the air.

A group of men sprinted from a van twenty yards ahead of them. They fired wildly. The response from the highly trained squad beside Rusty was precise and deadly. Four men staggered and fell. The fifth turned and ran back towards their van. He clambered inside and drove straight towards the defensive line of cars.

A sustained burst of heavy machine-gun fire brought the van to a standstill. Its driver now stared unseeing at the roof of the cab.

Across the cattle grid, they came. More and more vehicles. More and more men.

Henry looked at the casualties around him. Medics were at full stretch treating the injured.

Men sporting field dressings remained at their posts. Smoke, burning cars and dead bodies covered the lawns.

Henry Case moved towards the forward defensive lines. Should they abandon them? Could they continue to hold the line? Hayden Vincent was furthest forward; his crew halved.

"We need help, Henry," he shouted, "can you spare more men?"

"I'll help you myself," yelled Henry, picking up a gun from the floor next to a body.

He recognised the fallen agent. He had returned from Nigeria for retraining. Another two weeks, and he was due to join a team in Dover.

Hayden and Henry rallied their men and kept up a steady rate of fire at the advancing gunmen. The gunmen fell back, and others came forward to attack another defensive line. Hayden watched as the sheer weight of numbers took its toll; the cordon broke.

Phoenix and Rusty spotted the danger. Their squad moved forward beyond the orangery. They prepared to shoot anyone who crossed that line.

Hayden and Henry forgot those ahead of them for now. The gunmen were in a deadly crossfire.

There were no more headlights in the lane. Forty minutes of fighting ended. The cars and vans, still mobile, retreated across the cattle grid and back to wherever they came.

Henry began the sorry task of assessing the damage.

The Grid's attack left Larcombe with sixteen dead and several dozen casualties.

In London, Tyrone O'Riordan would soon learn his first attempted D-Day failed to destroy Olympus. His thugs had been bloodied. Over forty gunmen would never fire another gun. Nobody knew or cared how many wounded were rescued as the attackers left.

Henry's heart sank as he walked into the stable block's medical centre. He found Bazza Longdon, the senior trainer among the dead. He had been at Larcombe with Thommo Thomson since the beginning. Thommo kneeled beside his mate's body. There were no witty remarks tonight.

Henry walked past trainees, stewards, gardeners and drivers. Every one of them had given their lives for Olympus. At the end of the row of bodies, he saw the figure of Hayden Vincent with his head bowed.

"Oh no," said Henry. He put an arm on Hayden's shoulder. Tears rolled down the man's cheeks.

Athena cleared Kelly Dexter to withdraw from active duty on Monday. She had been six months pregnant.

"Why was she even here?" asked Henry.

"Did you ever try to tell Kelly she shouldn't take risks?" asked Hayden, "she loved this place. Nobody could tell her to stand aside."

Henry saw a doctor nearby. He read Henry's unspoken question and shook his head.

There had been no chance of the baby's survival. Henry sat on the floor and wept.

Phoenix and Rusty toured the grounds. The perimeter patrols had resumed, but it felt that the danger had passed. The ice-house was no longer on lockdown. Artemis had spoken with Rusty. Phoenix called Athena to tell her he was safe and the Grid's thugs beaten back for now. He admitted there had been casualties. There was time enough tomorrow to give her the details.

Sarah Case found Henry in the stable block. They clung to one another.

"Thank God you're safe," she said. "Now, I must do my duty."

As Sarah moved from corpse to corpse, the room fell silent. Her prayer sounded simple enough. The same prayer, sixteen times over, became a message of epic proportions.

In the main building, Sir Julian Langford and his wife Claudia sat with Mike Purvis. News of the dead and the casualties were relayed to them by Giles Burke.

"William Hunt imagined this might happen one day," said Sir Julian.

"He prayed Olympus never suffered this scale of a loss," said Mike.

"It was inevitable," said Claudia. "In 2006, when his advert in the Times first appeared, things were bad in the UK. Since then, things have grown ten times worse. This battle has to be a turning point."

"If Phoenix can achieve what he hopes for on Friday, we may look back on last night as just that. A fresh start. A new dawn.

Monday, 26th January 2015

As dawn broke, the clean-up began; they cleared bodies and burned-out vehicles from the lawns. They removed the defensive lines. The garage was two men short, but they strove to get enough vehicles ready for use.

If the wrecks had to become barricades, they would drag them out of the garage by a tractor. The medical unit had seriously wounded men to treat. The walking-wounded were back at work wherever they could.

Henry met with Phoenix and Rusty at seven o'clock to decide what to do with the men the Grid left behind.

"Sarah thinks we should return them to their loved ones. We're not barbarians."

"We don't know where to start," said Rusty, "and it raises too many questions. We can't rely on the police force turning a blind eye."

"I can't believe the police weren't called about the gunfire last night," said Phoenix, "surely Bath isn't overrun with Scotsmen?"

"I'm not the only one around here," said Rusty, "but we didn't waste drinking time on fireworks in my day."

"We must find a new place to bury the dead, near the estate's church. Sarah can consecrate the ground. We'll get a message to O'Riordan that their dead received a proper burial. It's more than they deserved, but Sarah's right. It will stand us in good stead on Friday if we can show the police we're not animals."

"Who's notifying the families of our people who died?" asked Henry.

"Athena returns from Burnham-on Sea later this morning. She knows the numbers but hasn't heard we lost Kelly Dexter and Barry Longdon. If she needs help, I'll get her to call Zeus and Hera. They need to know what happened. No doubt Zeus will want to call an emergency meeting to discuss the outcome of Friday's meeting. With this shift in direction, the eleventh of March is too long to wait to get everyone at the Olympus top table on board."

At lunchtime, Athena drove through the gates of her home. Patches of scorched earth told the tale of the battle of Larcombe Manor. A single church bell tolled in the distance. She wondered what it meant.

In her car seat in the back, Hope looked and listened.

Where was Daddy? Mummy told Grandad he was alright, but she needed to see him. Her face broke into a big smile as she spotted him by the big door.

Daddy looked tired and sad. Rusty stood beside him with Artemis.

They looked sad too.

"Artemis will look after Hope," said Phoenix. "We need to talk."

"The bell?" asked Athena.

"We are burying the enemy dead," whispered Rusty. "Sarah Case is officiating. Henry is on bell duty."

Artemis took Hope to their apartment. Her thoughts were with Hayden Vincent.

Phoenix broke the news of the full cost to Olympus of last night's fighting to his wife in their apartment. Athena looked out of the full-length windows of their lounge. The lawns and gardens were unscathed.

In the distance, the ice-house still held the massive intelligence infrastructure that drove the Olympus Project. The damaged areas would recover.

Athena wept for Kelly and Bazza. Olympus had lost two of its stars. She grieved for those who died for the cause, but Friday's meeting promised a brighter future.

Tyrone and Colleen O'Riordan licked their wounds. The attack had not destroyed the Olympus threat. Colleen blamed her son.

"You should have sent more men," she yelled, "you were so cocksure you had enough. Why didn't they stay until they finished the job? Who decided to pull out? If it cost a hundred men, finishing them would have been worth it."

"They buried our dead," said Tyrone, "I never expected that."

"That shows how weak they are," Colleen shouted. "If it been done right, we could have shoved the bodies into that big house and burned it to the ground."

"I heard from the Alliance last night," said Tyrone.

His mother was crazy. She never listened. Tyrone didn't tell her he had one last throw of the dice.

Epilogue

Friday, 30th January 2015

Rusty drove Phoenix to West Bromwich. Athena had decided they were best suited to discuss terms with the police chiefs. She stayed at Larcombe with Hope and waited for news.

"This still feels odd," said Rusty, searching for a vacant space in the visitor's car park.

"It offers Olympus a way forward," said Phoenix, "an opportunity to leave a legacy for the organisation."

"That's deep, even for you, mate," said Rusty.

He parked the car, and they got out.

"This is an important day, Rusty. The next few hours could give law enforcement real teeth again. This Assistant Chief Constable and his colleagues from across the country want to step away from the current ineffective system. Of course, there will be stiff opposition, but we can overcome it with public support. The protests in recent months show the majority have had enough. It's time for a change."

Inside the police headquarters, an officer took them upstairs to a meeting room, where they met with a group of high-ranking officers. Then, two hours later, they made their way downstairs again.

They had achieved everything they had wanted. Phoenix had considered every caveat their new colleagues suggested and, with Rusty's agreement, had accepted.

As they walked through reception, Rusty looked at his friend. Phoenix had been magnificent in that meeting. The confidence with which he made their case surprised him. Athena and the other Gods would be proud.

As they reached the door, a group of uniformed police officers entered the building. One stood back to allow Phoenix through. The others laughed at their fellow officer holding the door and pushed their way inside.

"Sorry, sir," said the young officer to Rusty with a grin. "I blame the parents."

They both heard a single gunshot.

Rusty raced towards the car park. Phoenix lay on the ground.

The young police officer raised the alarm and caught up with him.

"Shit. There's a lot of blood," he said. "Where's the shooter?"

The car park filled with armed officers; there was no sign of the gunman or a paramedic.

Rusty applied pressure to the wound. He tried desperately to stem the flow of blood.

"Hang on, Phoenix," he shouted. "Help's on its way."

Phoenix struggled to put his right hand on his friend's wrist and shook his head.

"I'm getting too old for this," he said. His hand slipped away.

Rusty realised Phoenix was gone. Tears filled his eyes as he hugged him.

A motorcycle paramedic sped into the car park.

"It's too late; he's gone," said Rusty.

"Let me check you over," said the paramedic after confirming that Phoenix was dead.

"This was his blood," said Rusty. "I'm fine."

"Maybe my mates did you a favour, sir," said the young policeman. "The delay at the doorway saved your life."

The ACC had now arrived on the scene. He took Rusty to one side.

"We've got CCTV cameras covering this area. We'll get the bastard that did this. Please tell your people this changes nothing. We remain one hundred per cent committed, and I'm sure you are too. It reinforces what we both believed. Organised crime and their establishment allies will go to any lengths to stop us from working together."

Rusty nodded and shook the ACC's hand.

"I must get back to his wife and family. I need to tell them in person. Can you keep a lid on this with the media for twelve hours?"

"You have my word," the ACC replied.

"I'll arrange for the body to be collected as soon as you've completed your investigations," said Rusty. He called the nearest Olympus team leader.

Rusty made the long, lonely drive back to Larcombe Manor. The news he carried from the Midlands was bittersweet. Olympus now had a new purpose, which was Phoenix's legacy. He would no longer see it come to fruition.

Saturday, 31st January 2015

Tyrone O'Riordan was not a happy man. The assassin had only killed one of his targets.

The media reported a lone gunman murdered a civilian in cold blood at the West Midland Police Headquarters in West Bromwich. There were still no details of who died. One thorn in the Grid's side was eliminated; another survived. His final throw of the dice had fallen short of the mark.

His friends in the Alliance had wanted both Olympus agents killed, just as he had. They financed the hit, so Tyrone knew they would be unhappy with the outcome. He needed to rebuild bridges if they were to continue their partnership.

February - April 2015

Maria Elena returned from Estepona on Monday evening after the attack. She refused to stay away from Giles any longer. The nanny looked after Hope while Athena planned the funerals of Barry Longdon, Kelly Dexter and her unborn child.

Minos and Alastor assumed responsibility for the other Olympus men who had died. As those arrangements were progressing, Athena learned of Phoenix's death. Another funeral to attend at Larcombe Manor. Where else could it be held? Phoenix didn't exist.

Athena endured many dark days after Rusty's return that Friday afternoon. The danger had always been there. She and Phoenix had both understood that. It didn't make the pain any easier to bear. She still caught Hope standing by the window, looking for her father to come home.

On Monday, the second of February, Rusty stamped his mark on the new Olympus with a visit to the City of London. He killed Tyrone and Colleen O'Riordan. He blew open the safe in the bedroom of Tyrone's flat and discovered damning documentation on the Grid. There were details of the burgeoning cooperation with the far-right group.

On Tuesday, Giles Burke hacked into the Glencairn Bank and froze the Grid's assets. But, without the shield of the bank to protect the money laundering, it exposed the soft underbelly of the network.

Zeus acted as Phoenix had forecast. He called an emergency meeting. Ten Gods gathered at Curzon Street, in London, on Wednesday, the fourth of February. The two newcomers, Chronos and Hebe, were welcomed. Aphrodite returned once more, bruised but not broken. Ambrosia was in mourning but managed to seat herself next to Zeus.

Zeus received unanimous support for the vision of the new Olympus Project. Athena would return to the table in time. Phoenix was gone, never to be forgotten.

Apollo proposed Rusty should take his place. Zeus dubbed him Perseus, the slayer of monsters.

In mid-February, Athena had the scan confirming she was expecting a son. There was only one name that suited the occasion. He would be called Phoenix.

Perseus promised to train Hope and Phoenix when the time came.

Artemis, Sarah and Maria Elena plotted to add to the number of students. There would always be monsters. The world needed heroes to slay them.

The tide had turned. Police now had the tools to wage the fight against organised crime with the help of Olympus.

Callum Wood received a call from Zara Wheeler at the end of March. She offered him Phil's old job. He had never fancied moving into the new headquarters at the end of the year, so he accepted.

Callum found a folder on his desk when he arrived on his first day at Larcombe Manor. He learned that the double murderer he sought was a Russian gangster contracted to kill Phil Hounsell. He had been eliminated.

The three Albanians responsible for the robberies and the killing of Wayne and Bridie had been hunted down and killed in Tirana. They recovered a substantial sum of money.

Callum was tasked with identifying a list of charities he thought should benefit.

Callum wondered what he'd let himself in for; he decided he wasn't an old dog yet. He could learn new tricks. Working at Larcombe Manor promised to be interesting.

The far-right conspirators revealed themselves as the Alliance Party in the run-up to the election. Giles Burke, Minos and Alastor provided more than enough to discredit them. The distorted transcripts from the BBC Monitoring Service revealed in January had wounded them. Proof of one hundred thousand pounds paid to Tyrone O'Riordan for the services of Steve Nash, even without a direct link to the Alliance, was confirmation these people didn't deserve the public's vote.

The Alliance Party made no impact at the General Election.

Another danger had passed. The UK could look forward to a brighter future.

It was as Benjamin Franklin had said:

"Justice will not be served until those who are unaffected are as outraged as those who are"

On a grey February day, a low-key funeral occurred in the little estate church at Larcombe Manor.

Olympus laid Phoenix to rest.

His identity remained a secret.

Everything had turned full circle.

Colin Bailey was invisible, just as he had been in the beginning.

More by Ted Tayler

vinci-books.com/fataldecision

He thought he'd left his life as a detective behind, but the past has a deadly way of catching up.

Gus Freeman, a retired Detective Inspector, has spent three desolate years after the loss of his beloved wife, Tess, to a sudden brain aneurysm. An unexpected lifeline emerges as his former boss rekindles a flicker of purpose within Gus, presenting an opportunity to lead a youthful Crime Review Team.

In the first of this new series, the team delves into the chilling annals of a cold case that has lain dormant since June 2008.

Turn the page for a free preview…

Fatal Decision: Chapter One

Saturday, 28 June 2008

"It's not right, is it?" muttered Daphne Tolliver, "a widespread ground frost last night with the school summer holidays upon us. Global warming, my backside."

Bobby looked up at her from his position on the comfortable couch in their front room.

"Nothing to add, little man?" said Daphne, shaking her head. "Thought not. As long as you get fed and watered, taken out to do your business, you don't give a toss, do you?"

Conversations were limited when you were widowed and spent long periods alone with only a Cocker Spaniel for company.

Daphne Tolliver was sixty-eight years old and widowed a decade earlier. Her late husband, Wally, keeled over in the bar of his favourite haunt, The Ferret in Newton Bridge. It turned out that Cribbage League matches could be as tense as a Champion's League Football Final. Who knew?

Wally's sudden heart attack wasn't fatal, but the induced coma he was treated to on arrival at the Royal United Hospital in Bath only delayed the inevitable. Daphne's younger sister Megan ferried her back and forth to sit by his bedside for five days. Megan never complained, despite the small fortune it cost to park. She knew Daphne would remember to offer to contribute in time. Her sister's head had been all over the place for several weeks. It was difficult enough with time to prepare for a loved one to pass, but Wally's death shocked everyone.

Daphne's parents always showed their daughters the love that went hand-in-hand with being part of a close-knit family. Mum and Dad set the tone while they lived, and the Sumner girls continued the theme throughout their lives.

Both daughters married young. Megan Morris, as she became, raised three children with her husband, Mick. All three were now married, with five grandkids between them. Daphne doted on them, whether children or grandchildren, especially when babes-in-arms.

Daphne and Wally never had children. Not for want of trying. They never bothered to find out whether pure bad luck or a problem with one or the other. Instead, they accepted it as their fate and played the cards life had dealt.

The couple spent an equal amount of time together and apart, with their various hobbies and interests. Of course, children would have been a bonus, but they had each other, and that was more than many others they could think of who lived around them.

They came from a different generation, her sister Megan often remarked. If couples today had trouble getting pregnant, they called straight round to the fertility clinic chasing an appointment. Always too keen to find someone to blame, Daphne thought. Somehow, she and Wally survived forty years of marriage without extra mouths to feed.

Wally followed his father's trade as a printer. He talked of retiring at sixty-five as his father had done and planned to spend his well-earned leisure days with Daphne. Those days never came. Maybe fewer pints of lager in The Ferret and other pubs might have helped. A Mediterranean diet could have benefited him, too, instead of the traditional English grub that served his ancestors well over the generations.

Days after his sixtieth birthday, he was halfway into his third pint of Stella Artois with the cribbage match evenly poised. He picked up the five cards dealt from the table — the Jack of Spades, the Four of Hearts, the Five of Diamonds. Wally couldn't believe it. He spread the remaining cards in his fingers. It couldn't be, could it? He held the Five of Clubs and the Five of Hearts too. Ever since playing with his friends in this Cribbage League, he'd always struggled to maintain his place on the team. As often as not, he was a reserve and fetched and carried drinks for the warriors at the table.

He had a chance to shine in this vital game within the overall match. He watched the dealer reveal the cut card. Wally's heart leapt as the Five of Spades landed on the table. The highest-scoring hand in this format of the age-old game.

"Come on, Wally," came the cry, "get on with it."

Sadly, Wally's heart didn't carry on leaping. It stopped.

The landlord called Daphne with the dreadful news. She had rung Megan straightaway, and Mick Morris drove them to Bath. They arrived to discover the ambulance still waiting to hand over its patient. The crew inside were working on Wally in the meantime.

Daphne had never accompanied Wally on his nights out with the boys. She preferred to stay at home and watch her choice of TV programme without him grabbing the remote to switch over at a critical moment to check the latest football scores.

As she walked from the living room they had shared for so long to the kitchen, she realised today was another Saturday. When you retire, every day is the same. It's so easy to lose track. When they were first married, Wally played football in the winter and cricket in the summer. Every Saturday, he dashed off with his mates.

Several of those friends were in The Ferret the night he keeled over. He always referred to those occasions as nights with the boys. It was strange to think that each of them had been approaching sixty or a few years older when he died. Yet, because they had known one another for fifty-odd years, they were still boys in their heads. Over the decades, those young sportsmen matured into armchair experts who kept active playing skittles, bowls and cribbage.

Daphne resigned early in the marriage to having three or four evenings every week left to her own devices. Then, of course, there was the cleaning to do, and many a night, she stood as she watched a film while she caught up with their ironing. Megan's little ones enjoyed Auntie Daphne arriving for a spell of babysitting too, so Mick and her sister could have a night out. As a result, filling her evenings had rarely been a problem.

When her niece and nephews grew older, Megan and Daphne travelled into Harrington End for a Quiz Night at the Waggon & Horses or played Bingo in the village hall. A simple life. No dramas. Typical of how country folk muddled through in their quiet corner of the West Country for generations.

Daphne saw clouds gathering as she peered through the glass curtains at the kitchen window on that late June morning. The darker variety that suggested a rain shower might be due. There are no guarantees, except if you decide against a coat or an umbrella. Daphne knew a downpour would start at the furthest point from home on those occasions. Regular as clockwork, just as she and Bobby turned to head home to Braemar Terrace.

The phone in the living room rang. Daphne scuttled back to answer.

"Hello?"

"Only me, Daphne," said Megan, "just checking. Are you still okay for tomorrow?"

"Sunday lunch at the Waggon & Horses?" replied Daphne. "When have you ever known me to resist the chance of enjoying their scrumptious carvery?"

"Righto," said Megan, "we'll pick you up just before twelve. What have you got planned for later today?"

"Keeping an eye on this blessed weather," Daphne told her. "My bet is we'll have a shower this afternoon. I might wait until it's blown over and take Bobby out for a long walk this evening."

"Don't forget to take your umbrella, will you? To be on the safe side," laughed Megan and ended the call.

Daphne didn't admit to her sister that today's extra exercise was the anticipation of another inch on her waistline after tomorrow's Sunday Big-Plate Special. However, it never ceased to amaze her how much food other people piled on their plates. The ones who could least afford to be eating to excess often sneaked back for second helpings.

Daphne was well aware these occasional lunchtime treats were Megan and Mick's way of checking she looked after herself. Not just that she eat a roast dinner on a

Sunday, but she wasn't depressed not having Wally around the house. Fat chance of that, Daphne thought.

Phone calls like the one just ended had become the norm following his funeral as Megan suggested new interests in which they both could get involved. Daphne knew Megan meant well. She was just sisterly, but sometimes, Daphne yearned for quiet. That's why Bobby had become so important.

When she and Wally worked, it wasn't sensible to own a dog. It wasn't fair to leave it at home for hours on end if one or both of them dashed out again as soon as they arrived home. So after she retired from her full-time job in the Post Office, Daphne asked Megan to accompany her to the local kennels to pick a puppy.

"I just want a friendly companion," Daphne said, "not one of those ferocious, fighting dogs or one mistreated."

"A rescue dog, you mean?" Megan replied, "I thought you might enjoy that."

"I haven't got the patience," said Daphne. "Something not too big, that's good with children. I couldn't stand the grandkids not visiting because it barked throughout the day, or worse still, nipped at their ankles."

They had spotted Bobby, the Cocker Spaniel, within minutes of their arrival at the kennels in Clatworthy. He gazed at the two humans walking his way and endeared himself to the newcomers. Bobby's amenable and cheerful disposition soon made him a joy in the home. He was never more content than when pleasing Daphne. As the weeks passed, he was as happy to snuggle on the couch with his mistress as he was to race around the garden with Megan's family.

It was only natural Daphne found adjusting to life without Wally difficult. Megan and her family did what they could, and her work colleagues were brilliant in those early months. In a small town Post Office, everyone knew everyone else. So, the posties had a cheery word, and the counter staff did their best to raise Daphne's spirits and involve her in any social evenings they organised. That left other nights and weekends when she might have moped, but Megan usually covered those.

Every Royal Mail branch across the country could have done with more customers in the latter years of the last century, and Daphne's was no exception. The announcement that their branch would close in 2002 accelerated her retirement. That prompted the usual wail of protests from the people most affected. The elderly, the infirm, and those on benefits which could least afford the six-mile bus trip to the next town. They expressed their concerns to the authorities.

Their response was sympathetic, if non-committal. Akin to the now-familiar reaction to sudden death of saying 'sorry for your loss'. After two years with the axe hanging over them, her former colleagues learned they had sold the site. A branch with a much-reduced staff would open in one of the small units in a precinct on the Westbourne Estate.

"Poor devils," Daphne thought when she heard the news, "moving from a popular site on Church Street to a precinct on a run-down council estate.

Daphne wandered from the living room to the kitchen. She had been right; those clouds held rain. It rattled insistently at the windowpanes. She decided to prepare herself a meal and wait for those white, fluffy clouds she saw in the distance to blow across the valley. In an hour, what remained would be a fine drizzle. The sort that hung in the air and got you wetter than a downpour. When she and

Bobby left the house, the showers would be over. Her view of the distant hillside held the prospect of a fine evening.

Wally had always loved this view from the back of the house. He never spent much time at the kitchen sink, where she now stood, but from the upstairs bedroom and garden, the valley stretched before them to the hills separating the town from Shaw Park and Clatworthy.

The couple rented a flat in town for the first two years of their marriage. When they moved to Braemar Terrace in 1960, the two-bedroomed mid-terrace property had been as much as they could afford. They always planned to move to a bigger place. No children meant that a move became a lower and lower priority as time passed. So they stayed put.

Their row of six cottages on the main road out of town had been built just before the outbreak of the First World War. Different neighbours came and went over the years. At the outset, the cottages were occupied by elderly couples in no rush to go anywhere. Their next stop was the churchyard in town or the crematorium four miles away. It was a waiting room. Wally and Daphne used to chuckle over it.

Before they knew it, they became an elderly couple and found the other cottages changed hands more rapidly as younger couples moved in, improved them and turned them over at a profit. Wally didn't see the point of adding refinements to what they had. He was content to keep everything as originally intended. His one concession was to keep it in good decorative order, inside and out.

There were always lots of cars parked outside her front windows these days. Wally cycled to the print works and often when going to his various sporting activities. Wally couldn't see the point in learning to drive. His father never did. He relied on one of his sporting pals to give him a lift when they played out of town. He and Daphne caught the bus if they needed to visit the bigger shops in Bath.

Years had passed since that rural bus service stopped. Daphne couldn't remember when. After it disappeared, Megan or Mick always helped if she needed to travel further afield.

After she retired in 2002, Daphne realised it wasn't just Wally she missed. She had bought Bobby for the company but felt she ought to do something positive with this spare time. So, she volunteered at one of many charity shops that opened in town. They took in items donated by the public for areas seeking Emergency Disaster Relief.

At first, Daphne worked two hours on a Monday morning. When news broke of a natural disaster on the other side of the world, she joined others pitching in for hours required to cope with the rush. It was heart-warming to see that the British public still dug deep to help those in trouble despite the troubles at home. On Boxing Day 2004, an Indian Ocean tsunami was caused by a massive earthquake. Within hours, killer waves slammed into the coastlines of eleven countries. Despite a lag of up to several hours between the earthquake and the tsunami's impact, it surprised many victims. No tsunami warning systems had been in place. The death toll approached a quarter of a million.

Daphne and the team of volunteers prepared emergency food, water and medicine packs. The donations came from the public and various organisations across the West Country. When the big rush ended, she returned to Braemar Terrace, curled up with Bobby on her lap, and wept.

"I wanted to make a difference, Bobby," she said, "but so many people never lived to receive the help we've sent out there. It was too little, too late. I'll look for something less stressful."

So, she placed an advert in the window of Patel's newsagents, offering a cleaning service. Soon, two other part-time employment opportunities presented themselves.

Despite the massive influx of immigrant labour in the UK's big cities and agricultural heartlands, they ignored this corner of the West Country. There wasn't much call for Lithuanian car-wash staff in Harrington End. Husbands still washed the car themselves at the weekend or left them dirty.

Daphne noticed the occasional Polish barmaid in the Waggon & Horses, and a girl from the Balkans often begged on the High Street with her three kids in tow. That was the sum of it. It just went to show. The grass wasn't always greener on the other side.

Her advert's first response came from the local primary school caretaker. They wanted someone for an hour every weekday in term time. That little job kept her busy from three to four in the afternoon. Then, one evening, she received a phone call from a lady with a very posh voice.

"Mrs Tolliver, I presume?"

Daphne stood. She wasn't sure why, but lounging in the armchair didn't seem right. The woman sounded positively regal.

"Yes, that's me," replied Daphne, shunning the urge to curtsey.

"Joyce Pemberton-Smythe speaking,"

Joyce was the local MP's wife. Leonard Pemberton-Smythe currently owned the large Manor House that stood a mile out of town on Lowden Hill, a local beauty spot. Her husband benefited from the presumed cessation of gang warfare after multiple deaths in the town in 2001. The murder of Councillor James Crook also helped his cause. But, despite Labour governing the country, pockets of the West Country remained staunchly Conservative. The other parties edged closer to him in that 2001 election, but Pemberton-Smythe survived by the skin of his teeth.

As campaigning for the 2005 General Election began, his much-trumpeted hard-line approach found ready support in the constituency. He promised to take up the cudgels James Crook had relinquished. His constituents confirmed the tide was turning against Labour, and Leonard won with an increased majority.

Like most politicians, he couldn't stop himself from getting his name and face in the media. As someone hot on crime and big on family values, Leonard was invited onto every relevant TV programme plus irrelevant ones.

His wife Joyce explained Daphne's duties, subject to acceptable references. She added that Leonard owned a flat in London where he stayed while the House was sitting. He only returned to the bosom of his family at the weekend. When not required at Westminster in the summer recess, they collected their two sons from boarding school and spent the holidays at their French home.

Alright, for some, Daphne thought when she spotted an article in a weekend supplement two weeks later. The 'little place' in France Joyce referred to turned out to be an eight-bedroomed chateau in fourteen acres of rolling countryside.

Daphne arranged to visit the Manor for an audience with the lady of the house the morning following that first phone call. She wore her best dress and cleaned her shoes. Daphne presumed the elderly gentleman who answered the front door was the butler. For one moment, Daphne thought he was about to send her to the back of the house, to the servant's quarters. But, as she learned later, Crompton was more of a jack-of-all-trades to the Pemberton-Smythes. He allowed himself a brief smile and ushered her into the spacious hallway.

"Welcome, Mrs Tolliver. Your prospective employer is in the conservatory waiting to serve you coffee. It's the last door on the right along the corridor. Good luck."

Daphne thanked him, trotted down the corridor and tapped on the glazed panel of the door. She could see Joyce Pemberton-Smythe sprawled across a rattan chair, reading a copy of Cosmopolitan. When she heard Daphne's tentative taps, Joyce looked over her half-moon glasses and invited her in with a desultory hand wave.

When she left thirty minutes later, Daphne had another cleaning job to fill her dwindling spare time and learned more about the occupants of the Manor House. Crompton, who didn't appear to have a first name, organised visits from gardeners, window cleaners and tree surgeons. He was an excellent chef but had decided that his eyesight wasn't enough to cope with the cleaning any longer.

"We lost a Sevres porcelain vase," wailed Mrs Pemberton-Smythe, "late eighteenth century. It stood on the mantlepiece in the main hall for decades. Clumsy Crompton flicked his duster a trifle too energetically...."

"Oh, dear," Daphne sympathised.

"Smithereens, darling. Utterly kaput."

Daphne promised to take great care of their ornaments. Joyce gave her a look that suggested they were objets d'art, not mere ornaments. Despite that minor hiccup, their conversation flourished. Daphne soon realised the coffee was more for her host's benefit than a means to put her at her ease. She was sure Joyce suffered from a right royal hangover. As for those references? Joyce couldn't wait to agree on terms and ring for Crompton to give her new cleaner a quick tour of the building and return her to the front door.

"We'll see you next Monday then, Mrs Tolliver," said Crompton as they emerged into the sunlight. He walked with her across the patio to the top of the steps to ground level.

"Call me Daphne," she replied.

"Of course," he said. Unfortunately, Daphne received no offer of a reciprocal change of name for himself.

Megan was ecstatic when she learned of Daphne's new appointment.

"Look at you," she chirped, "working at the big house for the toffs."

"It's too big for them," Daphne replied, thinking over what she'd seen on her tour with Crompton. "She's there on her own during the week. He pops in when he feels like it. The boys are away at school during term time. It's not a real home. They've got lots of nice things, but you wouldn't swap what you and Mick have for that place."

"Their money wouldn't go amiss, though," laughed Megan.

Little more remained to be said. Daphne continued to work at the primary school. She moved on from Emergency Disaster Relief to a local cancer charity housed in the Old Police Station. It wasn't as stressful. She volunteered several hours a week sorting through donations of quality unwanted goods, pricing them and dressing the window and store displays. She had performed her cleaning duties at the Manor House except for the holiday breaks. Years later, she wondered how she had the nerve to call herself retired.

Fatal Decision: Chapter Two

Bobby barked and interrupted Daphne's reverie.

It was one of her younger neighbours revving his car engine. A throaty little number it was too. Her brother-in-law, Mick, said it was all fur coats and no knickers. Quite how that related to a car's look and its performance, Daphne couldn't fathom.

"This won't do," she said as she busied herself in the kitchen, "we need to be busy."

The sound of cupboard doors opening and a tap running alerted Bobby to mealtime. He padded through to find his food bowl filled with something interesting. As he made short work of its contents, Daphne placed his water bowl beside him.

She watched her faithful companion double-check that both bowls were scrupulously clean. Then he sat and stared at her.

"Waiting for your treat?" she teased and handed him a dental chew.

That would keep him occupied while she prepared her

meal. Her thoughts returned to the enormous lunch awaiting her tomorrow. Tonight, she could make do with the last piece of quiche plus a salad and a slice of crusty bread. That was more than enough.

The evening proved better than expected as the dark clouds had disappeared. The sun kept its warmth late into the evening in June. It was ideal walking weather, so Daphne checked herself in the hallway mirror. A light jacket and a scarf were what she needed — no point changing again today. Her grey hair was shorter these days and didn't need much more than a quick brush. She still treated herself to a dab of lipstick each morning; that was her only guilty pleasure these days.

Daphne's pink summer blouse and navy blue slacks had seen excellent service over the years, but nobody took much notice of an elderly lady walking her dog. If anybody got a second look, it was Bobby.

"Bobby?" she called.

Bobby sighed, left his comfy rug, and shuffled from the kitchen to stand beside her, wagging his tail. His mistress hadn't mentioned 'walkies' yet, but surely they should venture out soon?

Daphne fetched Bobby's lead and attached it to his collar. With a final check that her white chiffon scarf was tied neatly and tucked beneath the lapels of her navy blue jacket, she opened the front door and off they went.

As she left Braemar Terrace, she met the teenage son of Mr and Mrs Brightwell, who lived in the end cottage. He was doing wheelies on the pavement. Daphne needed to step into the gateway of his home to avoid getting knocked over.

"Careful," she cried at the youngster. Carl Brightwell

peered back over his shoulder from under his sky-blue hoodie.

"Look where you're going, you old bat," he shouted as he bounced off the kerb and sped towards the town centre.

"Charming, Bobby, isn't he?" muttered Daphne. "Still, we won't let him spoil our walk, will we?"

Daphne Tolliver took the footpath across the meadow and climbed the stile that brought her onto Battersby Lane. Bobby struggled with the concept of stiles and merely ducked under the wooden steps and wriggled through. Daphne had to avoid the lead getting tangled. Once completed, they stood on the narrow pavement on the other side.

Daphne faced two options. They could turn right and make their way across the next two fields. She could let Bobby off the lead there to run free if there were no cows in the field. The farmer knew of the footpath, and an electric fence always kept his herd at least ten to fifteen yards away from any walkers. That wouldn't have stopped Bobby from dashing across to the herd for a closer look. On the other side of those fields lay the main road that led back into town. A well-lit, well-maintained pavement brought them back to Braemar Terrace.

Her second option was to continue with her original plan. Walk through the woods and to thread her way back to the main road via the open grassland of the park. Bobby was soon safely re-attached to his lead. The evening remained warm.

Daphne sensed someone's presence in the shadow of the hedge on the other side of the road. They must have crossed the fields opposite and crossed the stile further up the road.

Simon Attrill was a big boy, but his size and mental age

hadn't kept pace with one another. That was how Daphne thought of the poor lad. She always chose to think of people in the best light. He was twenty years old, with a mental age that would be permanently stuck at eight. When she started her cleaning job at the primary school, Daphne overheard several small children calling names as they left the playground, running helter-skelter for home. They were nasty to Simon, who was passing by the school gates.

Simon's parents didn't know how vulnerable his name would make him when they had him christened. It was a freak accident on the slide at the park that altered their lives forever. Simon had clambered to the top, and as he waited his turn, he leaned over the side to call out to his best friend as he ran back to the steps for another go. A moment's loss of concentration and Simon fell to the hard grass surface below, landing on his head.

"Simple Simon," the little devils chanted outside the school gates that afternoon. "Simple, Simon."

The sun disappeared behind a light cloud. Simon's face lit up when he spotted Bobby and ran across the road towards them. It was no surprise that he loved dogs. They were never cruel to him. Simon had heard that Daphne had told the headmistress what had happened that day. The teacher admonished the children, and their parents received a letter. The kids were even nastier to him after that. He didn't go into town in the evenings now. Boys like Carl Brightwell did more than call names if they spotted him. They punched and kicked him and stubbed out their cigarettes on the back of his hands.

"Hello, Simon," said Daphne.

"Where are you going?" he asked.

"We're heading for the woods, and then we plan to walk

back through the park to join up with the main road. Bobby hasn't been out for a walk today. Too frosty this morning."

Simon didn't hear her. He knelt on the ground with Bobby slobbering over his face.

"Bobby likes me, doesn't he?" he asked.

"He likes everyone who makes a fuss of him," laughed Daphne. "I'd better get moving. Those clouds are building again. I thought we'd seen the last of the rain for today."

"Rain, rain go away," said Simon.

The big lad stood by the stile and watched the pair disappear towards the woods.

Daphne glanced back as they reached the narrow pathway into Lowden Woods.

Simon Attrill hadn't moved.

"Such a shame isn't it, Bobby," she said, "not a bad bone in his body. There's no justice sometimes."

Bobby had forgotten Simon already. He strained at his lead as dozens of unfamiliar and exciting scents reached his hyper-sensitive nose.

The leafy lane burrowed its way through the many acres of well-established oak trees populating the lower reaches of Lowden Hill and weaved through more recently planted beeches and sweet chestnuts. The gathering clouds added to the gloom as Daphne and Bobby walked further from the roadway under the overhead canopy of branches in full leaf.

Daphne wasn't unduly worried. They used this route in the past when time allowed. She had Bobby with her; nobody else was in this part of the woods. But, since they left Battersby Lane, the silence had been deafening.

Another two hundred yards and they would reach the open ground of the municipal park. No doubt there would be others enjoying the summer evening. Even if they, too, were keeping a weather eye on those clouds. No cause for concern.

Bobby stopped dead in his tracks. Was it a strange smell or a noise he didn't recognise? It certainly unsettled him. Daphne also sensed someone ahead. Not in the lane. They were somewhere to her left. Close by but hidden from sight. She was sure it was two people. Those weren't words she could hear. They were more urgent, guttural grunting sounds.

Daphne couldn't resist pushing through the undergrowth, even though she dreaded the sight that might confront her. She dragged a reluctant Bobby, who seemed to understand nothing good lay behind those bushes and brambles.

Meanwhile, Holly Dean was dealing with her little Princess in the park. They had left her parents' home on the Greenwood Estate twenty minutes earlier at seven o'clock. The twenty-year-old shop assistant planned a brisk walk around the park with her Bichon Frise puppy before the rain returned. Her little bundle of mischief had done its business. Holly was dutifully dropping the waste bag into the bin by the side of the path when she thought she heard a scream.

Holly looked around her but couldn't see anyone in trouble nearby. She saw other people in the park, further away, who now looked in her direction. No doubt, they also wondered what they thought they had heard. Holly realised the noise must have come from the woods. She turned towards the tree-lined path and took a few tentative steps, clutching Princess to her chest.

The rain began to fall once more. Holly hesitated. Should she run home now? It might not have been a genuine scream — just teenagers mucking around.

The second agonised scream sent shivers down her spine.

Holly swallowed hard and bravely trotted into the lane. The rain was coming on harder now — an absolute downpour. The canopy of branches stopped Holly from getting drenched, but behind her, she heard the excited shouts of other park visitors as they raced for shelter. At first, she could hear nothing except the storm above.

Then suddenly, there was a noise behind her. Someone dashed a hundred yards away from the bushes and headed for the park. Holly turned and made out a figure wearing a blue anorak with the hood raised. She couldn't tell whether it was male or female, but the speed at which they disappeared convinced her they were young.

"Hey," she wailed, "what's happening?"

The lane was empty once more. Holly risked a glance from where the young person had come. She saw nothing. Branches were rising and falling like the wings of geese in flight as they were buffeted by strengthening winds. The grass squelched under her trainers as she edged among the trees.

Another faint noise reached her ears; it sounded like a dog whimpering.

Holly held Princess tighter as her puppy shivered with fright. Holly knew how she felt.

At the edge of the clearing, beyond two mighty oaks, she spotted a Cocker Spaniel, its lead trailing on the ground behind it.

Back and forth, it scampered, urging Holly forward into the open space beyond. In the park, people who were now sheltered under the trees heard the young girl's screams in the distance, and soon several men started running to her aid.

They found Holly Dean, Princess and Bobby standing at the foot of a giant oak tree.

Daphne Tolliver lay on the soggy grass, her unseeing eyes gazing at the heavens.

Monday, 26 March 2018

Assistant Chief Constable Kenneth Truelove sat in his office at the Wiltshire Police Headquarters in Devizes. He had just read through an updated file on a crime that had remained unsolved for far too long. A germ of an idea formed as he reviewed the case; perhaps it was time for a different approach.

The brutal murder of Daphne Tolliver left a lasting legacy in the quiet West Country town. Almost a decade had passed since the frenzied attack, yet townspeople still avoided the once-popular beauty spot where she died. The locals continued to talk about the motiveless attack on the defenceless pensioner. Daphne had been a widow for ten years and lived a quiet life. She came from a close-knit family and gave as much back to the community as she ever took from it. Why on earth would anyone want to kill her?

The ACC was aware some murders went unsolved, and killers got away. However, in the past decade, new scientific techniques offered a way of tracing those that slipped through the net.

Screams coming from the wood were one of the few clues to one of the most gruesome murders his county had ever seen. Daphne was walking her dog through Lowden Woods when someone battered her around the head with a rock. Despite one of the most extensive investigations in the county's history, they never established a clear motive. Finally, the detective in charge, DI Dominic Culverhouse, admitted to the press it may have been a case of being in the wrong place at the wrong time.

A Miss Holly Dean heard Daphne's screams at around twenty-past seven as she walked her dog in nearby Lowden Park. Miss Dean went to investigate and overheard Mrs Tolliver's distressed dog among the trees. She then discovered the bloodied body, and her panicked cries alerted members of the public.

Emergency services arrived and contained the crime scene as swiftly as possible. But, unfortunately, the weather that evening was dreadful, and there was no doubt vital clues got washed away by heavy rain or trampled underfoot.

A huge murder hunt followed, and officers took hundreds of statements, but nobody ever faced charges for the savage attack. Culverhouse focused on identifying a youth seen running into Lowden Park from the woods seconds before Miss Dean found the body. Did Mrs Tolliver know that person? Was it a teenage male or, indeed, a female? Could a young girl have carried out such a vicious attack, and what could have been her motive? The police were baffled.

A witness from Braemar Terrace, where the victim lived for many years, saw Mrs Tolliver walk past her window with her dog, Bobby, just before seven o'clock. The two were a common sight in the neighbourhood. The young mother recalled this occasion because the lad next door, Carl Brightwell, almost collided with Mrs Tolliver as he left his home on his mountain bike.

"They had words," she reported, "but I couldn't make out what was said because of the new windows we had installed in the Spring."

Even ten years ago, Carl Brightwell had a reputation in town for being a little toe rag. He was fast becoming a person of interest to the police. The witness confirmed Carl wore a sky-blue hoodie when he rode past her window. The lad was in town at the time of the murder. Over a dozen witnesses placed him in McDonald's with his mates. They were annoying the other customers, and at half-past seven, the shift manager Kief Dariwhal lost patience and asked them to leave.

As soon as they stood outside in the pouring rain, Carl and his cronies overturned the outdoor furniture and emptied the industrial-sized wheelie bins. They then started throwing chairs against the windows and found it amusing to smear rotting food on the advertising boards. Customers trapped inside with their young children pestered Mr Dariwhal until he rang the police.

The county's finest were busy responding to the incident in Lowden Woods, and two hours passed before anyone visited the fast-food outlet. The Police had ignored a frantic second request for someone to attend.

Before DI Culverhouse moved to Portishead and the Avon and Somerset force in 2013, he organised a reconstruction of the Tolliver murder. Another potential witness came forward. A man bird-watching high on Lowden Hill had seen someone in Battersby Lane. He was following the flight of a sparrow hawk with his binoculars when it swooped towards the ground. He lost it for a second, and as he searched left and right, he spotted a man and woman in the lane with a dog. They appeared to be chatting amicably. The man was playing with the dog. He had no doubt the couple knew one another. The bird-watcher had switched his attention back to his hunt for the sparrow hawk and didn't see the couple again.

Culverhouse knew the man in Battersby Lane couldn't have been Brightwell. The person in the blue anorak in Lowden Woods had to be the killer. His team spent hundreds of hours looking for the suspect without success. There were no other credible leads after five years. The Detective Inspector had given an interview to the crime reporter from the Wiltshire Times.

"We reckon Daphne's killer was a local lad who knew the area well," he said. "Several clothing items are being re-examined by forensic scientists for evidence that we couldn't test for back in 2008. That might lead to a breakthrough. I would urge any of your readers with information about the murder to come forward. In particular, anyone who may have been confided in by the killer since June 2008."

Dominic Culverhouse moved onwards and upwards within months of that interview. His successors had added nothing significant to the case file since that time. There was a report from a national newspaper in which an investigative reporter suggested Daphne Tolliver could have been a victim of a serial killer. He believed there were similarities to unsolved murders in Devon, Dorset and Hampshire.

Truelove had flicked through that article and decided against casting it aside. Like Culverhouse and his murder squad, he believed these deaths were unconnected to the killing of Mrs Tolliver. Whether they were themselves connected was for officers from other forces to determine. The main similarity was that they were women killed while walking their dogs. Their ages ranged from sixteen to fifty. A knife was involved in those other three cases. One couldn't rule out a serial killer using a different method to dispose of this potential fourth victim, but it didn't feel right.

From the outset, the lack of an apparent motive hampered the detectives. Daphne Tolliver's death wasn't a result of a robbery, and there was no sign of sexual assault. She didn't have an enemy in the world if you believed her family, ex-colleagues from the Post Office, and the primary school where she was a cleaner. Add in the glowing terms used by volunteers at the charity shops and in the letter from the Manor House; then, it was certain the lady was loved and well-respected.

So, why did someone pick up a rock and bash in her brains? It was a mystery to ACC Kenneth Truelove. But he knew just the man to unravel that mystery.

Gus Freeman was sixty-one years old. The retired Detective Inspector lived in Urchfont, a village five miles out of Devizes towards Salisbury, where Freeman had worked for much of his career. The ACC knew his reputation as a thief-taker. An honest-to-goodness copper who was considered these days as 'old school'. It wasn't a compliment since it marked them down as a dinosaur. Many other competent detectives had 'not wanted on the journey' tattooed across the forehead. The results were there in the headlines of every daily newspaper to show the folly of that policy.

ACC Truelove knew the tune for the police service's new anthem, but he sometimes struggled to remember the words. If he played things close to his chest, he hoped to convince his superiors that this idea was a modern initiative with all the diversity and forward-thinking they craved.

Kenneth Truelove reckoned Freeman's dogged determination and a knack for winkling out that valuable nugget of information others missed would work well on such a case. But, first, he had to convince the old bugger it was a proper job, not one created out of pity.

Freeman's wife, Tess, died from a brain aneurysm six

months following his retirement. He was still coming to terms with his enforced solitary existence. She hadn't had a day's illness throughout their thirty-five years of marriage. The ACC took a deep breath, picked up the phone and dialled.

After four rings, the answerphone kicked in.

"*Patience is necessary. One cannot reap immediately from where one has sown.* I'm not here, so leave your number, and I'll decide whether to bother calling back."

Truelove shook his head. He knew Freeman's reputation as an oddball, but he had to give him ten out of ten for originality. Then the beep ended the existentialist philosophising, not-so-warm, welcoming message.

"It's Truelove here," the ACC said, "call me when you've got a minute, Gus. I'm sure you don't need a reminder of the number."

The message was delivered. Now he had to wait. An Assistant Chief Constable's duties didn't allow time to muse over Freeman's call message. He had to create the vision and set the direction and culture for the county force. He was part of the Chief Officer Team, building public and organisational confidence and trust. It was the responsibility of that Team to enable the delivery of an effective policing service.

There was never a dull moment, but it was all bollocks.

Deep down, Truelove knew it, but he wasn't old enough to take his pension. Instead, it was time to do a John Redwood and at least try to remember the tune. There were meetings to attend and visions to be created. Freeman would call back sooner or later. Of that, he was confident.

Gus Freeman sat in the lounge of his retirement home. That was how Tess had termed the two-bedroomed bungalow when they moved here from Downton just over five years ago. They had planned for his police career to end as the dinosaurs were made extinct.

Her pastoral role at the Wiltshire College in Salisbury had been something she enjoyed too much to quit for the foreseeable future. The College was formed in 1992 when a College of Art & Design and a Technology College merged. The Campus lay on Southampton Road. It offered degree courses in association with Bournemouth University and vocational courses for school leavers.

Tess was a Wellbeing Advisor and was required to work a combination of twilight and night shifts on a rolling shift pattern. Tess might work from three to midnight or ten to half-past eight, but that never inconvenienced the couple. Before she took on this role, Tess suffered over two decades of Gus being called away at a moment's notice when another crime occurred on his patch.

Anyway, it was only ever the two of them to consider. Neither wanted children.

What mattered most to both of them in their career was job satisfaction. Gus got his pleasure by solving those crimes and seeing criminals in prison. Tess had taught for many years but gradually felt stifled by constant changes in curriculum and teaching methods. She got more fulfilment from providing a safe and secure environment for her students on Campus.

At Christmas and the end of every school year, when many left altogether, she returned home with a hundred cards from students who came to think of her as a surrogate mother. Someone they confided in when things got on top of them.

Tess took it in her stride. It didn't make her any more maternal. She shrugged when scooping up those cards to be recycled.

"I don't think I could even put a face to most of these names," she would sigh. "I was just doing what the job entailed."

Gus wondered how prepared those kids were for the outside world. He could never recall his teachers providing a safe and secure environment when he attended school. He couldn't imagine sending any of them a card at Christmas either. They may not have remembered his name after he left at sixteen. But he would never forget the names of those who wielded the cane with glee or whacked pupils with a blackboard rubber.

It seemed so long ago now. Gus couldn't wait to leave school. After six months labouring on a building site, he'd started evening classes to help gain the qualifications he needed to join the police at eighteen. His father warned him against it.

"You'll never be off duty, son," he cautioned, "and forget any friendships you've formed. They will never last once you put on that uniform."

Gus wanted to prove his father wrong, but he knew he was right within six months. Then, within a year, the opportunity to change things disappeared when his father died of lung cancer at fifty-three.

He completed his training in August 1975, and his first posting was to Amesbury. Two years later, he moved into the City of Salisbury. It was an excellent time to be a young copper on the beat. There was plenty of variety. He was encouraged to take his sergeant's exams. Despite being reticent about his academic prowess, Gus surprised himself by passing the first time and decided he had just been a late-developer. He wished those cane-happy teachers could see how he turned out.

Gus Freeman minded his own business, taking a leak in the toilet one morning when someone stood next to him. They said a vacancy was about to be advertised in the team of detectives.

"You should apply, young Freeman."

"I'm not on the square," he told them.

"Even better," he was told. "Mark my words, that job has got your name on it. Nobody else need bother to apply."

Gus didn't need to be told twice. He grabbed an application form as soon as the advert appeared on the notice board. Detective Sergeant Gus Freeman began thief-taking in February 1978.

Gus met Tess in The Swan at Stoford that summer. He was enjoying a few drinks with colleagues on a warm July evening. Tess arrived with a group of teachers celebrating the end of the summer term. The new one began no more than six weeks later, yet Tess returned to work wearing an engagement ring.

Tess and Gus saved hard over the next eighteen months. She had been a late arrival, and her parents were already in their late sixties. They had next to nothing put by and were unable to contribute much. It seemed they faced a long engagement. Almost two years after they buried his father, Gus stood by the same graveside and watched his mother's coffin lowered into the ground.

"No big mystery to solve for the cause of death," he said to Tess later as they stood in the bar of The Duck Inn in nearby Laverstock. "She smoked forty a day Capstan Full Strength since she was fourteen, the same as Dad."

The modest home he had grown up in came to him in

his mother's will. Gus and Tess set about re-decorating and ridding the place of the effects of decades of nicotine. She continued to live with her parents. Times may have changed, but Tess was adamant.

The couple were married in Salisbury Registry Office on Bourne Hill in 1980. The detective and the teacher then manoeuvred through thirty-five years of marriage, avoiding the icebergs that brought disaster to many others on the same journey.

Tess lost both her parents within the first five years.

"It's the two of us against the world then, Gus," she would say whenever a problem arose.

Then, after forty years of service, Gus had been called into the ACC's office. He asked whether he had considered retirement. He was three weeks into an investigation concerning allegations of sexual assault over several years at a care home. It had been a traumatic experience and promised to get even murkier. In a moment of weakness, Gus hinted that once this case ended, he might be glad of the chance to spend months scrubbing himself until he felt clean again.

Fatal Decision: Chapter Three

Tuesday, 27 March 2018

The message from the ACC came as a surprise. Gus had listened to it when he returned home yesterday evening after a tiring day. It made a pleasant change to hear a human voice behind that nagging red light flashing on his phone display.

Gus had been pestered in the past by so many computer-generated calls. He often let the number of stored messages reach the maximum of thirty before blitzing the lot without even a cursory check. The chances of missing a vital call were miniscule. It was almost sure to be PPI; his computer would crash the next day or another wrong number.

There were excellent reasons there wasn't a cat in hell's chance of the first two applying to him. As for the third option, Gus didn't enjoy conversations with people who thought he was their best friend or loved one.

The last episode lasted seven or eight minutes. Time lost; he'd never get back.

"Hello?" he'd answered brightly. He always tried harder to be jovial on a Sunday evening. It made him feel better about not attending church.

"Hello? Is that Dorothy?"

"No."

"Oh, is she there?"

"No."

"When do you expect her back?"

"I don't."

"Oh, has something happened to her?"

"It's possible. Perhaps you should call Dorothy to check."

Gus ended the call and made it as far as the drinks cabinet before the phone rang again.

"Hello," less upbeat this time. More unimpressed of Urchfont.

"Dorothy?"

"Still not here."

"That is 01380...."

"I know my number, and that's not it. You must have mis-dialled."

"Oh, I'm so sorry. I'm sure I wrote it down correctly."

"Don't worry. I think you may have switched the sixth and seventh numbers. Take care when dialling again."

"Thank you. You must think I'm a silly old fool."

"Not at all. Good evening."

He got further this time. As the single malt had slid from the glass and across his tongue, the phone rang again.

"The sixth and seventh numbers," he answered.

"How did you know what I was going to ask?"

"A lucky guess."

"I don't know you, do I? Your voice sounds familiar."

"It may be because we've spoken several times this evening."

"You've been so helpful. Gosh, look at the time. Dorothy will have gone to bed by now. Would you mind doing me a big favour? Could you tell her I can't make our bridge club this Thursday?"

That might be difficult, Gus thought, but the caller had gone. He had poured himself a generous measure. He felt he deserved it. After five minutes of sitting by the phone, he decided it was safe to sit and enjoy his drink undisturbed. That proved impossible.

He wondered how his phantom caller mastered counting cards to achieve a tricky five no-trumps on a Thursday afternoon. These bridge clubs involving elderly ladies were hotly contested affairs.

When he wasn't analysing that thorny problem, he scribbled the names of any potential Dorothy that had crossed his path on a scrap of paper. Women who lived in villages between Devizes and the parts of Salisbury Plain that were covered by the 01380 STD code.

Once a detective, always a detective. No matter how hard he racked his brains, it remained a concise list.

Gus gave up after his second drink and went to bed, having resolved to buy a phone with a caller display. He never wished to entertain another wrong number while at home. Most numbers got short shrift these days anyway, but if they seemed familiar, then he could at least weigh up the pros and cons of returning their call.

Weeks later, on a breezy Tuesday morning, the sun did its utmost to brighten his mood. He had to admit he was intrigued by last night's message. A call back wouldn't take much out of his morning. He planned to get across to his allotment. He needed to continue the work he'd put in yesterday.

They were on the threshold of Spring and a new gardening season. It didn't always feel it earlier in the month when the UK endured the tail-end of 'The Beast from the East'. It had been freezing, with daytime temperatures never getting above freezing. The strong easterly winds had delivered widespread snow to many parts, and as usual, everything ground to a halt.

Three weeks further on, temperatures were on the increase. The longer days triggered new growth, and the majority would survive as long as Gus offered his early sowings protection. This milder, unsettled spell was forecast to carry through into April.

Gus had applied for an allotment soon after moving into the village. Retirement was bound to deliver spare time. He and Tess could only take so many holidays outside of term time at the college, and visits to National Trust properties at the weekend didn't come cheap. They needed rationing.

Events changed that within six months. Although Gus struggled to motivate himself immediately after Tess's death, gardening was therapeutic. The patch of land's solace became crucial in his grieving process.

Yesterday, he had put the finishing touches to his winter pruning and started his digging. There was always something. He wondered again what Kenneth Truelove might want. Gus didn't want it to stop him from getting in his early potatoes.

There was nothing for it. Gus picked up the phone and dialled.

A bored-sounding woman answered.

"Can I speak to the ACC, please?" asked Gus, "I'm returning his call. Ex-Detective Inspector Freeman."

She asked him to hold, then treated him to a quick burst of 'Wouldn't It Be Nice' by The Beach Boys while he waited. Gus held the phone at arm's length.

"Truelove here. Good morning, Freeman."

"The cuts haven't bitten too deep, I see. You've still got a secretary."

"Vera is a Personal Assistant," replied the ACC, "and several of us share her services."

"Things *have* changed since I left."

"It's clear that you haven't, Freeman. You understood what I meant."

"Might I also suggest a change of background music? Something by The Police would be more appropriate. After all, Brian Wilson allegedly took an incredible variety of drugs in the Sixties. Is that the right message?"

"I'm a busy man, Freeman. I called because I have a matter to discuss with you face-to-face. So how are you fixed tomorrow afternoon? Let's say, two o'clock here at HQ on London Road."

"Two o'clock? Do I need to drive there with the traffic snarl-ups that the road suffers? OK, but I might be late. It depends on how I get on with my Ulster Classics."

That comment puzzled the ACC.

"I'm sure that means something to you, Freeman. Get here as soon as you can. I can hardly discipline you. Look, I have a serious proposal to put to you. So, please try to leave the levity in the countryside when you travel in tomorrow."

"Message received," said Gus.

Grab your copy...
vinci-books.com/fataldecision

About the Author

Ted Tayler is the international best-selling indie author of the Freeman Files and Phoenix series. Ted lives in the English West country, where his stories are based. He was born in 1945 and has been married to Lynne since 1971. They have three children and four grandchildren.

His thought-provoking mysteries appeal to readers of Sally Rigby, Joy Ellis, Pauline Rowson, and Faith Martin. His action-packed thrillers are a must for fans of Mark Dawson and J C Ryan.

Gus Freeman's cold case investigations are carried out with reasoned deduction rather than bursts of frantic action. In each of the 24 books, unsolved murders are accompanied by romance, humour, and country life. The core message in the 12 Phoenix novels is that criminals should pay for their crimes. Unfortunately, the current system fails to deliver the correct punishment, so Phoenix helps redress the balance.

Acknowledgments

The love and support of my family; without them, this would have been impossible.

www.ingramcontent.com/pod-product-compliance
Ingram Content Group UK Ltd.
Pitfield, Milton Keynes, MK11 3LW, UK
UKHW040119190326
469155UK00004B/1244